COLD
HARD
TRUTH

An unputdownable crime thriller with a breathtaking twist

REBECCA BRADLEY

DI Claudia Nunn Book 4

Joffe Books, London
www.joffebooks.com

First published in Great Britain in 2023

Cover art by Nick Castle

ISBN: 978-1-83526-174-3

PROLOGUE

The streets had been Dean Bird's home for the past three or so years. Time was a different concept when your days merged into one long struggle of trying to stay fed, hydrated and warm. Particularly on nights like this. A low wind chilled the air and brought the temperature down another notch or two, pushing and needling through the clothes he did his best to keep dry. Because, Jesus, wet clothes and cold weather, they sure didn't mix. But today, the quiet, low wind was subtle. Most other people, they probably wouldn't even notice. Wrapped in their nice full coats.

Not that he was bitter.

He was where he deserved to be.

The light wind found the holes and the gaps in what he'd managed to dress himself in, and it swirled beneath and wrapped Dean in a hug.

He shivered.

His bones rattled.

Days and weeks, even months, were impossible to keep track of . . . but the seasons, they helped. You could roughly work out a year by the seasons. Winter was always the hardest and summer the shortest.

How he loved the summer.

In the summer, he wouldn't be traipsing across town like he was now, looking for a new place to sleep because some headcase had stolen his box. In summer, Dean could have slept on the ground and it would have been warm enough for him. Three years, see, you get used to it. There are so many things you can get used to.

Even in summer, he'd never have stood up to the younger guy pushing him around, telling him he was taking his bed. Better to walk away. Now he had to find somewhere off the ground and sheltered from the wind.

But summer . . . people were happier in summer. They smiled at him; they stopped to say hello.

They saw him.

At the time he needed it most, in winter, it was like he turned invisible. People hurried past him with hands in their pockets and their heads down.

He'd been one of those people. Dean couldn't remember a time he'd ever stopped to speak to someone like he was now, on the street. He couldn't remember because it had never happened.

Dean Bird had been a jumped-up wanker.

He blinked.

He'd walked as far as Bingham Park. He wasn't sure how.

His shoulders ached, his legs hurt and his feet were sore. In fact, he couldn't remember the last time he'd looked at his feet. It was probably something he should do.

Bingham Park would offer shelter. Somewhere to hide from the wind and a chance to rest from the pain of his own body.

For Dean Bird, there were days he wished he'd go to sleep and not wake up again. Not that he was suicidal. That primal urge to live kept him going, but how long would it continue? How long can someone wake up to a world where survival is the goal, rather than living?

The park dampened the sounds of the city and the sounds in his head. It was dark and it was peaceful.

Dean no longer cared his bed had been taken from him. He'd spend the night here and would return again every

2

evening, until he was moved on. All he had to do was walk a little further in, so he wasn't in sight of anyone who would report him.

Now that a resting spot was in his sights, the small bottle in his pocket provided a reassuring weight against his leg as he hobbled onwards.

He spotted a bench. Somewhere to sleep off the ground, with more than a layer of cardboard and newspapers to stop the cold seeping into his bones. He was ageing and could barely take it anymore.

If he were younger, he'd have kicked the arse of the wanker who stole his bed, but he was too long in the tooth to go toe to toe with a young 'un. Fuck, his fingers couldn't even work properly. In his heyday, the lad would have walked a mile around him, standing proud in his desert fatigues.

It had been a long, long fall from there, though.

Dean paused and rubbed his knee. Emotion brewing in his throat at the memory he'd allowed out, now threatening to overturn him. He shoved the image that had come unbidden to his mind's eye back into its locked box, straightened with a wince and shuffled on.

He really did need to look at his feet at some point. Maybe just changing his socks would help.

A good sleep would help and that bench was perfect. With his trusty blanket in his backpack, he'd sleep better than he had for a while. But . . . Dean scrunched up his eyes. He couldn't make out what he was seeing. At fifty-seven, he had the body of an old man. That was what living on the streets did to you. Add that to the trauma of . . . well, he'd closed that box for the evening. The point being, he couldn't tell what he was seeing. He was too far away yet, and it was late, though the moon was high in the cloudless sky and broke the bleakness of the dark night. There was an indecipherable mound on the bench.

Maybe someone had dumped their rubbish. Or, worst case, someone had beat him to his bed, again.

The little hope Dean Bird had carried drained away. The backpack and bottle felt heavier, weighing him down.

All he wanted to do was sit where he was and cry. If his past had taught him anything . . .

Dean ground his teeth.

. . . it was that it wasn't over until it was over.

He put his hand in his pocket, touched the smooth coldness of the glass and trudged forward. The mound on the bench becoming clearer with every step. It was no rough sleeper like he'd ever seen before. She was young. That wasn't the issue. There were plenty of youngsters on the street. Shame on the government for that one. It was the way she was dressed. Too clean-cut.

Maybe she'd been out partying and had stopped there on the way home and fallen asleep.

Dean had to find out if she was here for the night, because if she was, she'd need his coat. She'd freeze to death dressed like that, and a girl of her age wouldn't die on the streets on his watch, even if it meant he might. He'd had his share of chances. Her life was only starting.

With dirt-encrusted fists, he rubbed tired eyes. All he'd wanted was a bed for the night. Somewhere to rest his head and leave behind the horror of life. It obviously wasn't to be tonight. He was destined to wander, both in the world and in his mind, when all he wanted was the darkness.

The bottle shifted against his leg.

If a drunken snooze had brought her here, then the girl needed waking so she could return home. Outside — this kind of outside — was not a place she needed to be. It was not a place she wanted to experience, especially at her tender age.

He shuffled closer and blinked a few times to clear his vision. There was something odd about the way she was . . . sleeping?

Dean Bird's old instincts flared. Red and hot around him. A live wire alert to danger.

No one slept with their arms crossed like that. Especially if in a drunken collapse.

He spun on the spot, or more specifically, staggered. His old-man eyes searching for the slightest movement, his ears listening for the threat of assault coming from the night, the treeline, the bushes.

His heart exploded in his chest and he gasped for breath. The fear of threat, of attack, jacking up every nerve in his body. If there was anyone out there, watching him, watching them, Dean couldn't locate them as his body betrayed him, lighting up like a New Year's firework.

Doubling over, with his eyes closed, Dean heaved air in as naturally as he could, until his heart beat steadily and his limbs stopped shaking. Rising, he looked again at the girl and then around them.

It was quiet.

Just him and her.

She hadn't moved as he'd approached. As he'd panicked.

He had to help her.

Dean moved closer. It was impossible to tell if her chest was moving in this light, but no one stayed so still when being approached in the dark. Her face was so pale it glowed in the moonlight.

His breath came faster and he started to shake again.

He could do this. Dean wrapped his arms around his body and patted his arms the way a mother might pat a child on the back. 'It's okay. I'm home. It's okay. I'm home. It's okay. I'm home.'

After another couple of deep breaths, he reached out and tenderly rubbed the girl's shoulder. 'Hey. Wake up. You don't want to sleep here all night.'

She wouldn't respond, but he had to try. He shook her a little harder in an attempt to rouse her, but still she didn't move. 'Shit,' he whispered under his breath. 'Shit, shit, shit, shit, shit.'

This was a whole world of shit, because Dean Bird's life of hiding was officially over. There was no choice here but to do the right thing.

Underneath the clothes in disrepair, the months of ground-in dirt, the disgusting stink of the unwashed, the bottle in his pocket and the old man's declining body, stood the man Dean Bird had always been.

5

CHAPTER 1

Gabby — six hours earlier

Gabby lounged on the bed. One elbow bent, her hand propping up her head, which felt as heavy as a boulder. She closed her eyes and blew air out through her lips.

'Stop. That tickles.' Ivy, sitting on the floor, flapped her hand around her ear.

Gabby stretched her long legs further down the bed, trainer-clad feet ruffling the thick pink knitted blanket slung across the end. 'I'm so tired. Why do they even make us do PE at our age anyway? Isn't it supposed to be for little kids?'

'You know, if my mum came in and saw your trainers up there, she'd lose a few brain cells.'

Gabby grinned. 'Would we even notice?'

Ivy laughed. 'It's a good job she's not in.'

'What you even doing anyway? I thought we were digging into your mum's gin. You know, to fend off the total and utter boredom that is life.'

'Yeah, yeah, course. I have half a bottle hidden under some clothes in my drawer after last time. Let me finish this.' Ivy's fingers flew over the screen of her top-of-the-range iPhone.

Gabby dropped dramatically on to her back. 'Oh God, Ivy. Not that again.'

'It's important.'

Gabby huffed.

'You know it is.' Ivy's voice was quiet.

Gabby rolled on to her side and pressed her chin on to Ivy's shoulder so she could see what her best friend was doing. As usual, Ivy had her TikTok account open. It wasn't the profile that everyone at school thought belonged to Ivy Henthorn. Regardless, everyone at school was friends with this profile, plus thousands of other people outside school, too. They just didn't know Ivy was behind it. 'Seriously? Isn't it time you closed that down?'

Ivy tapped furiously, ignoring her. Sliding between the video website she used and the account. Typing in the story she wanted to tell over the appropriate visual.

Gabby leaned further forward to see what Ivy was typing. 'What is it this time?' She narrowed her eyes and focused on the script.

Mr Joseph is popular with his students, but do they and their parents know the full story behind their favourite teacher? For I have news that will upset many of you.

We all know what it takes to succeed at the prestigious Wellington-Bell school. We've seen both students and teachers alike wash out, unable to weather both the strict personal and professional guidelines designed for the success the school wants to foster. But at what cost?

Because on Saturday, Mr Alexander Joseph, the blue-eyed boy, was slumped and out of it, after partaking in the very illegal drug marijuana.

'You can't write that without proof, Ivy!' Gabby sat up and swung her legs over Ivy's head until she was sitting upright at the side of her.

Ivy turned, a frown puckering her chin. 'You know me better than that. Of course I have proof. I don't just take

7

the word of whoever emailed me. There's photographic evidence. I'm attaching it. It'll appear at the end of the video of the outside view of the school with the story over it. Then, bingo! You can't rush genius.'

Gabby shook her head. 'Ivy, you can't keep doing this. You're destroying lives.' She rose and stalked to the drawers Ivy had indicated earlier. Pulled open the bottom one, shoved a hand in and triumphantly yanked out a half-drunk bottle of gin.

There were a couple of tall glasses they'd brought water upstairs in. With a clank, Gabby settled the bottle on top of the drawers and picked up the tumblers, opened the window and threw the water out. There was a high-pitched screech from below.

Ivy suddenly looked up. 'What the hell?'

'Oops?' Gabby giggled.

'Who?'

Gabby gingerly edged towards the window again and peered over the ledge, then waved a hand. 'Oh, don't worry, it's only Jasmine.'

Ivy rolled her eyes and dropped her phone on to the bed.

Gabby splashed gin into both glasses and handed one to Ivy. 'Here's to little sisters.'

Ivy laughed. 'I'll get it in the neck later, you know.'

Gabby slugged the gin back in one. 'Ivy, you need to stop.'

'You threw it, and besides, it was only water. I'm sure she's not scarred for life.'

Gabby shook her head. 'Ivy, the TikTok account. You need to close it. You're hurting people.'

Ivy gulped her shot back and blinked furiously. 'How can you say that? You know why I do this.'

Gabby grabbed the bottle by the neck and dropped on to the floor beside Ivy, pouring another measure into each glass. 'He paid for what he did to you. That post went viral like nothing I've ever seen.' She leaned into her friend. Shoulder to shoulder. 'And all the other girls that came forward after, it was . . .'

The boulder in her throat squeezed the words down, but she fought on. Eased the pathway with another slug of clear liquid. 'It was brutal and brilliant at the same time. Those boys didn't know what was coming or what the hell had happened. To see them so defenceless, to watch them as their power was stripped away . . . It was so cool, and I was there for it.' Hot tears pricked at the back of her eyes. Gabby didn't dare look at Ivy now.

'You did that, Ivy. You took your power back, and you took back the power for all those girls and gave it to them.' The words were a whisper now.

The bottle clinked as she poured another shot. Ivy shook her head.

'But it changed. *You* changed, and you never noticed.'

'Is this about—'

'It's about you!' Gabby shouted.

Ivy's eyes widened.

'You can't see what you're doing. How you're hurting people. You're doing this for fun now. Please, you have to stop.'

Ivy brought the phone up to her chest like a shield and wrapped her arms around herself as though it could protect her. Her face was pale; tears were running down her cheeks. 'You have no idea what it's like to be hurt that way by a boy. You're strong. You'd never hide behind a keyboard, because you'd never let it to get to that point, and if it did, you'd kick their arse. I'm not like unbreakable you, Gabby.'

Gabby's phone vibrated in the pocket of her shorts. She fished it out and read the text. 'My mum. I have to go.'

She finished what was left in her glass, actually feeling a little unbreakable as the alcohol buzzed lightly through her system. She'd drunk more when one of their group had a house party at the weekend. She leaned down and hugged her friend, nose pressing into the top of Ivy's head, which smelled of coconut and holidays. 'You're as powerful as you want to be. You get to choose.'

Gabby's phone vibrated again. The name *mummy* flashed on the screen. 'Someone's having a hissy. I have to go.' She walked to the bedroom door.

'Is Toby okay?'

Gabby shrugged. 'Fine, the last time I saw him. He's just being a baby.'

'He had an operation.'

'His tonsils out, Ivy. It's nothing. Snip, snip.' Gabby laughed as she made scissors with her fingers before opening the door.

A deep bass thundered down the landing from Theo's bedroom, Ivy's older brother. 'It's time to shut that account down, Ivy. Come on, bestie, end that profile. Live your best life with me. Catch up with you up later. Love you, see you soon.' She blew Ivy a kiss and skipped down the wide curving stairway, oblivious to the events that would follow.

CHAPTER 2

Claudia

It was over. Or that was how everyone not personally involved, perceived a moment like this.

How was she supposed to feel, though? As Claudia put one foot in front of the other, towards the heavy oak double doors of court three, she couldn't pin down a single emotion. She'd expected to be overrun with them at this point, overwhelmed by the final judgement. Sobbing in a heap, elated, furious. But as she neared the doors and escape, Claudia couldn't tap into herself at all.

She was numb.

Families shuffling out of the courtroom behind her were quietly in tears. There was nothing done with any volume in the court building. Work was carried out in a revered hush. Relatives hugged one another, offering mutual support. It had been an emotionally, hard-won verdict.

There was still sentencing to get through, but finally, after putting them through the pain of a lengthy three-week trial, it had taken a jury of his peers only a single day to find Samuel Tyler guilty.

At the end, he'd screamed and shouted at those who'd judged him. Then looked directly at Claudia as the court officers led him away, protesting his innocence at the brutal murder of her stepmother, Ruth Harrison.

It was over. She could forget it all. Everything she'd been through. This was the poison that had been hanging over all their heads. Time to move on, move forward.

Her dad, pushed on one of the doors and, with a quiet swoosh, it glided open. Claudia walked into the wide carpeted corridor, leaned back on the wall with a sigh and watched.

Her father waited with his hand on the door to allow everyone through. He was thanked with a discreet nod, a pat on the shoulder and even something as small as a blink from the most exhausted of the victim's family members. Finally he released the door and walked over to where she waited for him, arms wrapped protectively around her body.

The families of Samuel Tyler's victims huddled in the corridor. Claudia understood why they were here and hadn't immediately rushed out. To leave would be to say it was all over and they had to move on with their lives. Staying meant they were still immersed in their lost loved one's life. Plus, the press was waiting outside the courthouse doors. No one wanted to face that, Claudia included — and she was somewhat used to them.

Samuel Tyler was shrouded by infamy. He'd killed several women, before finally kidnapping, and killing undercover police officer Ruth Harrison. Spurred on, apparently, by a childhood trauma he believed he was putting right. He was a dangerous man and Claudia hoped the guilty verdict brought these families some peace. The sentencing, in a few weeks, would put an end to everything.

She looked to her father, who was also watching the families. His hands were in his pockets and his shoulders loose.

'You okay?' she asked.

He turned to face her. 'It's over, Claudia. He's finally going to pay for what he's done. I'm more than okay.'

So why was she so out of kilter? It was as though she were watching everyone else here from a distance.

Her dad touched her arm. 'How are you?'

Claudia shrugged. 'It's been a long time coming.' Murder investigations and the trials that followed were a legal process that dragged on. The system was not built for speed. It was archaic and had never moved with the times. It was one set of actions after another, with weeks and months between each, once it hit the court circuit. These families, of which she and her dad were one, had waited a long time for this verdict. Maybe that was why she felt so detached.

She was used to being here as the senior investigating officer, supporting families going through this and providing information and understanding. Yet what real understanding had she really known, up until this point? Being here now, she realised she'd blundered through these very same situations in different cases, offering what she thought were words of comfort and support, but really were cold, hard sentences filled with nothing but protocol.

Now she was intimate with this side of the judicial system in a way she wouldn't wish on anyone.

'But it's over; we can move on.' Her father's gaze fixed on her. There was something intense in his stare, as though he were trying to convey some hidden meaning.

Claudia returned her attention to the other families. They were moving away. Returning to their lives, away from the courthouse. Away from the terror of facing a murderer every day. She should probably do the same.

Her father was still watching her.

'Dad?' They had a strained relationship at times. Regardless of their relationship status, they had to be there for each other through this. Ruth was family. They both hurt with her loss.

Her dad blinked. Rubbed his face. 'I'm sorry. Tired, is all. I think I need a walk. Clear my head.' He looked around the corridor. It was empty now, other than a familiar face striding towards them. 'Do you mind?'

She didn't mind at all. In fact, she could do with the space herself. If he'd needed her after this, she'd have been there for him in a heartbeat. But in all honesty, she was glad he wanted to walk it off alone.

'No, it's fine. Go. Call me if you need anything, yes?'

He placed his hand on her shoulder. 'Of course. Thank you for being there through all this, Claudia. You know I couldn't have got through it without you.'

She nodded, words failing her.

Maddison Sharpe, her DCI, walked up to them. 'How are you both?'

'You'll have to excuse me. I'm just leaving,' said her father. He turned and, without another word, left Claudia and Sharpe alone in the corridor.

'Is he okay?' Sharpe asked.

'It's been a lot to process.'

'I'm sure.' Sharpe shoved a hand in her bag, and pulled out a pack of cigarettes.

There was no point telling her boss she couldn't smoke in here. She was well aware.

'Fancy a stroll outside?'

Claudia allowed herself to be propelled towards the exit, the way the families of the other victims had already gone. To run the gauntlet through the melee of press. It had to be done at some point. If not now, then when?

Sharpe pulled a single cigarette out and returned the pack to her bag. Claudia hated the smell of cigarette smoke, but always seemed to find herself in the vicinity of Sharpe when she had one lit. It was surprising how often her own clothes smelled of smoke, for a non-smoker.

As they approached the glass doors in a companionable silence, Claudia saw the huddle of reporters. Her dad had forced his way through, as had all the other families. They were packing up, believing everyone had gone. Cameras were being loaded into safety bags. The reporters had their backs to the doors, chatting to one another as they gradually moved away.

Sharpe held her arm out across Claudia like a barrier. 'Give them a minute.'

They waited until eventually the pavement was empty. One minute, it had been filled and raucous, and the next, as if it had never happened.

They opened the doors into the cold fresh air of early March. Spring was in sight, but winter wasn't yet giving up its fight for dominance. The day was clear and blue, but the temperature low and frosty.

Claudia pulled her coat tighter around herself and wrapped her scarf around her neck.

Sharpe lit the cigarette in her hand. Smoke drifted into the air. 'Albie's for a coffee?'

Claudia couldn't think of anything better than a hot drink right now. Though one with a nip of something stronger in it wouldn't go amiss. 'Are you back at work after this?'

'Yes, but don't worry about that. Connelly's in, and they have my number if the wheel comes off.'

Claudia's team was fairly new, created to investigate more complex cases than usually came through the door, thereby freeing up time for the Major Crime teams. But they'd run a few cases together now, and in that time, they'd all grown close. Her people would not allow the wheel to come off, no matter how depleted they were today, with her and her father here at court and Russ still off sick.

Traffic rumbled past as they walked quietly, each in their own world, towards Albie's coffee shop. Claudia shoved her hands in her pockets and hunched her shoulders up to her ears in an attempt to keep warm. She'd be glad when spring did actually show its face. She'd had more than enough of the winter now.

The independent coffee house was close to the court. It had a friendly ambience, and was well-liked by police and solicitors alike. After ordering drinks and a croissant each, they settled themselves in the corner. Claudia noticed Sharpe also instinctively sat facing the door. It was the cop in them. Being aware of their surroundings.

'So, how are you?' asked Sharpe, as she broke the end off her croissant and popped it into her mouth, her brightly polished nails glinting from the strip lighting overhead.

How honest should she be, to the woman who had some control over her work life? Show too much of her inner feelings, and Sharpe could think her incompetent. Be too stone-like, and Sharpe would know she was glossing over everything, and would just push more. Bloody woman.

'Glad it's over,' she said.

Sharpe took a sip of her coffee. 'I imagine. But that doesn't tell me how you're feeling, does it?' Her focus was laser-like now, and Claudia's skin heated up under the pressure.

She stared at her own untouched croissant. 'A little detached. Like I should have all sorts of emotions, but they're just not there and I'm not sure why.'

A small bell over the door tinkled, and both Claudia and Sharpe turned their attention to the man who'd come in. In his twenties, he had a large shoulder bag slung across his body. His hair looked like he'd jumped straight out of bed. There were some lads who spent hours creating the style, but this lad had the dishevelled appearance of a student, which made her think it was genuine. He made his way to the counter. Ordered a coffee and sat at the long high bench that ran along the front window, where he pulled out his laptop and started work. Definitely a student. Sheffield was a university city. It was difficult to walk five minutes within the city centre and not bump into a student.

Sharpe turned her attention back to Claudia, pulled away another piece of croissant and held it above her plate. 'And Dominic?' Straight back to topic, without missing a beat. This time the subject was her father.

Claudia stifled a sigh. The woman was relentless. 'He seemed okay. Like this was the end of it. Which it is. But yes, he's okay. Like I said, glad it's over.'

'Keep up the work with your therapist.'

Claudia didn't respond.

'Are you still staying with friends?'

Claudia thought of her blackened house. Her home. 'No. I've moved into a rental because of the size of the job. The fire caused so much damage that once I had someone come in to assess it, it became clear I'd be living elsewhere for a long time. The structural stuff needed dealing with first: trusses, floors, load-bearing walls. Then the whole building needs rewiring from scratch.' Claudia sighed again and ran a hand through her hair, sure it resembled a crow's nest after the day she was having. Maybe even as bad as the lad in the window. She hoped not. 'Basically, they're building a new house. It's a good job it's a detached property and no one else's home was damaged.'

Sharpe's croissant was close to finished. Claudia had no idea how the woman stayed so slim. Mind you, Sharpe was known to leave work late in the day in her gym gear. Exercise probably counted for a lot. Claudia was a runner. It helped with the stress of the job. She'd been doing a lot of running of late.

'I'm just glad you came out of it in one piece. Even if you needed a little recovery time.'

Was she really in one piece? The last year had been hard on all of them. It was a miracle any of them were still functioning.

'Claudia?'

She'd drifted off. 'Sorry. In my own head.'

Sharpe shoved the last piece of croissant into her mouth. Waited until she'd chewed and swallowed it before she spoke again. 'You don't have to be afraid anymore, Claudia.'

She snapped to attention then. 'I'm not afraid. What do I have to be afraid of? I'm a serving police officer. A detective inspector.'

How true was this? What *did* she have to be afraid of? Who was she convincing? Herself or Sharpe?

In response, Sharpe eyed up the croissant that lay untouched on Claudia's plate. 'Are you eating that?'

Claudia shook her head. Sharpe lifted the pastry and, again, broke the narrow end off and pushed it into her mouth. Claudia picked up her coffee, put the mug to her lips. It was hot to the touch, and the familiar scent under her nose was soothing.

'Look,' said Sharpe, finally, 'You've been waiting for this verdict for a long time. Tyler has denied killing Ruth this whole time. You must have feared a not-guilty verdict on her murder, if not the others, no matter the level of evidence against him. The tension you and Dominic have carried must have been enormous. That's all I'm saying.'

Sharpe paused there, glancing away, then back. 'You can let it go. Tyler is gone. You don't have to attend his sentencing if you don't want to. He's going down for a very long time. You and Dom can live your lives. You don't need to be afraid he'll get away with it anymore.'

Claudia rubbed her head, emotions a tangle in her entire body. Sharpe talked sense. It was all true. She should feel a sense of calm and freedom, and yet she didn't. Nothing was making sense, and she couldn't put her finger on it. 'You're right. Though I might attend his sentencing. The final nail and all that.'

The croissant was disappearing fast. 'I get that. Do what you need to. You always have my support.'

Claudia leaned back in her chair, coffee in hand, and considered Samuel Tyler, the man who had been convicted of killing her stepmum and best friend. Her unease was confusing her more. Why *wasn't* she elated with the guilty verdict?

CHAPTER 3

Gabby

It was clear from the blunt few words of her mother's text messages that she was unhappy about something. That she'd had to send Gabby a second message to call her home would not have gone down well.

Gabby's mother was used to having everything go her way, to getting what she wanted. When you were a world-famous solo violinist and paid the big bucks for your magical fingers, and your every whim was catered for, being highly strung was part of the job description.

When at home, the great Charlotte Hunt put as much effort into the role of mother as Gabby presumed she did as violinist. After all, motherhood was also a part she'd chosen, and she could never be seen to fail. Her profile was public — globally so.

Gabby smoothed her sweater and hoped her father was home, then she unlocked the door and entered.

'Gabby?' Her mother strode from the kitchen, heels clacking on the tiled hallway floor, blonde hair flowing behind her, as though she had her own personal wind machine.

'Is Toby okay?'

Her mother batted the question away with her hand. 'He's fine. That's not why I—'

Satisfied there was no drama with her brother's health, Gabby walked in the opposite direction to her mother, into the kitchen and towards the fridge. 'Is there anything to eat?' She was ravenous. 'I could eat a scabby—'

'Gabrielle Eleanor Hunt, you stop right there.'

She'd used that *tone*. The one that said she wasn't messing around, and you were expected to pay attention.

Gabby would have been more worried if the tone hadn't been overused during her childhood. Her mother used it to control her when she was young — at which point, it had done its job and terrified her. Her mother had continued to use what worked, but as Gabby aged, she lost her fear of *the tone* with regular use.

Gabby opened the fridge.

The thing was, her mother loved what she did. No, not the parenting, but the music and everything that came with it. The worldwide recognition, the touring and the massive fanbase. Who wouldn't love their own set of fans? The praise and love they rained down was her security blanket; it was the way she monitored how healthy her career was. Plus, she also adored the first-class travel, hotels and the money.

When she came home to Gabby, Toby and her father, it wasn't the same. In the early years, there were sticky fingers, tears and tantrums. It definitely wasn't a first-class package. So her mother had introduced *the tone*.

It was clear her mother was home: the fridge was filled with smoothies, salads and vegetables, as well as a change in the milk. Gone was good old full-fat and in its place was almond milk again. Gabby shifted things out of the way searching for the KitKat she'd dumped in there the day before.

'Gabby, I'm not messing around. My career could have been damaged. And what are you doing in there?'

She grabbed the chocolate like a prize and held it aloft as she pulled back, closed the door on all the unhappy food and looked at her mother properly, for what was probably the first time since she'd walked in. 'What's wrong?' She split the foil and snapped a finger off the KitKat bar, shoving it into her mouth.

Her mother reddened and shoved her phone into Gabby's face. The screen was on, but it was so close that she was unable to see what her mother was fussing about. There was nowhere to escape to, as her mother had now pinned her to the fridge.

Gabby put a hand up. The one without the chocolate in. She would not risk losing that. Her stomach was in full complaint mode. 'If you want me to see something, then don't push it up my nose.'

Her mother huffed, checked her screen was still awake and this time handed it to Gabby. 'This TikTik thing . . .'

Gabby splurted wet chocolate on to the phone screen.

'Gabrielle!'

'Yeah, sorry.' She wiped at the chocolate with the sleeve of her school jumper.

'That's no better.' Her mother's jaw tightened.

'It's just . . . *TikTik*, Mum?' she laughed.

'I don't care what you call it. I care that someone saw fit to denigrate me on the stupid little app.'

'You're on TikTok?'

'Not voluntarily, no.'

Gabby broke off another finger of chocolate and started chomping. 'So it was a bad review, huh?'

Her mother turned her back on Gabby and ran a hand through her hair. Whoa, if her mother was messing with her hair, it was not good. Surely she was used to critics by now.

'It is not a bad review.' Her mother faced her with tears in her eyes. 'Someone posted on this TikTik app that I . . .'

'TikTok,' Gabby said absently.

'Whatever,' her mother sniped. 'I wasn't aware until a junior member of the orchestra playing before me, nervously brought it to the attention of Ollie.'

Ollie was her mother's agent. His bald head and round face reminded Gabby of that actor who did movies and was also known for cooking around Italy, of all things. He was old, though, so she could never remember his name.

'Ollie was frightfully kind,' her mother continued.

Ollie was always kind. As far as Gabby could make out, he hadn't let the success of his clients go to his bald head. Whenever she met Ollie, he was dressed simply in jeans, T-shirt and trainers, with a smart blazer. And he had a million different blazers. Gabby loved his blazers. Ollie was not afraid to go for a short walk on the wild side, as far as his blazers were concerned.

'He promised we could ride this out, and that no one used this silly app, but I'm not so sure, Gabrielle.'

No, Gabby wouldn't be sure she'd trust Ollie on that one, either. He was obviously trying to be kind to her. She lowered her voice. 'TikTok's kind of a big thing now, Mum.'

Again the phone was thrust at her. 'Have you seen this?' Her mother's voice rose to near hysterical.

Gabby looked around. Where was her dad? And where was Toby, for that matter? Even in bed, surely he could have told their mother all about this.

To be in with any possible chance of watching what her mother wanted her to see, Gabby took the handset away from Charlotte and moved it into frame.

Her mother was right; it was on TikTok.

Gabby watched the video play. It was a black-and-white neutral video of a mother with a young child playing together in a park. The mother swinging the child around in the air, and the child laughing wildly.

A deep ache that Gabby hadn't been familiar with for some years made itself known. She swallowed it down hard.

But there was something familiar about the video. Though wasn't there about all TikTok videos? People simply did the same thing over and over again.

It wasn't the video that upset her mother. It was the story written over it.

The numbers have been worked out, and global solo violinist star and queen bee Charlotte Hunt has spent more time

working on establishing her career than she has on nurturing
her children and building her family. In a time when women
can have both career and family, does it matter which way
the clock skews?

'Do you see what I mean?' Her mother's voice was rising. 'How do we take this off the internet, Gabby? People are judgy.'

There was no thought for the impact the video would have on her daughter. Her mother was circling the wagons on her career.

'They will judge me because of this. They judge from behind their keyboards and phones. It already has hateful comments attached.' Her voice was louder in volume and pitch as she continued. 'You have to take it down, Gabby. This is your fault. Do you understand me?' Her stare was flint-hard. Sparks were a risk, and then they'd both burn where they stood.

But Gabby wasn't afraid of the heat. A cold chill wrapped itself around her as her mother set the blame squarely at her feet. 'Mum?'

'How else, Gabby? How else do they know my life like this? The internet, this is your world.'

'No, Mum.'

Her mother screamed, 'You have to take it off!'

She was serious. She believed Gabby could remove the video and take away her shame.

Was it shame? Or was it fear that she'd lose her fans?

'Mum . . .'

'Don't look at me like that.'

'But I can't. It's not my account. I'm sure you'll be fine. People who watch your concerts aren't the type of people who watch TikTok videos.'

'This.' Her mother waved an arm around their surroundings. The large kitchen. The huge fridge Gabby had practically been inside of as she searched for food. 'This didn't get here by accident.'

She'd heard this sermon a thousand times. How lucky she was, when all she really wanted was her mum to be at home like her friends' mothers. Like Ivy's mum.

'You're used to a home like this because your father and I work the way we do.'

There it was.

Charlotte waved at the phone still in Gabby's hand. 'But that, the video you think is insignificant, it can pull me down, and it can pull down all that is around you.'

Gabby didn't care about the house. But, she sighed inwardly, she *did* care about her mum.

'You have to take it off, Gabby.'

Emotion welled in her mum's face. Gabby wasn't quite sure which emotion. Her eyes were damp, her complexion paler than usual and her chin set at an odd angle.

Gabby shook her head. While this might not look good for her mum, it would only be temporary. She looked down at the TikTok again, but this time, she paid more attention.

Shit.

'What is it? You can remove it?'

'No, I . . . I . . . I'm sorry, Mum . . .'

Charlotte snatched the phone from her hand. 'I expected you to be more help. You always have your head in your phone. Remember what I said about the life you lead. It can always come crashing down around you.'

And if it did, would her mother blame her? It would be utterly unbearable to live with her mother if this video somehow brought her mother's career to a grinding and humiliating stop. Music was all she lived for. Here she was giving Gabby an opportunity to help, and Gabby was saying she couldn't. That lack of support would be forever held against her if the worst happened. And Gabby couldn't bear that.

She thought of the username she'd seen on the TikTok account. The user who'd posted the video about her mum. The video that her mum was going spare over. In Gabby's mind, it wasn't a huge deal. Her mother would likely sail through it unscathed, but the fact was, her mother didn't feel unscathed, and in turn, Gabby didn't feel unscathed. That video could bring Gabby's world down around her.

She shoved the rest of the KitKat in her pocket, oblivious to the possibility of it melting. There were bigger things to worry about.

Gabby recognised the TikTok user, but she'd stopped viewing that account some time ago. The videos weren't her thing. The only reason she'd watched in the first place was in a supportive capacity. By not watching, she'd missed this. It had been posted three weeks ago.

The user of the TikTok account upsetting her mother right now was her best friend, Ivy.

CHAPTER 4

Theo

His mother's face was flushed. Owen was standing beside her, playing the calm parent. Not that Theo would ever consider him a parent.

'I don't understand how you don't know where she is, Theo.'

'Ivy's a big girl. I'm not her keeper.'

Her glare could melt rock.

Owen tried for peace again. 'I'm sure she'll be in soon, honey. She's a sensible girl.'

His mother spun on him. 'You've been home half an hour, and yet you didn't even notice she wasn't in the house. Now you want me to believe you have the situation figured out?'

Ouch. That one had to sting.

'And you can take that smirk off your face, Theo.'

The smirk was removed.

'I ask you again, how can you not know she's left the house?'

'Because his music is so loud.'

Theo tried not to roll his eyes, but . . . Owen. It wasn't that Owen had been a cruel stepfather, like the movies liked to depict. No, Theo wished he had it in him. Owen barely took up his own space, never mind anyone else's.

His mother was the one who wore the trousers, which made Owen appear even more ineffectual. Though there had been the rare situation where Owen's temper had risen, and it hadn't been pretty. *Not pretty* was an understatement, Theo had been pretty damn terrified. As well as goddamn thrilled, at the same time, that this side of him existed. But it stayed hidden, so the man they lived with was boring old Owen — so beige he blended into the background.

'Theo!'

Theo jumped.

'Are you going to answer the question? Your sister?'

He mumbled.

His mother sighed. 'You're trying my patience. Please, Theo, pull yourself together. Tell me what you know.' She looked at her watch. It was a calculated move, but one that worked all the same. It was ten thirty and she'd held her concern, her worry and her temper for long enough.

He scratched his head. 'Yeah, I had my music on. It was loud. I can't have heard her when she left. When I went to my room, I left Ivy, Gabby and Jasmine in the kitchen. We'd all been in there getting something to eat.'

'Yes. I saw the evidence on the kitchen island. And that's it? So your defence is, that as far as you know, both your sisters could be missing, including the seven-year-old?'

The muscles across Theo's shoulders tensed, a deep ache throbbing over his back and into his neck. 'Jasmine's . . .'

'Do you think I'd be this calm if Jasmine wasn't in the house?'

No. If Jasmine wasn't in the house, then that terrifying side of Owen would be loose, because Jasmine was his actual daughter. Unlike the two hand-me-downs he'd inherited.

'I'm sorry,' he said instead.

27

His mother rubbed her hands over her face, and Owen pulled her into a hug, which she allowed him to do. It was rare the two of them were physically affectionate in front of him and Ivy, and Theo fidgeted from one foot to the other as he waited.

Owen released her, and she returned her attention to him, a little calmer this time. 'I don't need you to be sorry. I need your help in locating Ivy. Tell me, what did she say in the kitchen?'

What could he say? Jasmine was the little whiny kid she always was. Ivy was kind to her, and Theo ate with them, but pretty much kept to himself. He always had done since the thing with Ivy. The snaky little bitch.

All he could do was shake his head. 'Mum, she didn't say anything. Jasmine was . . .' He shrugged.

'What?'

Theo pushed the balls of his palms into his eyes. What could he tell her to get her off his back?

'Theo, what about Jasmine? What are you trying to say?'

Jesus. He wasn't trying to say anything. 'Nothing. Nothing. I'm not saying anything. Jasmine was whining, and Ivy and Gabby were cheering her up like always.' His voice rose, loud in his head.

In contrast, his mother lowered hers, which was more alarming than when she shouted. Which, in fairness, was rare. 'Detail when you last saw her.'

He clenched his hands, which were now down by his sides. 'I'd eaten my pizza. Ivy and Jasmine were still being . . .' He wrinkled his nose and top lip at the memory. 'They were doing that thing where Ivy pretends she's all girly and loves Jasmine's stuff and is interested in it.'

'Theo.' Owen's hackles were up now.

His mum stretched her hand out to him and he took hold.

'And you?' Even quieter.

'I went to my room, put my music on and gamed for a bit.'

'You didn't hear the girls come upstairs?'

Theo slunk away from his mum and Owen, and sank on to his bed. 'I had my headphones on for the game. I didn't hear anything.'

'Ivy's being a typical teenager, Verity, she's testing her boundaries, but I can see it's hurting you. If it'll help, I'll go and look for her. I won't be long.'

Finally his mother turned away, still holding on to Owen. 'I'll call Charlotte, and all Ivy's friends, and see if she's with any of them. She'll be in big trouble when she—'

The door closed quietly. Theo turned the music back up to block out the tension that reverberated through the house.

Jasmine easily fell asleep while reading a book, like the goody-two-shoes she was, and once she was asleep nothing would wake her, so his mother never bothered him about the volume of his music. His mother's only issue was when he had an assignment due or, as was the case now, exams coming up.

His mother was seriously rattled, and all screwed up in knots because she'd come home from work and Ivy wasn't in the house. That wouldn't have been so bad, but there was no note to say where she'd gone, no text message, and she wasn't responding to her phone. So now his mother was too wrapped up with Ivy to care or even notice whether he had done, or was doing, any revision.

Theo lay back, head on his pillows, and closed his eyes.

The music wasn't loud enough to block out the noise in his head, but he definitely couldn't turn it up any further. Not tonight.

Theo had lied to his mother and he could never tell her the truth.

CHAPTER 5

Dominic

It hadn't taken long to rally the troops. And as soon as work allowed, all his old team were sitting in the Head of Steam public house with Dominic, to raise a glass to the guilty verdict.

The team sat on wooden chairs around a long table pushed against the wall. These tables lined the longest wall opposite the bar and business was good. The room was alive with chatter and laughter, and the sound of glasses chinking and wooden legs scraping against the floor.

Dominic hadn't turned to the Complex Crimes Task Force team. No, he wanted the people he trusted around him. Those who had worked the initial case with him. The one that had resulted in . . . well, this.

Dominic didn't want to dwell on the reality of what this was. He slugged his beer back and slammed the empty glass down. The gas from the beer greeted the team as a loud burp.

Hayley Loftus, a Detective Constable from his old team scowled. 'You guys are always so disgusting.'

The men around her laughed and she shook her head. Rhys Evans, another DC from his old team, but one who had transferred with him to the new task force, put his arm around Hayley. 'You love us, really.'

Hayley smiled sweetly. 'In your dreams.'

The group laughed again. Rhys pulled Hayley to him, lifting two legs of the chair she was on right up off the floor. She grabbed the edge of the table quickly.

'I've missed you.' Rhys grinned.

Dominic stood. 'Who's for another round?'

A roar of laughter went up from a table closer to the door, a group of women with mostly empty cocktail glasses littering the surface in front of them.

* * *

Hayley unhooked herself from Rhys. 'Yeah, it's nice to be . . .' Her gaze lifted to Dominic.

He shook his head. 'Drink?'

'Sounds good.'

There was a chorus of agreement, and Dominic picked up the tray from the floor and strode to the bar.

'Shit.' Hayley looked at her friends and colleagues. 'I'm telling Rhys how nice it is to be together again, when we're here because Dom's wife's killer has been found guilty today.' She rolled her eyes. 'I'm such an idiot.'

'No argument here,' said Rhys.

'Don't worry about it.' DC Krish Dhawan, also on both teams, gulped down the rest of his pint, then continued. 'You know Dom, he doesn't take offence. Besides, he asked to drink with us, didn't he? It's clear he wanted to spend this evening together, so I believe he shares your sentiment.'

Hayley blew out a breath.

DC Paul Teague leaned forward. Like Hayley, he hadn't made it over to the new team, but had been absorbed into another one. 'He's going to drink us under the table tonight. We'll have to keep an eye on him.'

Krish pointed at Paul's half-drunk pint glass. 'I see you're already taking it steady. Orders from the wife?'

'There's no harm in pacing yourself. Like I said, it won't do any harm for at least one of us to be *compos mentis* as Dom spirals down.'

* * *

'You lot talking about me?'

They obviously hadn't heard him coming, and all bounced back like a pack of guilty children.

Dominic laughed and placed the tray, now laden with fresh drinks, in the middle of the table. 'Don't sweat it. It was expected.' He selected a pint and drank. 'Look, I'm okay. Don't worry. I just wanted to spend the evening with my mates. If I went home, I'd be alone, and I'd spend the night brooding. You're doing me a favour. Don't think I don't appreciate it. But stop fussing like old mother hens and let's drink.' He gulped more of his pint.

When he'd finished, half was gone. The rest of the team's drinks were still sitting on the tray.

'What're you waiting for?'

The evening wore on. The table stacked up with empty glasses, like transparent sentinels keeping watch over the proceedings, until they were removed by staff.

There was much laughter as the group reminisced about old times. Unimportant mistakes each other had made, including Paul being so forgetful he'd once turned up for work at eight a.m., when the shift had been changed to twelve p.m. — he had stayed rather than going home to come back again — and Krish's steel stomach, and the morning he'd arrived at work with a hangover and was so hungry he ate two-day-old Indian takeaway that had been languishing in the fridge, to no adverse effect.

Hayley held up her hands. 'No. No, no, no, no. We're not going there. We're not looking at me.'

Dominic watched her as the guys laughed.

'But it'd be so much fun.' Rhys grinned.

'I'm leaving before you can try.' She left her seat and headed to the ladies.

'I'll get another drink.' Dominic stood.

Paul checked at his watch, then Dom, who gently swayed. 'I think we should call it a night soon, don't you?'

'You're giving up on me?' Dominic rubbed his face.

Paul and Krish exchanged a look.

'No,' said Krish, rising from his chair and standing beside Dom. 'We're not giving up on you. But sleep might not be a bad idea.'

There was some more back and forth as the team tried to change Dom's mind.

Dominic pursed his lips as if deep in thought, swayed some more, then stumbled a step just as Hayley returned.

She grabbed hold of his arm and steadied him. 'Hey there. What're we doing?'

'Getting another drink, but I'm getting pushback.'

'Okay, then. Let's have a last one, and then call it a night. I think they're closing soon, anyway.' Hayley turned to Paul. 'Can you get them, please, and I'll sit with Dom?'

Paul jumped up, saluted her, and worked his way out from where he was near the wall.

Hayley, still holding on to Dominic, eased herself on to one of the two nearest empty chairs and pulled Dominic along with her. He dropped down on to the second with a heavy thud.

Paul arrived with the final round, and Dominic grabbed his. 'To guilty verdicts, and hopefully, long sentences.'

Glasses were selected and raised. 'To guilty verdicts,' echoed the group.

The bar had a strange tilt to it. Dominic probably should have had more than the couple of slices of toast he'd eaten before arriving. Food hadn't seemed like a top priority today. What had been important was drinking away the slippery darkness that threatened to engulf him. And drinking alone wouldn't drown out that darkness. No, it would only enlarge it. Allow it to smother him.

He'd had to bring his old team, his old mates. Those who'd been with him through everything.

Dominic leaned back and cradled the beer.

Hayley crossed her legs and leaned sideways on to him. 'You going to be okay tonight?'

The guys were talking among themselves. All frivolity gone. The night drawing to a close. As well as the room tilting, darkness curled around Dominic like a comfortable cloak. An old friend. He gulped down his beer.

'You should slow down now,' said Hayley.

Dominic angled his head to stare into her eyes, in an effort to offset the tilt of the room. Hayley smiled. He used to love the way she smiled at him. He leaned closer.

'Stop that,' she whispered.

How had his life got to this point? When had he gone down the wrong turn? He blinked hard. Tears sprang forward. Hayley opened her mouth as if to speak, but closed it again. She took the pint glass from his hand and placed it on the table. It hadn't been cleared in a while and looked like a party had been held.

'You know the last thing we did was argue.' A tear slipped down his cheek unchecked.

'That morning?'

'I don't even remember us breaking up, Hayley. Can you believe that? Time is a blur. It's supposed to be linlear, limlear . . .'

'Linear.'

'Yeah, that. It's supposed to be that. But it's not, you know. It swirls and bends and sweeps around, so you find yourself lost in the middle, not sure where you are or what the hell is happening next.'

Hayley gave a quiet sigh. 'A good night's sleep will sort your world out, Dom. It's been a tough day. But you can get through this.'

More tears fell. 'I don't even remember what we argued about, but I was so angry.' He scratched his cheek as confusion swept across his face. 'Where were you after it happened?'

34

'The argument won't have been important, Dom. I'm sure you made up during the day.'

He shook his head. 'You're not listening. When I got home from work that night. It was the last time I saw her.' The pint glasses were piled on the table and he couldn't figure out if any of them were his. 'That bastard took her from me.' He jumped up.

Krish leaned forward. 'You going to be okay tonight, Dom?'

'What, in my empty house, without Ruth?' Dominic slurred.

'We should probably get him a taxi,' said Paul.

The group gathered their jackets. Dominic waved a hand in the air and strode away from the table to the door.

Hayley grabbed her bag. 'Finish your drinks. I'll stand with him a minute, and then we'll get him in a taxi home.' She ran after him.

* * *

The temperature had dropped outside. It hit Dominic like a cold winter wind. His head buzzed and the pavement tried to rush up to meet him, but with his hand on one of the external pub columns, he maintained stability.

'Hanging in there?' Hayley materialised at his side.

Dominic attempted to focus on her, but there was a blur where she should have been. 'You never answered.' He had a minute. The guys were still inside.

Hayley stilled herself. Or as still as anything was around him right now.

'I miss you.' He pushed off against the wall, which caused Hayley to hold on to his arm a little tighter.

Her lips thinned. She looked back to the pub door. Dominic leaned in. Hayley had been a good thing. That familiar smell flooded his senses, her skin against his, her laugh in his ear. If he needed anything tonight, it was that.

'What are you doing?' Hayley leaned back. 'Dom. Don't.' Her voice was soft. 'You're grieving. This isn't what you want, and I've moved on. We were over a long time ago.'

A car blared its horn; a crowd jeered.

Dominic stiffened, suddenly a little more sober than he was a minute ago. He grabbed Hayley's hand. 'We were good together, Hayley. You know that.'

Hayley pulled back, freeing her hand. 'Dom.' Still quiet, not drawing attention to them.

Dominic glared at her. 'What the fuck?' He lurched forward and grabbed Hayley by her elbow. 'You practically promised this all night,' he hissed.

'Hey,' Krish shouted just behind them. His tone was light, but had a slight edge to it. 'Any sign of that taxi yet?'

Dominic dropped Hayley's arm, spun to face the guys, stumbled a couple of steps before righting himself. 'I think the taxi rank is down there, if I remember rightly, but it's been a while since I've been out on the lash.'

Paul stepped in between Hayley and Dominic, and wrapped an arm around Dominic's shoulders. 'Let's get you home, then.'

CHAPTER 6

Claudia

A headache was brewing behind Claudia's eyes as she stepped into the slippery Tyvek suit. At 12.35 a.m., Bingham Park was luckily empty other than the hive of activity created by officers and staff. The view across the lawns was concealed by the dark of night, the air of which was bitter as it blew the final hurrah of winter. Claudia's papery suit slid over her thick knitted jumper. There was no point wearing a suit to an outdoor crime scene at this time of the morning, and her usual warm winter coat wouldn't fit under the crime scene coveralls.

Claudia dug a thumb deep into her brow, trying to push the dull ache away. She wasn't sure how much sleep she'd managed over the last few weeks as the trial had run, and now she'd been called out in the middle of the night.

The headache was a reaction to a combination of sleep deprivation and the verdict, she was sure. She'd have it for the day, at least.

Claudia pulled the white hood over her head and strode towards the crime scene tape.

'Boss?' Krish was on a bench beside a rough sleeper who was likely to be their informant, if the telephone briefing had been correct.

Claudia inclined her head. She didn't want to be here tonight, and she wasn't up to answering the same question from everyone she came across.

The rough sleeper wrapped his arms around himself. It really was biting out here, and his coat was more of a padded shirt, with holes where the wadding was falling out. Sleeves of a dark-coloured jumper under the shirt were pulled down over his hands, further holes fraying the knit with strands of wool wafting around the tips of his fingers.

Someone should get him something hot to eat and drink while they took his statement. In a warm place inside. And maybe, for his trouble tonight, find him a couple of jumpers that weren't in such need of repair. She'd mention this to Krish, if he didn't do it himself anyway. Her team were a thoughtful bunch; she trusted the informant would be treated well.

Claudia continued towards the tape, crime scene tent and lights. She presented her warrant card to the uniform guarding the scene and manning the log, then she ducked under the tape.

It was times like this she missed her right hand, Russ Kane, who was currently on sick leave. She was used to walking into a crime scene with him. For all her desire to have him by her side tonight, there was still an unanswered message on her phone that he'd sent that afternoon, asking how she was. A question she had no answer to.

Claudia stepped inside the tent. It was like walking from night into day. The space was brightly lit by the high-wattage scene lamps. Claudia blinked to adjust to the change.

In front of her was another park bench. To one side, a suited-up CSI was photographing the scene, while two unidentifiable people in Tyvek suits had their backs to her as they worked. They blocked Claudia's view of the bench and the body that lay across it. The CSI lifted a hand in silent greeting. The two unidentified figures turned.

'Claudia.' It was Nadira Azim, the Home Office forensic pathologist, her voice gentle. 'How are you?'

This was the thing about the trial, facing people, answering their questions, and living through it all time and time and time again. Ruth's murder was like a shard of glass lodged under her ribs that she couldn't remove, but that others, however unintentional or even out of kindness, could prod and poke and dislodge, causing a recurrence of pain that she could do nothing to prevent.

'Boss?' The other white-coated body was Lisa James, another DC on her team. 'We weren't expecting you in until the morning. We thought you had the full day off after . . .'

Claudia could see Lisa's mind scrambling for the words, even as she hadn't responded to Nadira yet.

Lisa jumped in with both feet. 'After the trial.'

Opting for straightforward, Claudia noted. The best option. She liked this about Lisa.

Claudia shrugged, the suit crinkling in her ears from around her shoulders. 'I was supposed to be on leave until morning, but someone obviously forgot to take me off the on-call rota. As they'd already woken me up, I decided I may as well turn out. What do we have?'

A look passed between the two professionals as they parted to let her through. They'd noted her lack of response to the question about her welfare.

But how could she answer a question like that, so soon after the verdict, when she was still processing? Better to focus on the job at hand.

Laid out across the length of the bench was a young woman. Claudia tipped her head to the side to get a better look at her face. More of a teenager, actually. The quick telephone briefing she'd received had suggested a possible identification. At first glance, this appeared to be a run-of-the-mill murder, but as Claudia's team were the Complex Crimes Task Force, there would be more to it. Indeed, she'd been told that the identity of the girl's parents likely made this case high profile.

Lisa spoke. 'A rough sleeper entered the park looking for somewhere to spend the night. Instead of somewhere to rest, he got himself a shock when he found the victim. He had no phone to raise the alarm, but luckily for him, there was a guy out for a late jog. Fight with the missus or something.'

'A night for arguments,' said Claudia.

'So it would seem,' Lisa agreed. 'The jogger wasn't close, though. Our witness saw his headlamp bobbing some distance away and figured as he himself used to be a fit guy, he'd easily catch him up and ask him to call it in. Unfortunately for our witness, he's not as fit as he used to be. Life on the streets has had its effects, as he found out.'

Lisa winced a little. 'When Bird, the rough sleeper, finally caught up with the jogger, mostly by screeching for him to stop, he threw up at his feet before he could say he needed the police.'

'Jesus. I'm surprised the jogger stayed around.'

'He was jumpy when officers spoke to him. Said he was spooked by the shrieking man, as he put it.'

Claudia shook her head. It wasn't that the witness was shouting; it was the way he presented and the way he smelled that spooked the jogger. People were judgemental. 'He's been nowhere near the crime scene?'

'He says not. He moved away from the puddle of vomit a little and called three nines. Uniform were dispatched and attended, and the control room inspector pretty quickly matched up her description with that of a teenager reported missing a couple of hours earlier.' There was a brief pause, then Lisa went on. 'Has Dom been called out, too?' Her voice was quieter.

Claudia sighed. 'He has, but I spoke to him, told him not to come.' She wouldn't tell her staff that Dominic — she used her father's name when at work — was leathered. Grief-stricken from his loss and the trial, and was completely incapable of attending a crime scene. It was no one's business, no matter how well-intentioned. She moved the conversation back to the job at hand. 'I was informed this was something high profile. Who is she?'

Lisa looked to Nadira, then back at Claudia.

Claudia wished she would hurry up and make her big reveal. Her brain ached, like she was carrying a heavy stone that was far too large for her skull. The stone was being squeezed and it was agony. Claudia closed her eyes for a beat, breathed in, then out, and opened her eyes again.

Lisa was standing straighter. Her shoulders pushed back. As much as you can see shoulders pushed back in the sack of white paper they wore. 'We think it's Judge Verity Henthorn-Kimber's daughter.'

'Fuck.' Claudia looked around wildly, but they were contained in the tent. All she could see were the white shields of protection. 'Why the fuck did no one say when they woke me?' She waved an arm at the entryway of the tent. 'We need more uniform officers out there.'

'Boss?'

'When the judge hears her daughter might be here, the first thing she'll do is get in her car and come to the scene,' Nadira told Lisa quietly.

'That,' said Claudia. 'Jesus. What the fuck?' She ran her gloved hands over the hood of the protective suit. 'Okay, let's get to work.'

Nadira narrowed her eyes but remained silent.

'Lisa, tell the control room we need more uniform officers, please. Also make the request that no information be released to anyone at this time. I'll visit the family myself once we're done.'

Lisa gave a quick nod.

'Before you go, what do we know about the circumstances this girl went missing in? And what's her name?'

'Ivy Henthorn. Ivy has an older brother from the judge's first marriage, and they both go by their father's name. They have a younger sister fathered by the second husband. The judge reported Ivy missing just after ten thirty p.m. last night. She stated that the children were at home after school, and only the youngest saw Ivy leave. Everything seemed fine, and Ivy wouldn't tell her sister where she was going. Ivy should have been home for nine thirty, but didn't arrive. This is unusual.

The judge tried her phone but it went straight to voicemail. She gave Ivy another hour and then called us.'

'Did they know what she was wearing?' The child in front of them was wrapped up for the weather in ripped jeans, brown ankle boots, a cream jumper way outside Claudia's price range and an orange knitted scarf around her neck.

Lisa checked her folder. 'As far as I can see from the misper report, Jasmine remembered the orange scarf. Only because she coveted it so much. Officers described the judge as calm through a force of effort and allowing them to do their job. But she probably wouldn't be averse to pulling strings if she feels enough isn't done to find her daughter. Ivy is sixteen, five foot five and attends Wellington-Bell.'

'Of course she does.' Claudia looked down at the teenager again. 'Thanks, Lisa. If you can make that call, please, that'd be great.'

Lisa stepped out of the tent.

'She's posed,' Claudia said.

The girl that was likely to be Judge Verity Henthorn-Kimber's sixteen-year-old daughter was laid straight along the bench. Her arms crossed over her chest. Her long dark hair hung down towards the ground through the gaps in the slats of the bench.

'I agree. It's as though whoever killed her was sorry for their action. They took care of her in death.' As Nadira spoke, she removed a small paper bag, a roll of tape and scissors from her medical bag and proceeded to attach a bag to each of the victim's hands to preserve evidence on the journey to the mortuary.

'You think it was an accident?'

Nadira continued working. 'I can't determine exactly what played out here, particularly not from an examination at the scene. There is a blunt force trauma injury on her left temple, and a scrape on her knee, but there doesn't appear to be any defensive wounds. We'll know more when we examine her fully.'

'You think she knew her killer?'

Nadira sat back on her haunches. 'That's for you to determine, Claudia. I can only give you the facts this young girl's body offers me. You piece that together with the rest of her life, and I imagine you'll have your answer.'

Nadira was right, but Claudia had walked into this scene with a pounding headache, and she had a feeling this case would make damn sure it never let up.

CHAPTER 7

Theo

The glow from his phone was the only light in Theo's room. Darkness clouded the furthest corners, like the vignetting of photographs.

He'd kept out of the way since his mother cornered him earlier, but now his ears pricked as the doorbell chimed and his mother's voice rose in response.

The skin rippled as the hairs raced up his arms.

He'd keep his head down.

It was late, but no one cared what he was doing. They never did, as long as his sisters were okay.

It was all about them.

His top lip curled.

Theo was aware of the symmetry of his face. How attractive he was, and how the girls in his class loved his looks. Even when he snarled, they came flooding to him. It was like he could do no wrong.

Little did they know.

Theo returned his focus to his phone. He was so close to getting the girl to send him a naked selfie, but all she wanted to talk about was his damned sister. That was the last person

44

he wanted to talk about. Everyone loved Ivy; why would he join the fan club? She didn't need any more admirers. But this girl, she wanted to know if they'd had any news. When had he last seen her? How upset he must be . . .

Yes! Yes, he was so *upset*. He needed comforting. He needed comforting so badly. Only she could comfort him. And if she comforted him, he promised never to share the image with anyone. She was beautiful, and it would take his mind off everything that was happening.

Okay, she told him, *give me a minute*.

Theo's interest flicked elsewhere once she confirmed she'd send a photograph. It was more about the chase. About his ability to get girls to do as he wanted. Ivy told him he could charm birds from the trees.

There was a knock and Theo glared at the closed door, pulling the mobile to his chest.

His stepfather, Owen, poked his head in and cleared his throat. Theo rolled his eyes.

'Theo, the police are here. They have news. Your mother has asked that you join us.'

Theo's stomach twisted. 'Do I have to be there?'

Owen stepped into the room fully. The light from the landing created a column of soft yellow on the carpet. 'Theo, I'm afraid it doesn't look good. Your mother needs you.'

He actually wrung his hands. Theo had never seen this. He'd heard the phrase, but had never seen the reality of someone nervous enough to do it.

His phone vibrated against his chest.

The photograph.

It doesn't look good. The words bounced in his head. He didn't want to go downstairs. He wanted to stay up here in the dark. In his room.

'Theo?'

'Yeah?'

'Your mother.' Owen cleared his throat again. 'I don't think we should leave her alone. She needs you. You're old enough to be there. Theo, please. For your mother.'

The police were waiting downstairs, and his mother wanted him. Theo wanted nothing more than to stay where he was.

The phone vibrated again. She'd want a response.

Theo slid off the bed, bare feet landing on thick pile carpet. 'Okay.'

'You'll leave your phone here?' Owen indicated his hand.

Theo threw his mobile on the bed and followed Owen out into the light and down the stairs.

His mother was sitting on one of the sofas. There was nothing natural about her posture. Her body was rigid. Her hands clamped between her legs, she was tight up against the arm of the sofa, as though there was no space for her.

Owen went and sat beside her, pulled a hand from between her thighs and held on to it. He squeezed in reassurance, but his own body had turned taut.

Theo had never seen either of them like this before.

Two other people were in the room. Two women. A blonde and a brunette. They were casually dressed. The blonde in jeans and a jumper and the brunette in trousers and a jumper. Not what he expected from police officers, if that's who they were. Owen hadn't actually expanded on their way downstairs, but it was the only explanation.

Owen whispered to his mother and she looked over to him. 'Theo . . .' Her voice was soft and it almost broke on the one word. Her face — no, it was her eyes. They appeared sunken, darker, like she was turning into a skeleton in the space of only a few hours. 'Come and sit.'

There was an unusual stillness about the room, considering how many people were present. Waiting for the guillotine to drop.

A hollowed-out, bitter chill seemed to open up deep in Theo's stomach and he couldn't move.

The brunette rose from where she was sitting and led him to the side of Owen. For once, he wanted to stay by the side of his mother, but she clung to the arm of the sofa.

Theo, though eighteen and considering himself an adult, was truly out of his depth in this room. A room he was intimately familiar with — yet at this moment, it was as though he'd never been here before. He looked to his mother for answers. Her hands were clamped tightly between her legs once again. Theo mirrored her. His shoulders ached as the tension rippled through him, but he forced himself to keep still and focused.

The blonde broke the stillness, her voice like a fire-cracker in the soft cream sitting room. She was perched on the edge of the chair, her elbows balancing on her knees and her attention trained on his mother. The hollow ice cavity that had opened up in his stomach a moment ago widened and grabbed hold of his spine. The room closed in on him.

'. . . we believe she is your daughter, Ivy. I'm sorry.'

High-pitched wailing. He'd missed most of what the blonde had said. But that *wailing*.

Theo wanted to cover his ears with his hands like when he was younger and Jasmine had been born. He'd hated the sound of a baby crying. He'd bitched about her to his mother daily. She'd soothed him while at the same time soothing Jasmine.

But this wailing. It was so much worse.

Owen had his arms around her. Her face was mostly hidden by Owen's shoulders, but what Theo could see was contorted and red and her eyes were wild.

If she were an animal, she'd be shot. Put out of her misery.

The brunette walked past him with a tray of cups of something steaming. When had she left to do that?

China clinked. Owen patted his knee.

Theo couldn't track time properly. His hands were still clamped between his knees, but his mother's were now holding her head. The facade she always portrayed of calm, of being in control, was gone.

The blonde was still talking: '. . . identification. In your own time.'

Would anyone notice if he walked out and went to his own room, where he could . . . what? Text that girl back? He couldn't even remember her name.

But he didn't want to talk to her. He didn't want to see some stupid photograph she'd sent him. What an idiot she was for sending it in the first place. At eighteen, wasn't she old enough to know better? Hadn't her friends taught her anything?

He wanted his mother. But she was gone. Theo had never seen her like this. His mother, the judge, the woman the neighbours aspired to be and who they looked up to, who they wanted to be friends with. His mother was composed and immaculate in all circumstances, even when clothed in joggers and a T-shirt. Yet now, she was breaking into pieces in front of his eyes. It was terrifying.

Owen, the slimy little weasel, held on to her like she was a Ming vase, with tender hands, but a steel determination that he would not let go, for fear she might slip from his fingers. The muscles in his shoulders were taut under his long-sleeved T-shirt. It was pathetic to watch him cling to his mother. Where was Owen's emotion?

The wailing had stopped, but it had been replaced by a silent, but no less horrifying, sobbing.

Theo hadn't moved. His hands were still clamped between his thighs. How desperately he wanted to escape the room. 'Can I go?' His voice sounded weak, even to his own ears. A little boy asking permission.

'I'm sorry,' said the brunette to him. 'If you could stay and run through tonight's timeline, it'd be really helpful.'

He didn't want to help with the timeline. He wanted to flee this room and everything it represented. The icy chill had encompassed his spine, his insides hollowed out.

A slight squeeze of his knee and Theo opened his eyes, unaware he'd closed them. It was his mother. She'd reached across Owen and was touching him. Something deep inside her reached to him.

Theo flinched. His knee jerking spasmodically.

His mother's eyes widened and she withdrew her hand, only for it to be grasped by Owen immediately.

'We'd like to ask you all some questions, if we can?' the blonde said. 'The timing isn't easy, we understand. But the more we know and the sooner we know it, the better the chance we have of finding out what happened.'

His mother nodded.

'Owen,' said the blonde, piercing him with a look, 'you made the call to police when Ivy didn't return home.'

The brunette retrieved from her bag a small black hardback notebook that opened vertically rather than horizontally, her pen poised for note-taking.

Owen cleared his throat before speaking this time. 'Yes. Verity thought it better she search Ivy's room for any evidence of where she might have gone. She asked that I make the call.'

The brunette made a quick scribbled note.

'What time did she leave the house?'

That frigid feeling reached the base of Theo's skull. All thought seized up.

His mother shook her head. Tears slipped freely into her lap. 'I'm her mother. I should know. But Owen and I were both still at work. The three children were home together.' She waved a hand absently. The free one that Owen wasn't clinging to.

Owen had shed no tears, Theo noticed. Owen was probably grateful it was Ivy and not his own real daughter who was laid on a—

'But they're not really children, are they?' his mother continued. 'Not Theo or Ivy . . .'

The blonde handed her more tissues. His mother accepted them.

She was his mother. She was a judge. How was it that she looked this fragile?

'Jasmine is sleeping.' Her speech was broken and stilted as if the words were glass over her tongue. But the two officers waited and they listened. 'We talked to her earlier. She's only seven so she was in bed with a book by seven. It's hard to get her to put the book down and go to sleep.'

His mother wiped her nose. It was pitiful.

'Jasmine heard Ivy going downstairs. A friend had been in the house earlier but Ivy was alone then. Jasmine went to ask what she was doing. She saw Ivy was dressed to go out and wanted to know where.'

His mother gave that small smile that all mother's do when they're proud of a child. Not that he ever received it.

'You know what kids that age are like, so inquisitive, so many questions. We get frustrated by them all, but it's the only way they learn.'

'And what did Ivy say?' the blonde asked, pushing his mother forward.

She looked startled, like a rabbit in headlights. 'Oh, yes.' She wiped her face again. 'Ivy refused to tell her. She told Jasmine she had something to do and to go back to bed. It was time to turn her light off. She gave her a hug and, in Jasmine's words, skipped downstairs.'

The blonde focused in on him now. 'And Theo? Did you see your sister leave?'

The question wasn't accusatory like his mother's had been. It was soft, encouraging.

Theo shook his head.

His mother sighed and the sobs began again.

'Theo was in his room with his music turned up and didn't hear Ivy leave,' said Owen. 'So, it was any time between Jasmine going to bed at seven and Verity getting home at eight forty-five, because Jasmine has no idea what time it was, or how long she'd been reading, she was so engrossed in her latest book.'

The blonde hadn't taken her eyes off him. 'Ivy didn't tell you she was going out or where she was going to?'

Theo shook his head, which was already spinning and foggy all at the same time. He desperately wanted to leave.

'Just a few more questions, Theo. You never heard the door? It would really help if we had some kind of timeframe to work to.'

'Question' wasn't the right word. To Theo, this felt more like an interrogation.

'I'm sorry.' Theo couldn't sit still any longer. Ivy was dead. These conversations wouldn't change that. A time-frame wouldn't change that. He leapt to his feet and fled up the stairs before anyone could stop him.

CHAPTER 8

Claudia

After catching a brief four hours' sleep, Claudia was in back the incident room.

She wasn't sure it had been a good idea to go home. Her head was fuzzy and still pounding. It would be a day of ignoring the deep ache and just getting through it. And in thinking of the deep ache, Claudia remembered the therapy appointment with Robert later.

Quickly she tapped out a text cancelling. They had a job; she'd rearrange when she could. She hadn't wanted to disturb his morning with a call. Though if she were sitting in front of Robert, being challenged into honesty, she'd say she was using text messaging as avoidance.

She wasn't in front of Robert, though, and she had a high-profile case to focus on.

DC Graham Dunne walked in with a tray loaded with steaming mugs for all. As an ex-soldier, Graham was more than happy to dig in and make a brew when the team needed it. He was greeted with grateful thanks by his colleagues, who surrounded him like seagulls around a few dropped chips. They'd all returned home for a nap in the early hours, agreeing to the quick turnaround so they could crack on with the investigation. It was in these first few days that the most evidence would be captured, and you couldn't call anyone on this team a slacker.

Claudia had never been so happy for a mug of tea.

For what felt like the hundredth time, Claudia kneaded at her head, but it offered no relief. There was something about the act of trying, though.

'Headache, boss?' Lisa had caught her.

'Afraid so.'

'Paracetamol?'

'Ooh, yes please. I didn't have any in.'

Lisa rummaged in her bag and handed a plastic strip to Claudia who snapped two pills out and downed them with her tea. She held the strip out to Lisa, who waved a hand her way.

'Keep them. You might need them later.'

Claudia thanked her, pushed the strip into her pocket and grabbed a free chair. 'Okay, guys, let's get to it, shall we?'

Conversations stopped and phones were lowered. Dominic, she noted hadn't been involved in either a conversation or engaged on his mobile. He was slumped in the chair, pretty rumpled.

She'd try to have a quiet word with him and see how he was. It could be that he needed some time off. The trial had probably brought up a huge amount of emotion for him, just like it had done for her, and as usual, he'd be pretending all was well. He was not one to be honest about his feelings. Putting on a brave front for his colleagues, when the reality was he needed to recover at home with some peace and solitude. Time on the sofa with a good book or two, or a good box set, had never hurt anyone. Not that Dominic ever really seemed to get caught up in pop culture. That had been Ruth's thing. She'd dragged him into the twenty-first century; since her death he'd simply let all that go.

And with Ruth on her mind, Claudia needed to acknowledge the elephant in the room before they could get down to the morning briefing. Her father's daughter, she would have preferred to sweep the subject under the carpet, but her team cared and wanted to know she was okay. Better to set their minds at rest. That way, there would be less speculation and more work.

She closed her eyes and took a deep breath in, then out. 'Okay, let's talk about yesterday first.'

Her father crossed his arms and tucked his chin into his chest. The rest of the room was still.

'As I'm sure you're all aware by now, Samuel Tyler was found guilty on all counts, including Ruth.' Claudia's throat thickened. She picked up her tea and sipped at it.

The room waited. Her father's shoulders were hunched right up to his ears, jaw clenched and gaze fixed at the floor. She'd get this over with quickly.

'Obviously we still have the sentencing to go, but it was a big day yesterday. One we . . .' Her throat was really letting her down. She swallowed more tea and licked her lips. 'Me and Dominic . . .'

It was like there was a desert in her throat. Everything had dried up. Speech was becoming impossible. Her body was fighting against her.

'And the families of the other victims, we . . . it was a good day.' She couldn't say anything else. With a croak, she told the expectant faces she was okay and grateful for their support, then slugged back the rest of the tea.

'Now to the briefing.' She was glad to be back on solid ground. 'Thanks for turning out last night and through the early hours. Being on call isn't easy, but let's go through what we have, shall we?'

There was a visible relaxation as the team shifted in their chairs and made themselves comfortable.

'Ivy Henthorn, sixteen years, of Stumperlowe Crescent Road, was found by a rough sleeper on a bench in Bingham Park. Her family say there are no underlying health conditions. We'll need that confirming with her doctor. A blunt force trauma injury was visible on her head, and the position she was in when found appeared posed, which means we're treating this as a homicide until we know otherwise. Alek Sawicki has been allocated as the family liaison officer. He's been briefed and is with the family.'

'He's one of the best,' said Graham. 'He can handle a high-profile job like this.'

'Good to know.' Claudia scanned through handwritten notes in her Major Incident Notebook resting in her lap. 'Ivy's is a Cat A due to the potential for media intrusion, so it falls under the umbrella of Operation Symmetry.'

'Another random name pops out the hat,' mumbled Krish.

Claudia continued. 'A media release has gone out disclosing that the body of a young woman was found in Bingham Park, late on Monday, and police are treating it as suspicious. It won't be long before Ivy is publicly identified, so be alert.'

'We'll give them more?' asked Lisa.

'Yes. After the PM. Let's get through this briefing before we worry about how the media are going to portray us.' She placed the mug on the desk beside her. 'Ivy was laid out neatly and posed with her arms crossed over her chest, suggesting whoever killed her was remorseful. The post-mortem is scheduled for later today.'

'The killer being sorry . . .' Rhys waved a hand around in the air as if the words he wanted would suddenly be within his grasp. 'That mean Ivy knew them?'

'Let's not jump the gun. It may simply be that our killer is repentant.'

'How sweet of him.' Rhys's tone was the complete opposite of sweet.

Claudia raised her eyebrows.

'Yeah, I know. Sorry, boss,' he said, with no irony at all.

Dominic still hadn't engaged or contributed. She couldn't catch his attention. 'Ivy's bedroom was searched and her laptop seized. It's been delivered to the digital forensics unit. We've asked for a rush job, but we all know how snowed under they are. They promise it's been prioritised.'

There were grumbles as the team understood what 'prioritised' meant in real terms. Claudia moved them on. 'This was called in by a rough sleeper. Krish, you have the details?'

Krish flipped his pocket notebook open, bright-eyed and alert, as though he hadn't worked through the night and had only a few hours' rest. 'Dean Bird. He said the park isn't his usual place to kip, but he'd had an argument with another unhoused person at his usual spot, and rather than make it something bigger than it need be, he'd stormed off. Bird said he'd wandered for a while, walking his anger and frustration off, while at the same time thinking about the best place to get his head down. It's difficult to go into areas that are already taken. Sometimes it's like invading someone's home; other places you're warmly welcomed.'

'It's like any section of society, boss,' added Graham. 'You get the good and the bad, the kind and generous, and the angry and unreasonable.'

Claudia shook her head. She'd been made homeless by the fire, but she had insurance, she had money, wages. She could afford to live elsewhere while her home was repaired and made liveable again. How a country could allow people to sink to such depths that they had no other choice but to sleep on a freezing park bench was beyond her. And on top of those troubles, they then had to figure out the unwritten rules and laws of the street — that had to be beyond miserable. A wave of disgust swept through her. How could they sit here so privileged while people struggled to that extent?

She gave herself a mental shake. She couldn't think about the injustice of it now. 'What did Dean see, Krish?'

Krish closed the notebook and tapped it against the edge of his desk.

It was here they walked the fine line between sympathy for the rough sleeper who had stumbled on the murder of a young girl, and suspicion that he was a possible suspect, and it wasn't an easy line to tread.

'He said it was dark and quiet. He talked quite emotionally about how it's still winter out there, and how people aren't about at that time of night when the temperature drops, not when they have warm houses to stay in. He was extremely apologetic he couldn't provide anything helpful.'

'Did he corroborate that the jogger didn't go near the body?'

'Yeah. He said the guy wouldn't go anywhere near him, particularly after he'd thrown up, never mind going near the poor girl on the bench.'

It didn't matter your circumstances. Having *stuff* didn't make you the better person.

'We've seized the clothes from both Dean and the jogger?'

'All sorted. I personally dealt with Dean.'

'You know he's our first port of call, the first person we're going to look at in relation to this.'

Krish had worked enough homicides. In questioning Dean and seizing his clothing, they were working the crime scene and wanted to know if he was attempting to create a reason for being there and for having his DNA on the victim. It was policing 101.

Krish ground his jaw, and a pulse flickered in the tension.

Claudia frowned, not wanting his compassion to cross the line into bias in favour of the homeless man. 'We'll follow procedure, Krish. It's all we can do.' He needed the push. 'Submit his clothes to forensics, including the swabs.'

'Yes,' Krish hissed.

Claudia ignored the attitude. There were times each one of them became attached, for whatever reason. 'It goes for both Dean and the jogger. What did he say about approaching the victim?'

Krish worked his jaw. Graham dropped his head. Lisa found something to do inside her desk drawer.

'Dean said he saw the girl and thought she was asleep, because he would, wouldn't he? It's what he was there for. So, he shook her shoulder gently, because he was going to offer his coat. It was cold out and she didn't look warm enough.' His face was like stone now.

Claudia never took her eyes off him. They had to get through this.

'It didn't take him long to realise, and he backed away.'

'So there should only be contact trace on Ivy's right shoulder, and if we find other evidence, he hasn't provided a reason for it. That's what we're saying?'

'Those are the facts.' It was a growl.

'Okay,' Claudia smoothed out her tone. They'd established Bird was being processed properly. But was he also being cared for humanely? 'We sorted out warm clothes for him?'

Krish's jaw relaxed. 'We'd normally have provided him with some clothes out of custody, but I asked a uniform to sit with him a while and I popped home and grabbed him a few items I was intending to give to charity.'

'Krish . . .'

'I was!'

'I take it we have a way of contacting him?'

'Yeah. After I obtained his first account, I took him to Framework so he has a roof over his head, and I'm picking him up to take his statement today.'

'Can you also sort out the jogger's statement while you're at it, please? And confirm his story with his partner about the argument and clarify the timings. What time he left home, etc. You know what we need.' Claudia was aware the name of the jogger hadn't stuck in her mind.

'Will do.'

'You found somewhere to take Dean in at such a late hour?' Lisa was impressed.

'Yeah, a friend of a friend helped out.'

'Okay.' Claudia was glad Krish had taken care of Bird, but was still a little concerned with how much he was personally connecting with a witness. They had no idea how Dean Bird fitted into the picture yet. 'The crime scene manager recovered a phone from Ivy at the scene, so that's being processed, along with the laptop, as high priority.'

'Not a robbery gone too far, then,' one of the civilian staff offered.

Rhys smiled. 'Goes towards my "she knew her killer" theory.'

Claudia pointed her pen at him. 'Where are we on CCTV?'

He raised his palms. 'None in the park.'

'Check with all taxi companies that employ dashcams. If any of them were in the Bingham Park area last night between the time her mother reported her missing and Bird found her, they might have something. That's our timeframe, until we know anything more from the post-mortem. If taxis were in the area, we want the footage.'

Dominic still hadn't engaged. 'Dominic, as the person with the most sleep last night, you can take Ivy's parents to do the official identification this morning.'

Now she had his attention. His eyes burned into hers, emanating rage, his fists clenching in his lap. If he didn't want to be here, then he really hadn't needed to come in. He was a stubborn old mule. But he was here, and she'd use her staff as she saw fit. With more sleep than his teammates, they'd appreciate him doing this task.

Claudia exhaled, then continued. 'I'll take the PM later with Graham, but first, I think we need to build up a victimology.

'Ivy Henthorn's mother is, as you're aware, Judge Verity Henthorn-Kimber. I'm sure many of you have been in her court through the years. She's what we call "firm but fair". Owen Kimber is her second husband and Ivy's stepdad. Ivy's older brother, Theo, was present last night when we informed the family of Ivy's death. Then there's the youngest sibling, Jasmine Henthorn-Kimber, who is the child of the judge and Owen.

'Ivy's father died not long after her birth. A drunk driver hit him as he walked over a pedestrian crossing. There was massive internal bleeding, and he didn't make it through the night.

'Ivy never got the chance to know her father. The judge brought the children up alone until Owen came on the scene. Owen set up and runs a charity that supports children dealing with grief with the aid of music. It was how he and the judge met.'

'Owen's unlikely to be the target,' said Lisa. 'But do we think this murder has anything to do with the judge? Killing Ivy to send a message to Judge Henthorn-Kimber?'

'It's a line of inquiry we need to open up. Talk to her judicial assistant, get a list of all the judge's cases over the last five years that resulted in a prison sentence or in a defendant losing access to their family. On top of that, I want to see all the threats she's received. There has to be at least a few.' Claudia paused and assessed the team. 'Investigating the judge will be a full-time job on its own. We'll be stretched thin as it is, not least because we'll still be one down.'

She needed to visit Russ and see how he was doing. The hit and run had caused serious damage, and not just to his body. When she'd dropped by previously, Claudia could see the pain in the lines of his face, the set of his jaw through the stubble he'd grown, even if he tried to hide it from her. With a new case in their laps, it would prove difficult to call in, but she'd make time for him. They'd been through so much together, and he'd always been there for her.

'Lisa and I tried to obtain as much information about Ivy as we could during our visit but, as we all know, hearing one of your children has been murdered is rarely conducive to the necessary follow-up questions. Even from someone as high up in the judicial system as the judge. Her husband was a little more coherent, and—'

'Because he's behind it?' Rhys broke in. 'Someone cared enough, or was sorry enough afterwards, to make Ivy comfortable. It could have been her stepfather. Did you get a measure of him?'

Claudia sipped on her tea again. Attempted to get her brain in order. It was a valid question from Rhys, and these briefings were all about the team coming together.

What wasn't valid was whoever had failed to remove her from the on-call rota last night. After the emotional day, the long night and only four hours' sleep, her brain was a complaining puddle of fuzz. Which was why she was particularly grateful for her team this morning.

Everyone's input was important and no idea, question or suggestion was too out there. Claudia encouraged them to think outside the box. Though considering a parent wasn't exactly outside the box. However, when the stepparent was married to a judge, it certainly became a more delicate issue to approach.

She cradled the mug, warmth seeping into her fingers. 'Lisa? What did you think?'

'He was definitely less emotional than her mother, and that was picked up on by Theo, the brother. We know grief manifests in varied ways. His lack of outward emotion doesn't mean he killed her or isn't heartbroken at her death. He might be attempting to be the tower of strength he thinks his family needs.' She shrugged.

Claudia thanked her. 'To start, let's get the phone and online work completed on all the family.'

Lisa made a note.

'As I was saying—'

'Sorry, boss.' Rhys was apologising for jumping in with his question about Owen.

Claudia waved a hand to indicate that it was fine. Though the briefings were for the team to work through what they had and to gather everyone's thoughts, it was usually a process of working around the room and giving each officer and staff member their own time to speak. To Claudia, his small outburst showed his enthusiasm for the inquiry.

'We managed to ask about Ivy after Theo left the room. As you can imagine, being a teenager himself, he was fraught and struggling to hold it together. We went over the timeline. Theo being in his room with his music on and not hearing Ivy leave. Jasmine being the one to see her go. Ivy refused to tell Jasmine where, and sent her back into her room. The judge has, begrudgingly, agreed to one of us speaking to Jasmine today, with a timeframe of ten minutes, to confirm the veracity of this.'

Claudia assessed the team. The task required sensitivity, bearing in mind the parents would have identified Ivy and emotions would be fraught. 'Krish, can you do that, please?'

'Yes, boss. Gentle and quiet she goes.'

With that organised, Claudia pressed on. 'According to Ivy's parents she was a grade A student and loved school. She had no trouble and was universally liked.'

A groan rumbled from somewhere in the room.

'I get it; it's not often true. Parents see nothing but good in their children. We know that. And this viewpoint is particularly intense after a child's death, and they double down after a brutal death. Therefore, we take what they say with a pinch of salt and we build our own picture of Ivy Henthorn.'

Claudia looked to Rhys. 'But what Owen did share, for which he received quite an annoyed glare from the judge, was that Ivy's grades dipped a little less than a year ago. The judge quickly jumped in to remind us of the truth of the matter: that Ivy had been a grade A student at the time of her death, and that she was a teenager with teenage hormones. It was natural her grades would fluctuate.'

'A grieving parent seeing the good in her murdered daughter and clinging on to that memory,' said Graham quietly.

'Exactly. So today we'll visit Ivy's school and see what her teachers and school friends have to say. One of her friends, Gabby Hunt, was at the house after school, we can ask her if Ivy was having any issues.'

'Ooh,' said Rhys. 'We're going to Wellington-Bell? You're sure they're going to let the riff-raff in, boss?'

'Well, I can't promise they'll let you in, but I'm a dead cert,' said Claudia, to good-natured laughter.

Wellington-Bell was a prestigious private school with a high rate of pupils securing places at Oxbridge. If you had the money, the influence, and the drive for your children, you sent them to Wellington-Bell. But influence was imperative. Wellington-Bell was elite, only educating 610 pupils at a time. There certainly would be no light relief while they were there.

Claudia jumped out the chair. 'Okay, everyone, we've got plenty to be getting on with.' She glanced at Dominic who was still downcast, apparently unreachable. 'Dom, can I have a quick word, please?'

She walked to her office without a backward glance. She was fully aware of how peeved he was that his daughter out-ranked him, but Claudia wanted promotion and Dominic didn't really try, which in her mind meant he wasn't that interested.

Today, though, all she wanted to do was offer her support. At work, these barriers existed and it did no good to anyone pretending they didn't. The thing with her father was that he'd always be there for her. No matter how annoyed he might be. She'd been in some dire scrapes during her service, and her father was always the first one to run to her aid. First and foremost, he was family.

Today, she would be that for him.

CHAPTER 9

Dominic

Dominic followed Claudia into her office, aware all eyes were on them.

People had treated him with kid gloves since Ruth's murder. Well, that wasn't entirely true; they'd treated him with kid gloves once they'd ruled him out of their inquiries and trained their focus elsewhere.

All he wanted was for this to be over. To go back to a life where he could be the man he was before this happened. Strong, wilful and living life to the fullest.

Now Tyler had been found guilty by a panel of his peers, Dominic hoped he was close to that finish line. The last step was for Tyler to be sentenced, and then it was done.

People wouldn't see him and immediately think of what he must be going through. In most situations, people had short memories. They expected grief to be over, or at least hidden from view, within a couple of weeks. A loss due to a violent crime like murder allowed a little more visible griev-ing time. But the fact that Dominic's colleagues worked the Tyler case, or were at least aware of the status of the Tyler case, meant they tiptoed around him.

'Close the door.' Claudia sat behind her desk.

As her father, Dominic could pick up on the nuances of her tone and her body language. Things she might want to hide from the team.

She was tired.

He slumped into the chair facing her. What on earth had possessed him to drink so much last night? He hadn't been that out of control since his twenties. And he was far too old for it now.

Coming into work had been a struggle, but he'd appear weak if he didn't.

'I have to check you're okay?' Claudia jumped in feet first.

It tasted like there was a dead rat's nest in his mouth, even after he'd brushed his teeth twice before leaving the house and stopped at the shop for peppermint chewing gum. His head was filled with cotton wool wrapped in barbed wire. and his stomach was behaving like someone was dangling him over a cliff by his ankles. And Claudia wanted to check he was okay?

'I'm fine. Why wouldn't I be?' That was a stupid question. He was asking for her to take a deeper look at him with a response like that.

'Oh, I don't know, maybe because your wife's killer was found guilty at court yesterday, and today you look like you crawled backwards out of a beer barrel after being locked inside it for the weekend and having to drink your way through it. You stink. You do know that, don't you?'

'Say what you mean.' He couldn't keep the hard edge from his words.

Claudia folded her hands together on her desk and leaned forward. 'I told you not to come to the crime scene last night because I thought you needed some time to process the verdict.' She wrinkled her nose. 'This is you processing?'

Dominic rose from the chair, his hackles twitching. 'We can't all be perfect, Claudia.' He hated arguing with her. She was all he had left, but she could push his buttons. Why the hell had she followed him into this job? If she'd done something else with her life, he'd have a *normal* father–daughter relationship with her. Whatever one of those looked like, it certainly didn't look like the one he had with her now. The one where they both had the same, or similar, strains and stresses. They both worked the dark side of life, and the dark side of life seeped into your own world.

It couldn't be helped that the darkness of the criminals they hunted would rub off on them. You saw the damage they inflicted. The victims and the families, all the trauma. You had to be made of stone for it not to seep into your mind. Particularly brutal images would flash up behind closed eyelids in the dark of night. During moments of intimacy.

Dominic and Claudia's most recent trauma, before the fire at her house, had been the bloodbath in the woods. Dominic had seriously thought he'd lost her then. And yet he still couldn't bring himself to take off the brittle armour he wore around her.

'Perfect?' Her voice was quiet, as though he'd asked her what type of tea she preferred. 'You think I'm perfect?' There was a facsimile of a laugh. More of a bark really. 'My home has been burned to the ground. My second DS had to fight for his life. I have to process my own actions in killing a man . . . and, on top of all that, I'm still grieving Ruth. As you are.'

If only she knew. He was so tired of this pretence. The energy it took to keep it all together. She was his daughter; surely she'd stand by him.

'Look,' she continued, 'I need you to take Ivy's parents to identify her, but you can't go like that. You have to clean yourself up first. Judge Henthorn-Kimber will not be impressed if you turn up in this state. Shower, change and pull yourself together before you meet them. The judge lost her daughter last night. I don't want to get it in the neck from Sharpe or Connelly on your behalf.'

Dominic stalked to the door, ready to do as his daughter had directed.

'Dad?' Her tone was so quiet he barely heard it, but he stopped nonetheless.

Claudia didn't like to call him *Dad* at work. Dominic stopped, his hand on the door handle. He turned to face her.

'What can I do for you?' Her eyes shone with the threat of tears.

'I'm fine, Claudia. I'm sorry I turned up for work like this. I did drink too much yesterday after the verdict.' He shrugged. 'Not the best way to deal with it, but it was my way.'

Claudia tried a smile. One corner of her mouth crinkling. 'We're nearly there, Dad. Then you can maybe live your life again?'

Dominic stared out the glass windows that made up Claudia's office. The incident room beyond a hive of activity, chatter and camaraderie. His hand still on the door handle. 'You don't think I live my life?'

'I think it's been on hold for a while. It's like you've been waiting for Tyler to be dealt with. Like he's a physical manifestation of everything stopping you moving forward.'

Claudia would never know how insightful she was.

'You're right. Things'll change when he's sentenced and he's gone and I don't have to hear his name again. The whole thing has been like a millstone around my neck.' He pushed the handle down and the door opened a crack. The sound of their colleagues slipping through into the space between them.

'Dad.'

He stopped again.

'Do you want some leave? Do you want to go home?' Her words were rushed, tumbling over each other in her haste to get them out before he could respond.

Dominic pushed the door closed again. Colleagues and friends shut out. The cloistered weight of his daughter's expectations taking over the room again.

He'd done his best in the months since Ruth's death, to be the person everyone expected him to be. They expected grief and loss, for him to retreat at the start, so that's what he gave them. They expected anger, drive to right wrongs; he'd done that too. They expected him to be the type of man to throw himself into his work; that's what he'd done. But now, as it was coming to a close . . . what did they expect now? What would he expect of a friend?

It was a ridiculous question, because very few people lost loved ones to murder. Illness, yes — but a violent crime? No.

Here was Claudia, offering him time away. Was that as his daughter or as his supervisor? He didn't know. And he didn't know the expected response.

What he did know was that once Tyler was sentenced, he would request a transfer to a different unit. It just wasn't a good fit, him and Claudia on the same team. Maybe he'd broach it with Sharpe.

'Dad?'

'No. I'm fine.' He'd finish what he started, and then he'd maybe take time away and come back a new man to a new team and start afresh. With a team who hadn't worked with him through all of this. 'I'll get cleaned up and I'll take the family to ID the victim.'

'Her name's Ivy Henthorn.'

'Yeah.' Dominic opened the door and walked away from Claudia. Once he moved out of the task force, their relationship would stand on better footing. Who cared that he was hiding who he really was? That would all be in the past. He was very nearly there. He could practically taste it.

Or that could be the rat's nest in his mouth.

CHAPTER 10

Showered and changed, Dominic met Ivy's parents at the mortuary on Watery Street.

He climbed from the car and saw the couple sitting, hands clasped together, in the waiting room, already ahead of him.

The shower had served to drain away some of the hangover from the previous night, but he'd seriously hammered the ale. Dominic popped a couple of mints in his mouth, scooped his hand up, breathed into it and sniffed.

He'd pass.

Sharpe, like Claudia, had suggested some days off. He should have taken them, but he'd been too stubborn. He didn't want to appear weak, like Tyler had broken him. What he wanted was to give the impression he was powering through.

Today though, there was not much powering through. Dominic was in the clutches of hell. His stomach was an acidic bath and his head an impenetrable rock.

He pushed his shoulders back and walked in to do the job he was tasked with.

Judge Verity Henthorn-Kimber had presided over a few of Dominic's trials in the past. It was peculiar to see and speak to her in such circumstances.

In court, she wore the large flapping gowns that added illusion to the size of any judge beneath. The wig she wore covered pinned-back, tidy hair.

Today the judge was a different person altogether. Gone was the Royal Warrant-appointed judicial professional; in her place was a grieving mother. Her shoulder-length hair was lank around her shoulders and her skin was pale and sallow. The judge's appearance told a story of weeks of grief, and it had only been a matter of hours.

Beside her, Owen Kimber hung in better. Back straight, clinging on to his wife for all he was worth.

Dominic introduced himself. 'I'm so sorry for your loss.' He hated the stock phrase. Families knew you'd said it to the last person and would say it again to the next. It lost its meaning in overuse.

'I want to see my daughter.' The judge struggled to her feet.

Owen supported her every movement.

'Follow me, and I'll take you to see her.' He gave a quick nod to Glen on the front desk and walked Ivy's parents to see their child in a way no parent ever should.

* * *

On the way out, Owen half supported, half carried the judge to their car, parked directly outside on the street. She was silent and her face was paper dry. Dominic steadily walked behind in case they struggled, but Owen capably had his wife. He gently pushed the door closed and turned to Dominic. 'You'll find the bastard who did this?'

'We have an excellent team on the investigation, Mr Kimber, I can tell you that. As I'm sure you're aware, the inquiry has been moved from the usual MIT to our task force, which deals with more complex crimes, so we're particularly equipped to work the case.'

Owen Kimber gave a curt nod, strode around to the driver's side, climbed in next to his wife and drove away.

There was no word of thanks. Not that Dominic expected it from people like him. People who thought they had power over others, though Kimber's perceived power only came from the woman he married. She was actually the powerful entity in their marriage.

Though Dominic could admit, these thoughts were probably running through his mind because he was still a little peeved by all the issues on the Cunningham case. The investigation that had rocked the entire team and still had Russ off work, healing from his injuries. Those with influence over others needed to wield the weight of that control carefully.

CHAPTER 11

Claudia

Claudia had left Lisa in the office to deal with the Judge Henthorn-Kimber angle.

Dominic had run home to shower and change, but not before putting in a call to the judge, who had refused to be collected and had stated she'd make her own way to the hospital and meet him there. Claudia just hoped she hadn't made the wrong decision in sending Dominic to do the identification.

Verity Henthorn-Kimber might be Ivy's grieving mother, but she was also one of the busiest circuit judges in the city, and you put her offside at your peril. Which was another reason her team had been given the job in the first place. Connelly wanted to be seen to be putting his best officers on Ivy's murder.

Could Dominic be classed as one of Connelly's best officers right now? Claudia wasn't sure. He'd refused to go home, instead saying work was the best place for him. Claudia had no way to argue with him because she was also there. So she'd at least made him promise to clean up properly before he attended the hospital and met with the judge.

Dominic had bristled. But she'd had no choice. They were being watched from all quarters. And this was something she was finding a regular occurrence in this department. They took high-profile or difficult-to-solve cases, and everyone wanted to know how they were doing. Claudia was wondering if she'd made the right decision agreeing to head this task force.

Now Claudia forced her mind on to the present. She, Graham and Rhys had been granted permission to enter through the secure gates of the Wellington-Bell grounds and were slowly winding their way through the tree-lined approach.

'How the other half live.' Rhys was driving steadily towards their destination. 'You certainly didn't get a view like this when you walked into my old school back in Wales. We walked from our brick estate into a brick-built two-storey comprehensive.'

The driveway opened up and before them stood the grand school that was Wellington-Bell.

Rhys blew a low whistle. 'No wonder the fees are so high. I bet the maintenance alone is extortionate.'

A magnificent huge red-brick Victorian building rose in front of them and winged out to the side before disappearing back.

Claudia climbed out the passenger seat and slammed her door shut. The sound echoed as Rhys and Graham both did the same.

'Now that's what I call a beautiful building,' said Graham.

From beneath a deep arch in the centre of the building, a wooden door opened and a small man leaning heavily on a cane headed towards them.

'Let's get this done,' Claudia said quietly. 'You both know what we're here for and what we need. Do not be put off by any pomp and circumstance.'

She strode to meet their greeting party of one, the footsteps of Graham and Rhys a comfort behind her. 'Mr Drysdale?'

'Yes, yes.' Mr Drysdale stopped. As she reached him, his upturned face told a thousand stories. She'd never looked down at a man before, but Drysdale was short, stooped and elderly, and he leaned so heavily on his stick Claudia thought it might actually bend and snap in two.

He'd told her on the phone that he was the personal assistant to the headteacher, Ms Daphne Price, and he would be the one to show her team around when they arrived. The school did not want the students to be any more distressed than they already were.

Claudia said, 'Thank you for agreeing to meet with us.'

Drysdale, keeping his hold tight on the stick, shuffled around it, causing Claudia to step out of his way, until he was facing the school again. 'It is a terrible business. We are all rather at sixes and sevens. Ivy Henthorn was such a lovely child.'

'We're sorry for your loss.'

He was already walking away from them. The grey sky overhead released a few spots of rain. A threat of a heavier downpour to come, maybe.

'Let us get inside before we are soaked through, shall we?' His pace didn't quicken. Rhys threw a look at Claudia and she shook her head to keep him quiet.

Inside, the entrance was like a vast cavern. To the side was a long desk that matched the building in its grandiosity, and behind the desk a woman with completely grey curly hair piled up on top of her head. What was this, pensioners' week?

'Can you sign in with Mrs Honeycutt, please?' Drysdale lifted his stick and waved it in the direction of the woman at the desk.

Claudia complied, with the team behind her.

'Terrible business about Ivy,' Mrs Honeycutt said, as she tapped their details into her top-of-the-range laptop. 'And poor Theo. The pair of them were so close, I worry about him now Ivy isn't here. How he'll handle his emotions.'

'Did you know them?' Claudia asked.

Mrs Honeycutt raised her eyebrows. 'Oh, my dear, I know all the children here. They have to go past me to get in and out of the building, so I know most of their habits. Who is see-ing whom, and behind whose back. It's very scandalous some months, you know. At the end of the day, they are teenagers.'

Claudia could well imagine. 'Would it be possible to have a chat with you after my discussion with Ms Price, Mrs Honeycutt, please?'

'Oh, dear, call me Margaret, and yes, I'll be here. Poor Ivy was a love. I'll do anything I can to help. Mr Drysdale won't mind covering for half an hour, if the desk gets busy, will you, dear?'

Mr Drysdale, going by his stiffened posture, looked very much like he would mind covering Mrs Honeycutt's desk, but told her no, he would be happy to do so while she spoke with the officers.

He turned his attention to Claudia. 'Now to Ms Price. Though I am not sure you need three police officers to interview her. It speaks a little of overkill, does it not?'

His grey eyes pierced Claudia.

'I'm sorry,' she said. 'I thought I'd made it clear on the phone. We need to speak to Ivy's teachers and the students who knew her. I brought extra staff along so we'd be out of your way as fast as possible.'

Mr Drysdale moved forward, his stick clicking on the hardwood floor, like a click of a tongue in admonishment. 'Very well, Mrs Honeycutt can sort that out. If you would follow me.' The sound trailed off as he moved away from her.

Claudia nodded to her team and Mrs Honeycutt, whose face crinkled in a warm smile, then she followed Mr Drysdale down the wide corridor further into the building.

'Have you been Ms Price's PA for long?' she asked, once she'd caught up with him.

'I have been here most of my life,' replied the stooped old man. 'My father was the groundskeeper many years ago, and for that, he was allowed to send his only child to the school without payment. In my gratitude, I applied for the personal assistant to the head of the school position when it arose, and I have been here ever since.'

'How many heads have you seen come through the school?' If it wasn't for his crooked posture, Claudia was sure she'd have seen a smile play at the corners of Drysdale's mouth. There was something in the way he spoke next.

'Ah. Wellington-Bell headteachers. That is a question.'

Their pace to Ms Price was slow going as Drysdale clacked his way forward.

'There have been many heads and many changes over the years. Each head wanting to make their mark on the school. Stamp their authority and leave a lasting change for future generations to remember them by.' He stopped and faced Claudia. 'But this is the first time we have had a student murdered, Detective Inspector Nunn.'

She noted he hadn't answered her question, but had left her with more questions. But there was no time to press him for answers now. They were standing in front of a thick wooden door, complete with a brass plaque bearing the words *Head of Wellington-Bell*. Claudia supposed if they didn't put a name on the plaque, it meant they didn't have to change it with every new head that arrived.

Instead of knocking, Drysdale pushed the door open and stepped into an anteroom. It was large and airy, with ceilings as high as the rest of the building. Bookshelves lined one wall, and under the tall narrow windows was a desk with the nameplate *Mr Drysdale*. A door to the right held a plaque with Ms Price's name on.

Ms Price must have heard the outer door, because she opened her own and invited Claudia in.

'I can't quite get my head around what we've been told this morning,' the headteacher said, as she walked across her office towards a comfortable seating area at one side of the room, with a low-slung dark-wood coffee table between them holding silverware, a silver tray with a silver milk jug, a silver sugar bowl, a small silver box and two silver cafetières.

Claudia followed her and they both sank into the thick navy sofas. It was as though she were being wrapped in the arms of a cloud; the cushions were that thick and soft. She surveyed Daphne Price, the head of Wellington-Bell for the past two and a half years. The woman wore a black suit that fitted her perfectly. It most definitely was not off the rack. Beneath the suit was a silk shirt in a dark raspberry, and she clutched a slender blue folder.

As Claudia assessed Daphne Price, the other woman took the measure of Claudia. There was nothing hostile about the act; it was more a professional assessment.

When she was finished, Daphne Price leaned forward and offered Claudia a drink. 'We have a choice of tea.' She placed the folder down and lifted the lid on the small silver box. Or we have coffee.' Price waved her hand at the two cafetières.

'I'll have an English breakfast, please.' Claudia shifted to the front of the sofa in the hope it would consume less of her and she'd be able to hold her own in a conversation. 'I'm sorry for your loss. It must be difficult.'

Price shook her head as she made the drinks. 'Twenty years ago, we could have informed the students in a calm and clear way, while at the same time supporting them.' A tiny polished spoon clinked against china. 'But now, in the age of the internet and social media and mobile phones — small computers in their pockets—' a small sigh, another shake of her head — 'there's no containing it. The kids, they hear about it before you do. Their bodies are assaulted by emotions they have no idea how to process, while the adults in their lives have no idea what they are viewing, or what they're consuming, raw and brutal, straight into their minds. Like this, a loss of someone they knew.'

The lines around the headteacher's eyes deepened. 'We've lost our control.'

It wasn't said with malice or with a desire to cling on to the power of old; it was something else. 'They thought reaching into their phones seemed like an easy way to absorb the news of the day. That is, until they *became* the story.'

This woman in front of her was devastated — not just about Ivy, but about the rest of her students and her powerlessness to protect them from the trauma of Ivy's murder. The internet and the mobile phone had erased her ability to guide how the murdered girl's friends were informed.

This was a head who cared; Claudia had been told that she'd already organised a therapist on site, available for as long as the students needed it.

Price handed Claudia a cup and saucer. Steam rose into the space between them. Claudia shifted even further forward so she could reach the milk jug, and tipped a little of the liquid into her cup, which tinkled in the saucer as she attempted to hold herself still in the marshmallow-like furniture.

'What can you tell me about Ivy Henthorn?' Claudia asked.

With precision, Daphne Price placed her drink on the silver tray and gently tapped the blue folder with her neatly polished forefinger. 'Her student profile is in here. Shall we have a look?'

CHAPTER 12

Claudia doubted that the headteacher really needed a folder to inform her of Ivy's academic progress.

She imagined that as soon as she was aware of Ivy's murder Ms Daphne Price was completely on top of the situation. This included Ivy's attendance, performance, friendship groups, friendship issues and any family problems the school may be aware of. It might even extend to threats sent to the school, for Ivy or her mother. Because ultimately, the parents of the children here were of some wealth and power.

Price would need to protect the school, while at the same time be seen to support the authorities in their investigation. Because, again, the murder victim had a very powerful parent of her own.

Yet here she was, drumming her highly manicured finger on an extremely slim folder.

'You knew Ivy personally?' Claudia asked.

Price scooped up the folder and laid it in her lap. 'I've interacted with all the students in the school, Detective Inspector. It doesn't mean I know them all on a personal level. I tend to know the highest achievers in each year group, and those who may be at risk of slipping below our standards.'

They obviously had standards. Claudia wouldn't ask what happened to those students who fell beneath them. Not unless Ivy was one of those students. 'And where did Ivy fall in the achievement standardiser?'

Price's lips thinned.

Claudia reminded herself she needed to play nice with these people, as it was the easiest way to gather the information they held and gain their trust and support. Otherwise, it would mean the school putting up roadblocks at every turn, and then a need for search warrants that would make the whole relationship with Wellington-Bell, students and parents included, acrimonious. And Price had shown herself to be nothing but kind, as well as upset at the cruel murder of one of her students.

'I'm sorry,' she amended, 'I didn't know the correct language for it. I just meant, where did Ivy's grades fall?'

Price inclined her head. 'Ivy was a naturally gifted student. She was . . .' Price paused and appeared to search for the word.

Claudia waited. It was better to leave the silence, should it arise, as the interviewee tended to fill the space naturally. If Claudia jumped in now, then Price could forget her line of thought and something significant could be lost.

Price narrowed her eyes as she opened the folder on her lap. She flipped through the pages in front of her.

Claudia picked up her drink, careful to remain as unobtrusive as possible. To leave the headteacher to untangle her thoughts. Just why, though, was the question about Ivy's grades and ability causing Price such a problem?

The tea had cooled slightly. Somehow, drinking it from the china cup and saucer provided a richer flavour experience. There was a depth and cleanness to the fluid Claudia never usually noticed. Maybe china crockery was the way to go. She would do without the saucer, though.

Price straightened her spine. 'Ivy had been a gifted child from her very first days at Wellington-Bell.'

There was a sense of pride emanating from the words. 'She was lively and full of fun. Ivy wanted to experience

80

the world around her in all its technicolour and glory. The rules of the school seemed too constricting for her spirit. There were run-ins with staff, but . . .' Price's voice was soft as she remembered her pupil. 'Regardless of the energy she put into her extracurricular activities, Ivy never failed to top the class with her grades. It all seemed too easy for her. She shone.'

The headteacher's eyes glistened.

'She sounds like a wonderful girl,' said Claudia, putting her drink down.

Price shook her head. 'You mistake the emotion, DI Nunn, for the loss of Ivy. My time to grieve will come, once I've taken care of the children left behind. But there was something else.'

Claudia's attention pricked. 'Something else?'

Price shifted in her seat. Her shoulders tight. It was clear that wriggling like a five-year-old was not the done thing, but her emotions were getting the better of her.

'A little under a year ago, maybe ten months, there was a sudden and unexpected change in Ivy. It was just after her sixteenth birthday.'

Claudia waited, a chill filling her stomach.

'The once bubbly and vibrant girl disappeared, and in her place was a quiet, almost mousey child.' Price dipped her head and looked into the folder open on her lap.

'Did Ivy tell anyone of problems she was having?' Claudia hoped for an easy answer.

Price studied her, sadness in her eyes. 'It was immediate and sudden. An overnight and emphatic transformation.' She tapped the folder thoughtfully.

But Claudia knew the headteacher didn't need reports or grades to inform her about the change in Ivy Henthorn. Both women recognised instinctively what had happened to cause such a dramatic transformation. It was a horror that still too many of them faced — and here, it seemed, had Ivy Henthorn. Her parentage hadn't been enough armour to protect her. At the end of the day, Henthorn or not, Ivy was a young woman, and to some of the male population in the world that was enough.

Price continued. 'Her grades slipped, but it was only for a brief time. It was enough of a concern that we discussed the issue with her parents.'

'Was Ivy present?' Had she spoken out, or stayed hidden as many did for fear of reprisal?

Price folded her hands neatly over the documents she held that Claudia believed said nothing of the real story, but was simply a list of grades and behaviour patterns. What Claudia needed was the girl behind the numbers.

'She was. Ivy was silent during the discussion between her parents and me. If she spoke, it was only in response to a direct question from her parents.'

'And did she see Mr Kimber as a parent?' The inquiry was so new, Claudia wasn't yet sure what they were dealing with. Her line of questioning was becoming tangled, rather than linear, so she pulled out her notebook and pen and scribbled down the information she had so far.

'As far as I could see. The family appeared warm whenever I saw them together at school events, and that included Ivy and her stepfather.'

'And the meeting?'

'As with these things, I informed the family of my concerns and asked if they were worried or if there was anything ongoing at home that the school could help Ivy with. Her parents agreed they'd noticed a change and thanked me for alerting them to her altered grades. They asked Ivy if there was something they could help her with. She became tearful, but refused to provide a response, instead telling us she was fine and would get her grades back on track. She said she would sort everything out.'

'And did she?'

Price turned her attention to the huge floor-to-ceiling window to the side of them. The seating had been arranged so both parties were able to take in the view.

The head's office overlooked a courtyard where barren trees waited for spring to breathe life into their long limbs again and wooden benches were planted into concrete for chattering children to fill their seats in the warmth of the sun.

Yet as spring crawled ever closer Claudia wondered how the pupils and staff at Wellington-Bell would feel whole again after such a tragedy.

'Her grades rose, as she'd promised.' The headteacher's attention came back into the room. 'Though her personality never returned to its once bubbly and a little over-the-top character. There was always a small piece of her missing.'

That chill in Claudia's stomach froze over and hardened. 'And you never found out why?' Her voice was deadly quiet. 'No.'

The room stilled. The faintest hiss came from a far corner of the room. Claudia narrowed her eyes to listen. Then slowly the scent of warm vanilla drifted through the air. She tapped the pen on the notebook.

She had to focus. 'And recently?'

'Ivy had been on a level. More like the girl of before, but like I said, there was always a little bit of her missing. Those of us who knew her long enough could see it. To anyone who met her after that change, they wouldn't notice. Her best friend Gabrielle Hunt, Gabby, she's devastated and hasn't come into school today. They were two peas in a pod.'

They'd wanted to talk to Gabby today. She'd obtain her address from Mrs Honeycutt on her way out.

'Gabby's mother, Charlotte, is also Judge Henthorn-Kimber's closest friend. This whole thing is a travesty and has broken the lives of so many.'

The British stiff upper lip had so far held, but the headteacher of the prestigious Wellington-Bell senior school, Ms Daphne Price, was not hiding her human side well, as tears trembled, her jaw tight with the effort of reining them in.

Claudia rose and held out her hand. 'Thank you—'

A sudden loud but muffled thud stopped Claudia in her tracks. A dark shadow had flashed across the corner of her vision. Both women spun to the window beside them. On the glass was an uneven, oval-shaped smear that elongated slightly at the bottom, stretching down. A small patch of blood and a couple of feathers told the story of what had happened.

Price shook her head and the tears that had threatened began to fall.

CHAPTER 13

Mrs Honeycutt was exactly where they'd left her. As Claudia approached, she offered a pleasant smile.

'There's no need for you to cover the desk, Mr Drysdale. I can cope quite well on my own.'

Mr Drysdale didn't need telling twice. He clicked off with his walking stick down the corridor, and into the depths of the old school.

Mrs Honeycutt waved a hand at Claudia. 'Pull one of those chairs over, won't you? I do hate people standing over me. I'm getting older now and the students here are told I won't respond unless they're sitting. There's a sense of power imbalance, you see, if one of you is standing and the other sitting.'

Mrs Honeycutt was wise, and Claudia pulled a chair from the side of the great hall to the front of the receptionist's desk. 'Thank you for agreeing to talk to me,' she said.

'Do you know how many hours I sit here?' The receptionist pushed a wispy strand of hair, which had become loose, behind her ear, before answering her own question. 'No, I don't suppose you do. Anyway, it's always nice to talk to someone new.' Her tone grew serious. 'Even in such circumstances.'

How many more years would Mrs Honeycutt stay here? Even with grey hair, she didn't have the appearance of ageing rapidly. Still, she was well past the age of retirement. Some people just loved their jobs and loved the people they worked with. Claudia was grateful to have someone like Mrs Honeycutt here, who claimed to be the fount of all knowledge as far as the students were concerned. She offered her condolences again.

'It's a life taken far too young,' said the old woman. 'So much life to have missed out on.' Real emotion and knowledge of what she spoke of shone from her eyes.

'It is,' Claudia agreed. 'You're in the perfect position here to know what the students are up to, day in and day out . . .' Better to tell the receptionist how good she was than remind her of her own words. It would ease the transition to interview. 'What can you tell me about Ivy and her world?'

There was a small square box of tissues on the huge desk that Claudia hadn't noticed earlier. Maybe they hadn't been there, but were now necessary. Mrs Honeycutt reached out a pale and softly creased hand to pull a couple out. She dabbed at her eyes.

'I don't mean to upset you,' said Claudia. The first days of a homicide inquiry were emotionally draining.

'Don't you worry about me,' Mrs Honeycutt said. 'It's these young people we need to care about.'

The steel inside Mrs Honeycutt swelled Claudia's own emotion from recent events, though she held it in check. 'I couldn't agree more. What can you tell me?'

'She was the sweetest child. Her and Gabby Hunt were thick as thieves, as the saying goes. When Ivy went through whatever it was, Gabby was glued to her side and would never leave her.'

'It sounds like Gabby's the kind of friend you need,' said Claudia.

'Indeed. Gabby has the passion of her mother in her blood.'

Two boys cautiously approached the desk, one with a slip of paper in his hand. They paused a few steps behind Claudia. Mrs Honeycutt waved them forward. 'Come on, what do you have?'

'A dental appointment, Mrs Honeycutt.'

Mrs Honeycutt took the 'authorised to be out of class' slip from the boy holding it.

Claudia looked at the both of them, standing together, side by side, and then did a double take. The boys grinned at her.

'Identical twins,' Mrs Honeycutt explained the obvious. 'Okay, off you go.' She shooed them away. 'I take it your mother is collecting the pair of you?'

'She's outside,' one of the two halves of the same coin said.

'Wow,' Claudia exclaimed once they'd walked away. 'I've never seen identical twins — not in person — and they seriously are identical. How do you know which one is which?'

The receptionist laughed. The sound was warm and melodious, like hand bells on a summer day. There was nothing about this woman that Claudia disliked. 'When you've worked with children as long as I have, you soon learn how to identify them. Taron and Keagan have such distinct mannerisms, it's quite easy to tell them apart.'

'I am in awe of your talents, Mrs Honeycutt.'

The receptionist smiled. It appeared this was her natural demeanour; Claudia was not surprised she was the adult in the school who was aware of the activities of the children. She was genuine, kind and open. 'You're too kind, Detective Inspector, but I'm not sure you listen. I asked you to call me Margaret.'

'You did indeed. I apologise. Please, call me Claudia.'

Mrs Honeycutt deserved the deference her full title provided her, and yet she offered up her first name for use. Claudia smiled and hoped that message was passed on in her expression.

The receptionist inclined her head.

'You mentioned Theo when we arrived,' said Claudia, moving on. 'You were worried about his emotions and how he'd cope. His sister has been murdered. He'd obviously be emotional. Was there something else that concerned you?'

Mrs Honeycutt clasped her hands together on the desk. This was the first time Claudia had seen any kind of visible anxiety in her.

'As you said, his sister has been murdered. What other response is expected from him?'

'Margaret?' Claudia lowered her voice.

The kind and generous receptionist suddenly wasn't meeting her eyes.

'Margaret, please? If you know something, you need to tell me. Any piece of information could prove helpful in Ivy's inquiry. No matter how small.' It was a repetitive phrase, but a true one.

Mrs Honeycutt shook her head like she was trying to shake the memory out, freeing a few grey curls from their clips. 'Oh, I should have kept my big mouth shut.'

'No. Not true. Knowledge of the family dynamics will help support them.'

'Theo is a lovely boy.'

'I understand.'

Mrs Honeycutt wrung her hands more. Claudia waited.

'It was about the same time as when Ivy's grades slipped and she became introverted. There was a huge change in Theo . . .' She looked around the grand hall, but there were no students waiting for her support. Classes were on. There were no teaching staff in need of her assistance. There was nowhere for her to turn other than to face Claudia and continue.

'Tell me about the change.'

She shook her head again. 'This is about Ivy. It's not about Theo.'

'Theo's not in trouble, if that helps. But he's a teenager who will be facing a tumult of emotions he has no idea what to do with. We need to know, between us, how to support him with that.'

Mrs Honeycutt finally nodded. 'Yes. Yes, we do. I can't tell you if it was related, but Theo, he was rageful. He'd fly off the handle for seemingly the smallest slight. It was only under threat of expulsion, after he got into a bit of a fracas with a boy in Ivy's year, that he brought himself under control. I'd often see him and Ivy huddled in a corner whispering. You could see by her face that she was scolding him, and he'd stand and take it with his shoulders slumped.' She smiled at the memory of her lost student. 'The rage left him, but he was forever changed. They both were.'

That was interesting. The siblings changed at the same time? 'In what way was Theo changed?'

Mrs Honeycutt finally looked her age. Her skin took on a greyed tone and appeared translucent, whereas earlier it had bloomed with colour and life. More curls escaped and framed her face.

'I'm sorry,' Claudia leaned forward, elbows on knees. 'You know the children. This must be difficult.'

Tears glossed, unfallen, over the receptionist's eyes. 'Such tragedy. They should never have to experience it at their age.'

This was true. For all the murders Claudia worked, those of children were some of the hardest. Not just for the loss of what lay ahead for them, but in seeing the grief of those left behind. It hit harder, dug in deeper, and scarred indelibly.

She trod gently over the topic of Ivy's brother. 'It sounds like Theo and Ivy were close. Whatever happened at that time, I'd really like to understand so we can help them both, and in turn Jasmine, who will grow up in a world without her sister, and with her older brother forever altered and her parents not quite the whole they once were.'

The tears spilled over. Mrs Honeycutt dabbed at them with a couple of fresh tissues from the box. 'They were close.' She dabbed again. 'Whatever happened that angered Theo, Ivy calmed him, but the rage left its mark. He withdrew into himself, and if he ever did join in with anything, there was a distance about him. Something had hurt him and hurt him badly.'

The sound of bells rang out clear but short. Claudia questioned the receptionist with a look.

Mrs Honeycutt pasted a smile on her face, all thought of the broken boy gone. 'It's lesson changeover. They only have five minutes and they have to be as polite and tidy about it as possible. This is not a break, and it won't take long.'

As soon as the words were out of her mouth, the dull but persistent footfall of students filing in pairs from one direction and across the reception area thrummed like a low drumbeat on the hardwood floors. Heads bent together to keep the inquisitive chatter inaudible. It took only a minute, and they were gone as if they'd never appeared. 'That's impressive,' said Claudia.

'They're good kids.'

Claudia turned to Mrs Honeycutt again. The colour had returned to her face and her eyes were dry. The distraction of lesson changeover had given her the moment she needed to recover herself. Claudia hoped Margaret Honeycutt had a family and a life outside Wellington-Bell. 'So it seems.'

Though, with no real leads as yet, the truth was, there may well be a killer among them.

CHAPTER 14

It was getting late, and Claudia and Graham hadn't yet eaten. She checked her watch. They had fifty minutes until the post-mortem. Time enough to grab a bite on the way there.

The press was all over Ivy's murder. It was inevitable, because of who her mother was. So now, as the media reported every step the task force took, the public would assess and hold opinions, regardless of their level of policing knowledge. These were the times they worked in now.

Decisions taken not only had to be explainable, but had to hold up to public scrutiny in a way they never had been before.

And the first decision, Claudia attending Ivy's post-mortem, would be deemed special treatment not given to the public, but due to Judge Henthorn-Kimber's personal connection to the murder. What people wouldn't know was that SIOs were usually present during homicide post-mortems. But for Claudia, it provided her a real insight for their investigation, right from the start.

The post-mortem not only potentially told a story about the killer, it also informed the inquiry about the victim and their life in a more detailed and intimate way that friends and family either couldn't, or didn't feel was significant. Because no matter how many times you asked loved ones not to censor themselves, and to provide every piece of information asked of them, they still withheld when they considered it irrelevant. And in a murder inquiry, nothing could be excluded.

With a tuna mayo roll stuffed down her throat in the car park, and a cheese and onion for Graham, they made their way into the low-slung red-brick building. She was likely to suffer later due to the speed she'd eaten. But on the first day of a homicide inquiry, hurried sandwiches were about all they could manage.

As they walked into the Watery Street mortuary, Claudia brushed off the breadcrumb evidence of her meal.

Glen, who always covered the front desk with a kind word, asked how her day was. She stopped a moment and inquired after his son.

A smile opened up his face. The sleepless nights were obviously taking no shine off the new addition. Claudia couldn't help but share his infectious delight.

She had to walk away before he pulled out his phone, which she imagined contained many hundreds of photographs of the infant. Much as she'd actually love to see them — to her surprise — stopping to eat had already put a kink in their timeline.

Graham chuckled to himself as they walked away.

'You can stop that.' Her growling tone couldn't belie her growing smile.

'What's that, I hear?' Graham raised a hand and cupped it to his ear. 'Is there a clock ticking in this corridor?'

'If you want a positive annual review, Detective Constable Dunne, I'd get your hearing checked.' The grin she still gave him was increasingly like that of a wolf with its prey in its sights.

Graham simply laughed louder.

Smithy, the morgue tech, and Nadira were already present when Claudia and Graham pushed through the plastic double doors into the examination room.

Ivy Henthorn was silent and still. It couldn't even be said that she was waiting. The Ivy Henthorn that people knew and loved was no longer present. The cadaver on the examination table was here to tell the story of Ivy's life and her death, so those very people who knew and loved her could, maybe, get some peace. Claudia understood how difficult that process was, but also how imperative.

In working with the dead, she had come to realise the necessity of stepping back from their victims and understanding the science of what the post-mortem did. This didn't mean Ivy Henthorn's body wouldn't be treated with the utmost respect. They all had loved ones, and their lives would end at some point, one way or another. Those in Nadira's care were respected as much in death as they were in life.

'Hey.' Smithy raised a gloved hand.

'Sorry we're late.' No need to expand with excuses. They were late; an apology was necessary.

Nadira waved it off. The pathologist was standing at the end of the table, at Ivy's feet. 'Don't worry. I know what your day's been like. We've made a start, but you haven't missed anything. The young lady has been weighed and measured. X-rays have been taken and reviewed. There's nothing out of the ordinary. No breaks, old or new.'

On the worktop were all the bags, containers and labels required to exhibit Ivy's life. Graham was here as the exhibits officer, one of the most responsible roles in a murder investigation.

Claudia removed a pair of small-sized blue nitrile gloves from the box marked 'small' and Graham pulled from the 'large' box. The boxes attached to the wall in a line with other boxes, all offering varying sizes of gloves so technicians and pathologists could work easily.

Nadira worked her way up the young woman, searching for any visible injury, bruises, cuts, scrapes, injection points, scars — including old surgical scars — as well as tattoos and birthmarks.

At sixteen, there shouldn't be tattoos, though it wouldn't be unheard of to find them. Teenagers were ingenious at getting the things they most desired.

Nadira worked methodically and narrated her task for the digital recording.

Ivy had been wearing ripped jeans when found, and there was a scrape on her right knee, which Nadira swabbed.

At her hands, Nadira removed the paper bags she'd attached to preserve evidence, and swabbed and took clippings. Blood stained the pads of Ivy's right-hand index and middle finger.

The assessment of her head took time. Nadira stepped back, allowing Smithy closer access for photographs. She pointed: 'Can you make sure you get it from this angle as well, please?'

Smithy stepped into position for the shot Nadira requested. Photographs done, Nadira swabbed the wound at Ivy's left temple. Blood had run from the injury and dried on her skin. There was a smear through the middle of it.

Her fingers.

Ivy had not died instantly.

The post-mortem continued. Everything was as you'd expect for a fit and healthy sixteen-year-old with no medical history to speak of.

Nadira removed her stomach. An important task that helped pin down time of death, if there were any issues with that, and could also place the victim at a location if the food or drink was specific enough.

With the stomach on a tray, Nadira expertly used her scalpel and emptied the contents into a transparent container.

She leaned closer over the container. 'Do you smell that?'

Claudia didn't move. 'Not from here.'

Though she'd managed to get her squeamishness over post-mortems pretty much squared away years ago, it didn't mean she was completely happy with all parts of it. The PM was a necessary step in the investigative process, and that was how she approached them. People were never really meant to see each other from the inside, though, and stomach contents — well, you couldn't get much more *inside* than that.

'Claudia,' Nadira's voice was soft, as it always was. 'Come closer.'

Soft it may have been, but what she'd said wasn't a question. Nadira was doing her job, and Claudia was here to do hers.

Claudia stepped into position beside Nadira.

'Can you smell it now?'

Claudia was holding her breath. Seriously? Nadira wanted her to breathe this disgusting mess in?

'Can't you smell it?'

She tried not to roll her eyes. Instead, she released her breath and inhaled with as much gentleness as she could muster.

'Now?' Nadira had watched her every move.

Claudia shook her head.

Graham marched up and took a big, audible sniff. 'Alcohol,' he said, happy with himself.

Jesus. Both he and Krish had a steel stomach.

'Exactly. Thank you, Graham.'

He stepped back with a sly smile.

'So our A-grade student was drinking right before her death?'

'She was definitely drinking, but pinpointing how long before her death may be difficult,' said Nadira, as she returned to the table.

'I thought that was the point of examining the stomach contents. Or at least, the stomach contents are one of the points of reference.'

'The problem with a head injury,' Nadira continued to work as she spoke, 'is that they inhibit the secretion of gastric juices and the motility of the stomach, thereby messing up the digestive clock.'

Ah.

'But the point being—' Claudia steered them back to the disgusting container that Nadira had cruelly made them sniff; why would she do that, when she could tell them? — 'that Ivy was drinking.'

'Yes.' Nadira shook her head. 'Why do teenagers always do this to themselves?'

'My daughter's fifteen.' Smithy was completing the paperwork for the transparent container. 'I can tell you, I've never had to parent as hard as I do now. They think you know nothing, that you were never their age . . . and even if you were it was in the Dark Ages, *obvs*.'

They all grinned at the deliberate use of the teenage slang.

'And all her information and direction comes from her peers. They are simply just a herd, with no real-world brain between them, trying to behave like adults, way before their time. It's terrifying.'

'It's their brains,' said Nadira. 'Genuinely.'

She looked silently at Smithy. They'd obviously had this conversation before. 'Their brains aren't fully developed and matured until their mid- to late twenties. And it's why they're impulsive, and why we as adults slow down in that respect as we mature, because it is a physiological process, rather than them just doing this crazy stuff to piss the parents off.'

'Oh, there's plenty of that,' grumbled Smithy, and placed the container on a tray that would go elsewhere when the post-mortem was completed.

'Could the alcohol have contributed to her death?' Graham asked. 'As in . . .' He stopped, considered his thought process, then shook his head. 'I was going to say, as in could she have been drunk and fallen and cut her head, then I realised how stupid that was, because how did she get on the bench? Maybe she was still conscious after falling and hitting her head, and was able to climb on to the bench?'

'Good question,' said Claudia. 'Only Nadira can tell us the severity of the head wound, but if it didn't kill her straight away, if she lay on the bench to rest, do we really think she'd have crossed her arms like that?'

'There's less debris around the head wound than I'd expect if she fell onto the ground and injured herself,' said Nadira. 'Though I'm inclined to suggest, with the positioning of the wound, Ivy Henthorn was assaulted from the front.

You'd need to be on the comically tall side, or standing on the bench itself to cause that from behind.'

Claudia filed that note away in her head.

The post-mortem continued; Nadira worked methodically and respectfully. Finally it was over.

Nadira stripped out of all disposable items and thanked Smithy as she exited the examination room. Claudia and Graham followed her into the office. It was an office she shared with her fellow pathologists. As in police buildings, space was at a premium, so the office was kept immaculately tidy to preserve everyone's temper during busy shifts — which Claudia imagined would be most days. Smithy had stayed in the examination room to clear up both the examination room and Ivy herself.

Nadira relaxed into the chair behind her desk and grabbed a floral-covered water bottle. 'You need to keep yourselves hydrated. It's one of the most important things the body needs.' She took a sip.

'I doubt you see many deaths in here from lack of fluid, though, do you?' asked Graham.

'You'd be surprised,' said Nadira. 'It's the pensioners. The ones who live on their own. They forget to drink and can quickly become dehydrated. It's why, in the summer, people are reminded to check on their elderly family and friends and neighbours as much as they do in the winter.'

Graham pulled his phone from his pocket and tapped at it furiously.

'What are you doing?' Claudia asked.

'Checking on my mum.'

Nadira and Claudia laughed to see the big ex-forces guy worrying about his mum this way. Though, obviously, it was lovely to see.

Graham scowled, then put his phone away.

'Preliminary?' Claudia brought her notebook and pen out of her bag.

'As discussed on examination, the wound at Ivy's left temple would suggest she was assaulted from the front. It would be incredibly unlikely given the positioning of that specific injury for it to have been committed from the rear. There was also a noticeable lack of defensive wounds on Ivy's hands and arms.'

'Suggesting she wasn't expecting the assault, and/or it was someone she knew,' said Graham.

'That would track with how she was laid out on the park bench,' said Claudia, writing notes.

'Not just that,' said Nadira. 'The lack of defensive wounds on her hands tell us Ivy didn't fall and hit her head, because what's your natural instinct when you fall forward?'

'To put your arms out, specifically your hands, to stop your fall,' said Claudia.

'Exactly. Also, the wound was too clean for it to have occurred in a fall. If Ivy had fallen and hadn't put her hands out to protect herself because — let's say for argument's sake, until we get the tox results — she was so drunk she couldn't figure out which way was up, the head wound would be more of a scrape as her face collided with the park ground. It wouldn't be as clean. The wound would contain rubble from where she fell, and her skin would be broken and dirty. I'd also suggest more of her face would be messed up with a fall like that. Particularly her nose and chin, which jut out of the face, so are prone to getting injured.'

Nadira was wonderfully clinical and scientific in her appraisal of a job.

'We're looking at a murder,' said Claudia.

'You know I need to wait for all of the test results to come back before I can provide a definitive answer. But the points I've raised certainly point to a suspicious death that requires some investigation.'

'And the cause of death was the head injury.'

Nadira didn't respond.

'Come on, Nadira,' Claudia wheedled. 'You want us to investigate, but don't give us the tools to do so.'

'I need longer to examine Ivy's brain.' She sighed. 'There was visible bleeding on it, which indicates a TBI.'

Claudia stared.

'A traumatic brain injury.'

'Oh, yes.'

'But a TBI is a broad term that describes a vast amount of injuries that can occur, including bleeding, bruising and torn tissues. I need time to examine Ivy's brain to see the real impact of the blow to her head. The fact that she'd had a drink prior to the TBI will have factored into events.'

Claudia tapped her pen, not very patiently, on her notebook.

Nadira sighed. 'You know, you cops are seriously frustrating.'

'But I'm the nicest of them.' Claudia smiled what she believed was her best smile.

'You might be the most annoying,' grumbled Nadira. 'I know you have a job to do, and waiting for me to do my job frustrates yours.'

Graham clamped his mouth shut.

Nadira tapped her fingers on the desk. 'My preliminary findings are that Ivy was fit and healthy, other than some intoxication, which—' her tone was suddenly stern — 'I need to analyse.'

Claudia nodded in agreement.

'The only visible cause of death I can find is the TBI, which I've already put on record, but which needs further investigation. It's not like opening a book, Claudia; the answers aren't there, ready for you to read. My full report will take eight weeks, so I don't expect to find myself quoted until then.'

Claudia tapped her pen on the pad. 'Time of death?'

'Between nine and eleven thirty.'

'Thank you. Now we have a cause of death—' she paused, acknowledging to Nadira that it wasn't complete — 'and a time of death, we get on with the essentials: who killed Ivy Henthorn, and why?'

CHAPTER 15

Darkness had fallen hours ago. A pizza order had been delivered, and mostly empty boxes were stacked randomly on desks. The smell of hot pizza cheese, tomato sauce and meat wafted around the room.

You'd have a hunt on your hands if you wanted to find a slice going spare now. The sandwich had repeated on Claudia, as she'd predicted, and she was not in the mood for anything else. Graham, however, was moving from desk to desk and Krish had his phone out, screen pointed directly at Graham.

'Put that thing away before I make you eat it,' snarled Graham, a man built for food, not for the long, busy days of a homicide inquiry.

Krish laughed and sensibly shoved the phone in his pocket. He pointed to Lisa's desk. 'She's storing pepperoni over there.'

'Hey!' Lisa did not approve of losing the pizza she'd been hiding, as Graham found the box and held it aloft like a grand prize, to the sound of clapping from Rhys, who'd been quietly watching.

Claudia shook her head and laughed at her team. They worked hard, and she was grateful for them.

Dominic walked in.

Krish laughed some more. 'That's where your pizza went, Graham.'

Dominic shrugged and sat at his desk.

'Okay,' Claudia said, raising her voice a little in an attempt to get their attention. 'Let's pull the day together, see what we have and then I might, just might, think about letting you lot see what your homes look like.'

'Whoop!' More laughter. This time from Rhys.

They were clearly tired. So far past tired that they'd lost a part of their minds. She'd get this briefing over with as quickly as she could.

Gradually, the team quietened.

'Okay, no pun intended, but we'll not make a meal of this. We'll see what the day's brought us. I've had an email from the digital forensics unit to say they can't gain access to Ivy's phone. It's the latest model iPhone and it's protected. I presume you've sent off for what you can from the service provider, Krish?'

'Yep, that's all done and gone. Just a matter of waiting for them to come back to me.'

'Great. Thanks. And today?'

'First off, I had the chat that you requested, with Jasmine, and it's clear this is, obviously, the incident that will shape her life.'

It really was. Whatever future moves Jasmine made, whatever decisions, she would think of her sister. She would think of the police officers who visited the house; she would think of the way her family spoke to her and she would think of the way the police spoke to her. She would think of her return to school, and how she was treated differently. How people walked on eggshells around her or tried to push too close to be near the girl who had the interesting event to talk about. Her whole life would now be decided by her experiences and reflections on what happened to Ivy.

Krish continued: 'She held it together, as I presume her mum asked her to, and she told me what we already knew. The judge ushered me out pretty quickly. Refused to allow a full Achieving Best Evidence interview back at the station, so anything else the child knows she's keeping it to herself.'

'It's not ideal, but we'll let it slide for now and see where things take us. If we have to revisit the situation later, and apply more pressure, and get a more in-depth conversation with Jasmine, then we'll cross that bridge when we come to it. But thanks for doing that. You saw Bird as well?'

'Yeah, I went through a full interview and statement with him today. He appreciated the good night's sleep. His statement matched up with his first account and nothing new was thrown up.

'He'd never seen Ivy before. Not in the park, or in any of the areas he finds himself in through the day. He said people behave as though he's invisible, and the effect of that is he feels like he's invisible — so in turn, he pays people in his vicinity little attention. All he wants is to get through a day and then get through a night. It's a one-step-at-a-time kind of world for him.'

What an existence. 'The place you housed him . . .'

'Yeah, Framework, they'll support him and work with him to get something more permanent.'

Claudia sighed. 'And the jogger?'

'Oh yeah,' Krish laughed. 'His wife was seriously pissed with him. Seems it was more than just an argument. The guy had been caught flirting with a co-worker, and his wife was none too happy about it. She did, however, confirm that they argued last night, her husband went out for a run and he left about twenty minutes before his phone made the three nines call.'

Claudia considered this. 'It doesn't rule him out. There was time for him to have killed Ivy. He could have been running away when Dean caught up with him.'

'If he killed her, do we think he'd have stopped for Dean if he was running away?' Graham asked.

'It's a question we can't answer. We'll have to wait for forensic submissions to come back on that one. Do we know anything about his usual running routine?'

'We do.' Krish grinned. 'I've submitted his sports watch thing. We removed it with his clothes last night, and today his wife said he wears it constantly and it tracks everything. It holds all his running routes, his running times, the days and dates and even his heart rate. So I imagine if he was busy killing someone, his heart rate would be through the roof.' His grin was the *tada!* of grins.

'Or it could tell us that Bingham Park is one of his usual routes and there's nothing unusual in him being there,' Claudia said.

'Or that, boss.' The grin deflated.

'Good work with the wife's interview and the watch, Krish, thanks.' They needed to move on. 'Dominic?'

'I met the judge and her husband at the morgue, where they identified the body as that of their daughter Ivy Henthorn.'

'Thoughts?'

Dominic rubbed his face. He looked worn out. 'Yeah, Mum is absolutely devastated, as you'd expect. Her world has collapsed in on itself. Owen Kimber had to physically support her the entire time.' He screwed his face up.

'What is it?'

'I can't say there was anything definite; it might easily have just been me, but there was a vibe I didn't like about the husband. Yeah, we're reminded time and again that people grieve in different ways . . .'

There was a pause as the room recognised the comment for what it was.

'But still, he appeared one step removed from the process. It might have been that he was too busy supporting his wife, because man, did she need it. I wouldn't expect to see her in court for some time now. But he was almost aloof.'

Claudia tried to think about her impression of Owen Kimber when they'd issued the death message, but her focus had been primarily on the judge and on Theo, the teenager struggling with his sister's death. 'Okay, we'll keep that in mind. The phone work for the whole family is being submitted, so we'll see if that brings anything up.'

She'd brought her water bottle with her and took a drink. It was a moment to gather herself. Was it really only yesterday she'd been at court watching the guilty verdict come down on Tyler? And now they were knee deep in a homicide investigation. There had been no time to breathe, never mind to process everything. Okay, on with the show. The sooner she finished the briefing, the sooner she was out of there for the day.

'Ivy's school, Wellington-Bell, was interesting. Graham and I were only able to stay for a little over an hour, as we had to attend the PM, but I spoke to the head of the school, Ms Price, and the receptionist, Mrs Honeycutt.

'Ms Price confirmed Ivy was a grade A student and popular among her peers, but that something had occurred just under a year ago to bring her grades down, and also to bring Ivy herself down.

'It was a strange meeting. Without putting anything in words, Ms Price managed to convey what she thought had happened, and it has a high possibility of being the correct answer. The problem being that Ivy never admitted to any adult at the school what had happened. She just promised to raise her grades and she delivered.'

Lisa's voice was barely audible. 'Price thought Ivy had been sexually assaulted.'

It wasn't a question.

'It wasn't put into words, Lisa. I can't confirm what she thought. The head was composed and wouldn't say anything so definitive. Especially if it could bring the school into disrepute.'

'She'd protect a sex offender to preserve the prestige of her precious school?' Rhys spat.

Her team were passionate, with a fervent sense of right and wrong. It was that sense that had helped Claudia on more than one occasion. 'No, Rhys, you're not hearing me. Remember, *listen* to the women in your life.'

He clamped his mouth shut and a faint blush slid up his face.

'It's okay,' she reassured him. 'Ivy refused to say why her grades and her personality had changed. She refused to say why in front of her parents, when a meeting was called to discuss it all and to support her. What she did say was she'd deal with it and get her grades back on track, which she did. In that position, the school's hands were tied. There was nothing they could do. Who do they talk to? Who do they point the finger at?'

'And her personality? Her joy?' asked Lisa.

'No,' said Claudia, the sorrow of that one word sucking out the last of her energy. She sagged on the table she was perched on.

An unorganised moment's silence filled the room. It was heavy, rageful and contemplative, depending on who you looked at, who they were and who the loved ones were in their lives.

Claudia needed to push on and get them home for the night. 'Price told me Ivy's best friend, a girl called . . .' She opened her notebook and flicked through to the page she needed. Her brain was tired and wasn't holding everything. 'Gabrielle Hunt, known to friends as Gabby, wasn't in school today. I think it's important we talk to Gabby as she was at home with Ivy before she went out, so I asked Margaret Honeycutt at reception to let us know in the morning if she comes in. As the closest person to Ivy, Gabby might have some useful insight as to who Ivy might have gone to meet.'

She sighed, the case weighing heavy. 'I sat and chatted with Margaret. In her position at the front of the school, she sees all the comings and goings and knows all the students. She hears the breakups and make-ups as the kids are starting or ending their conversations coming in or going out of the premises, not thinking Margaret is interested. But that clever, intelligent woman knows everything.'

'Does she know who killed Ivy?' Dominic asked.

'I said she was intelligent, not clairvoyant.'

Rhys smirked.

She was tired, and that comment was uncalled for. Dominic would pull her up for it when they were not in a work setting. He said she was harder on him than the others because she was trying to prove herself independent. He could be right, but her mind was not able to sort it out now. 'Moving on . . .'

Dominic glared at Rhys, which only served to make his grin widen.

Claudia ignored the children in the room and continued. 'Ivy's Facebook page is already inundated with posts by Wellington-Bell students offering their grief for the world to witness. It's something we need to trawl through, I suppose, to see if anyone lets anything of interest slip out.'

'I'll look at it,' Lisa said.

Claudia continued: 'Margaret had something curious to say about Theo, Ivy's brother.'

She'd caught their attention. 'Around the time Ivy's grades slipped, Theo became angry and argumentative. His anger was directed at the boys in the school, and he was close to expulsion when he got into it physically with a younger boy, one in Ivy's year. This is until his parents stepped in.'

'Why didn't the head mention any of this?' Dominic asked.

'I imagine because we were there about Ivy, and she didn't see Theo's history as being connected, no matter what we say about needing to know every small detail of her life. It only came out because Margaret slipped up in her concern for Theo. She's worried the loss of Ivy will spin Theo out. It was Ivy who kept her brother under some kind of control, back when their problems arose.' Claudia rubbed at her head, the tiredness dense. 'We need to let Alek know Theo may be more volatile with grief than he's expecting. Let's not put him in any danger. Graham, you know Alek. Can you make that call before you leave, please?'

'Can do, boss.'

'It's a line of inquiry we need to follow up on. Ten months is a while ago. It may or may not be relevant to Ivy's murder, but we won't know unless we examine it. Opening old wounds won't go down well, so tread lightly.'

Lisa rubbed her eyes.

They were nearly done.

'Did we get anything else from friends, other students or teachers?'

Rhys checked the notes in his inquiry workbook. 'I was given the keys to Ivy's school locker and seized the contents, so we could check through them. So far, there doesn't appear to be anything of use. I interviewed a couple of teachers who all said the same thing. Ivy was a strong, bright personality and grade A student. They worried about her last year, but she turned it around. The students I managed to talk to matched up as well. I had the sense that some were polite because she was dead, but put it down to kids having their own friendship groups rather than anything more sinister.'

'We need to bear that in mind,' Claudia said. 'Graham?'

'Same as Rhys. I will say there was a lot of open grief among the students. I suspect at their age, for most of them, Ivy will be one of the first people in their lives to have died, if they haven't already lost a grandparent. Beyond which, she was murdered, which makes it all the more visceral for them. They don't know how to process their emotions.' He lifted the lid on the pizza box he'd taken to his desk and wrinkled his nose when he realised he'd eaten everything inside. 'I mean, adults struggle enough when a loved one or friend is murdered, so it's no surprise these kids are all over the place.'

'The head said she'd brought in a therapist to support the students, and they'd be on site for as long as needed.'

'A problem,' muttered Dominic.

Claudia rubbed her head. Why did it have to be him? 'So long as they're only talking about their emotions and not the murder, then there's no issue as far as the CPS are concerned. We just need to keep an eye on where the inquiry takes us.'

Krish was slumped in his chair, while Lisa tapped a finger lightly against her desk.

'Okay, get out of here. Great work today. We'll pick up again in the morning.'

Where there had been fatigue, there was now a burst of energy as computers were turned off and bags, car keys and coats collected, then a near stampede made for the exit.

Claudia gathered her own coat from her office. There was somewhere she needed to go this evening before she could collapse at home. She'd put it off last night, as all she'd wanted to do was crawl under her duvet. Today, no matter how tired she was, Claudia would make this stop.

CHAPTER 16

Claudia was exhausted, and she hadn't known what to do with herself. She was lost. It had been an exacting few weeks.

Eventually she found herself standing in the dark stains between streetlights, outside the home of her second-in-command, Russ Kane. If he knew she was hiding in the shadows like this, he wouldn't be happy.

The front of his property looked like any other on the street, and the street was like any other in the area. Nothing to tell it apart, nothing to remind residents or to inform newcomers of the horrors that had occurred here.

With a tightness in her chest, Claudia walked up the drive and knocked on the door. Russ opened it with a grin.

A light breath escaped from Claudia's lungs. It happened every time she visited. They'd shared this horrific event, and because of that, a fear lodged in her chest just before she set sight on him. Fear of what, she couldn't say. But it was like all the air had been sucked out of her for those brief moments, and pain sliced through her lungs as she waited for breath, for that second when she saw Russ safe and well, and she could breathe normally again.

'Are you just standing there, or you coming in?' He stepped back.

The sound of kids squealing assaulted her when she walked into her friend's warm home.

He laughed as she grimaced. 'Maisy has a couple of friends round to sleep. This is them sleeping. Something about dragons and princesses. The result of story time in nursery.' He winced.

Russ had told her that when the car hit him, he was so disoriented by the rapid assault of it, his brain had perceived the sound of the roar of the engine as being from a dragon.

Claudia placed her palm on his back briefly as they walked to the kitchen, where Russ's wife, Maura, was sitting with a mug and a book at the small table.

An expression Claudia couldn't place flitted across her face, but it was gone as rapidly as it had appeared. 'Hi,' she said. 'I didn't know you were coming. I'll pop the kettle on.' Maura jumped up.

She'd lost weight since the hit-and-run. They both had. Russ had been a rugged guy, but he was slim now. It didn't suit him. He needed to . . .

Claudia shook herself. It was none of her business. They'd all been through the mill. People would deal with it as they needed to. Maura and Russ would be taking care of each other.

Russ put his arms around Maura and kissed the top of her head. 'Don't worry about it, love. I'll make Claudia's drink. Sit, relax.'

Maura did the opposite of sitting and relaxing. She rose from the chair. 'The kids are making quite the noise. I'd better see that they're not about to bring the house down around our ears.' She smiled at Claudia. 'I'll leave you two to catch up.' She walked to the door. 'It was lovely to see you, Claudia.'

She placed a hand on Claudia's arm, but no sooner was it there than it was gone again and Maura was out of the room, a whisper of soft flowers drifting under Claudia's nose.

'Did I . . .' Claudia stared at Maura's retreating back.

Russ clicked the freshly filled kettle on and shook his head. 'No. Don't worry about it. Maura's extremely grateful for all the support you, Sharpe and the rest of the team provided when we needed it.'

'I was there that night, and then I was targeted and wasn't much use. The team did all the heavy lifting, Russ.'

The kettle thrummed quietly.

'You think that night didn't mean anything?' His voice was soft and low.

Claudia didn't have the words.

'That was the most terrifying night of Maura's life, and other than the medical professionals, you were the first person there for her.' He swallowed hard. 'She wouldn't want this to become common knowledge . . .'

Russ busied himself, selecting mugs from the cupboard, pouring milk, dropping teabags in. The kettle boiled, he made the drinks and he handed one to Claudia. 'Maura has been as badly affected by events as I have. It shook her to the core that our family could be targeted that way.'

He sat on one of the chairs around the table, cradling his own drink. The sound of the children upstairs still beating a dull soundtrack through the ceiling.

'Maura went to some pretty dark places after I was targeted and the car hit me. She worried that if people were prepared to go after a police officer . . .' He caught Claudia's eye. 'Two police officers . . .'

Because they'd gone after Claudia next, burning down her home with her still inside it.

'Maura wondered what else they were prepared to do to help their cause. Would they, for instance, go after the families of the officers involved in the case? The children? She was out of her mind, Claudia.'

'You didn't say.' Claudia's grip tightened on the handle of the mug.

'You had enough on your own plate. Not only were you injured, but you had to find somewhere else to live.'

'Oh, Russ.'

He smiled, but there was no joy in it. 'Things are levelling off. Maura sought therapy. There were several conversations with the top brass to reassure her that our family was their top priority, and very quickly it was all wrapped up. You got the guy.'

The smile didn't last long. It was fleeting.

'You didn't come to hear about Maura. Tell me how yesterday went.' Russ lifted his mug and sipped.

'Guilty on all counts, but you know that.'

'I do.'

'When he was led away though, Tyler was as vocal about Ruth as he always is, Russ. He's still denying killing her, which I find a little weird, and unnerving, if I'm honest.'

'Maybe he doesn't want to go down as a cop-killer.'

'But he'd be revered in prison for killing a cop, surely.'

'You're happy with the outcome?'

How did she answer that? 'I'll be glad when he's sentenced and I no longer have to think about him. These things drag on far too long. It's been an eye-opener, seeing it from the other side. What we put people through, or what the system puts them through.'

'And Dom?'

A high-pitched screech went up above them. Claudia and Russ lifted their chins to face the ceiling. Russ laughed. 'It's a good job Maura's already up there. They sound like they're murdering one another.'

'It sounds harder work than dealing with a pub brawl.'

Now Russ's smile was genuine. 'But it's worth every minute. A pub brawl might get you a black eye, and will definitely get you hours of paperwork.'

Claudia listened to Maura attempting to resolve the disastrous issue above them.

Claudia's ex-husband, Matt, was now married to someone else. Would she ever be in a place where she had the time to give to a relationship and then have children? Her biological clock hadn't started ticking yet, no matter what Graham said, but she was only too aware there was a certain amount of time to do these things. She was also aware that she wasn't even obliged to do the reproductive thing. It was a personal choice.

'Dom?' Russ prompted.

'Ah, you know Dom. Keeps his thoughts and feelings to himself. Took off pretty quickly after the verdict came back. I'll give him the space he needs.' She picked up her drink. It had cooled. 'What about you? How are you doing?'

Russ rose and turned his back on her. There were a few glass tumblers, small bowls and plates stacked next to the sink. Russ selected one at a time, turned the tap on, rinsed an item off and loaded it into the dishwasher.

'Russ?'

'Yeah, I'm healing.' The sound was dull as Russ spoke from the depths of the dishwasher.

'Any date on returning to work?' She missed him.

Claudia was the detective inspector of the Complex Crimes Task Force and Dominic Harrison and Russ Kane were both detective sergeants below her. Russ had come over to the newly created unit with Claudia from a Major Crime team they worked together. Detective Superintendent Connelly had decided Dom would work on the team with no consultation from Claudia. It wasn't the best of circumstances, supervising her father, but they worked with what they had. Russ was her right hand, though. She needed him back.

Russ methodically rinsed and stacked each item, keeping his back to Claudia consistently. So much so, she didn't know if he'd even heard her. She was about to repeat herself when he slammed the dishwasher door closed and turned.

He'd paled.

'Russ?'

'I'm sorry, Claudia . . .'

'Sorry?' Butterflies took off in her stomach. Today was not going well.

'I'm taking some time off.'

'You were hit by a car at speed, you've had surgery, you're recovering. No one expects you to rush back.'

Russ sighed and sank on to his chair again, tapped his fingers against his mug. 'It's not just that. I'm pretty much healed, but my doctor is willing to sign me off for longer with depression.'

Claudia watched his tapping fingers. The fluttering in her stomach dropped like a stone. 'Is there anything I can do?' It was almost a whisper.

'I need time with my family. I need time to think, to process. I need to figure out what I want to do with my life. And I need to be there for Maura.'

'You're not coming back.'

The room was silent other than the low hum of the fridge. Even the children had stilled.

Tears pricked at the back of Claudia's eyes. She would not allow them to fall. If they fell, it would add pressure to Russ and she wouldn't do that to him. She ground her jaw hard and dug her nails into her palm as she held on to the mug.

'I don't know. Will you be furious with me?' His eyes pleaded for forgiveness.

Russ needed no forgiveness. He'd been by her side through thick and thin; he was only in this position because he'd followed her into the breach without a single thought for himself.

'I could never—' The words were trapped in her throat as it closed in around them. She would not do this to him. She dug her nails in harder. A piercing in both palm and brain. 'Could never be furious with you, Russ. Though I think Ted might miss the bottle of whiskey at Christmas, and the team might miss the fans he magics up for them in the summer, because you're the only staff member to remember he exists in the building!'

Russ laughed. It was loud and infectious. Claudia joined him. He hopped up and wrapped an arm around her. 'You know I'd do it all again, for you.'

CHAPTER 17

The morning briefing had run smoothly. Everyone had actions to get on with. Mrs Honeycutt from Wellington-Bell had called halfway through, as requested, to inform the inquiry team that Gabrielle Hunt had not attended school for the second day running. The school were not concerned by the absence, considering the circumstances.

A HOLMES action like this would not normally be on Claudia's to-do list, but the task force were short-handed. Not only was Russ on sick leave, but one of their civilian staff had gone on maternity leave and another was ill with flu, and Claudia had ordered him to not enter the office under any circumstances. Better to be down one member of staff than the whole team, if he passed it on. He promised he wasn't capable and she wished him well.

It didn't help their situation, though.

The officers she had were either at the crime scene continuing house-to-house inquiries around the park, searching out and viewing CCTV footage if they found any around the park, contacting taxi companies who may have been in the area around the time Ivy was, or tied up obtaining written statements they believed were necessary from students and staff at Wellington-Bell. And this wasn't even a comprehensive list. Background checks needed completing on all witnesses. A request had been submitted for all the judge's cases and they needed to be trawled through, which would be hugely time-consuming.

Knowing Ivy inside out would be the crux of the investigation, and Claudia was interested to hear what Ivy was like from the person closest to her. She completed the urgent admin that, as SIO, she needed to keep on top of, then drove out to Gabby's house herself.

Claudia had no qualms, no airs or graces about her, that said she couldn't do this because she was a detective inspector. A task needed doing, and she was the only available resource.

Electric gates secured the property, a gorgeous detached cream build standing in a rich paved setting, with two solid cream posts accentuating the dark grey door.

The door was opened. A man with a balding head and cheeks flushed from a good life peered out at her. A belly hung over his jeans, covered by a striped blue shirt, and bare feet poked out at the bottom of the jeans. Dark hair curling on his big toes. 'Can I help you?'

Claudia produced her identification. 'Detective Inspector Claudia Nunn. I'm the senior investigating officer in the murder of Ivy Henthorn.'

The man Claudia believed to be Mr Hunt turned and looked into the house behind him, pulling the door ever closer to his frame.

'Mr Hunt?'

He returned his attention to Claudia. 'Oh, yes. Detective inspector Nunn, you said?'

'Yes.' Claudia shoved her ID away. 'I understand it's an emotional time. We've been informed by Mrs Price at Wellington-Bell that your daughter, Gabrielle, was best friends with Ivy, and that she stayed home today. I wonder if it would be possible to have a short chat with her?'

Mr Hunt pulled the door tighter to himself. So much so, he had nearly pushed himself out of the house.

It was clear the man was protecting those he loved, but Claudia needed to speak to his daughter. She hated to be pushy, but she had to get into the house. Gabrielle Hunt could be a material witness, if she was as close to Ivy Henthorn as Ms Price had alluded.

'It's important I speak with her, Mr Hunt. You and your wife can be present to support your daughter, but this is a murder investigation, and Gabrielle may hold information that could help. To put this off could allow a killer a head start. I'm sure you're aware of the—'

'Who is it, Lawrence?' A female voice came up behind him. Lawrence startled. 'If it's the press, just shut the door. Stop being polite, for heaven's sake.'

Lawrence froze, stuck between two strong women, both of whom were demanding he move in different ways.

'Mr Hunt . . .' Claudia pushed.

The door that had been protecting the inner sanctum of his home was yanked open and a woman, taller than Lawrence, slender, with skin like porcelain and the darkest green eyes Claudia had ever seen, stared right at her. 'Vultures. That's what you are. Vultures.' Her tone was clipped and sharp as glass.

Claudia retrieved her ID and introduced herself again. 'I'm sorry, I understand you're having a difficult and emotional morning. The reason I'm here is that the head at Wellington-Bell said Gabrielle was Ivy's best friend, and we were notified that she hadn't attended school the last two days. Otherwise we'd have interviewed her there.'

Claudia winced. The pursed lips of Mrs Hunt informed her that *interview* hadn't been the best choice of word.

It was cold on the doorstep. March was supposed to be when spring sprung, but it never did. It was always the last month of winter, and winter really wanted to have the last word.

What Claudia wanted was to get off the doorstep and into the warmth of the house. 'This isn't an easy time for anyone. Teenagers in particular. But I need a short conversation with your daughter. As Ivy's best friend, she's in a position to help us build a more nuanced, layered picture of Ivy. Obviously the adults in Ivy's life see her a certain way, but a person her own age could grant us a more personal insight, which could be extremely helpful to our inquiry. We're particularly interested in her last few days.'

Lawrence had been shoved back, out of the way. Mrs Hunt was in charge of the decision on whether to allow police to speak to their daughter and Claudia faced her down. The woman wasn't moved by her approach. It was time to bring out the brutal truth.

Claudia lowered her voice a little and dipped her head slightly, so as to not appear aggressive. She needed access to Gabrielle Hunt. 'If it were the other way round, and Gabrielle had been murdered, wouldn't you want the Henthorn-Kimber family to support our investigation?'

The arrow landed exactly where she'd aimed.

Mrs Hunt opened her mouth, no words forthcoming. Her hand clutched at the doorframe.

'I'll be as gentle as I can with her.'

Gabrielle's mother let out a deep sigh. Her whole body releasing the pent-up tension she'd obviously arrived at the door with, ready to battle journalists. Her shoulders sagged slightly as she nodded a silent consent and opened up the door to allow Claudia entry.

'It's Gabby. She prefers Gabby,' the girl's mother said, as she closed the door on the cold and cruel world beyond, because she wasn't wrong — at some point, journalists and hacks would descend.

The murder of a teenage girl at a private school was newsworthy, much as it was distasteful. But money and power made a story more salacious — and disgustingly, to the red tops, it made the murder one step removed from their readership. Therefore, the murder could be glamourised and picked over, more so than that of a young woman attending a community school, living her life the way the majority of the country could recognise.

For the second time since the murder, Claudia was led into a living room that was larger than the entire ground floor of her own home.

A home she longed to return to.

CHAPTER 18

Gabby

Her bedroom, large and spacious by any standards, was suffocating her, like a prison cell. The walls closing in. Oppressive, and crushing the breath from her lungs.

Gabby couldn't breathe. Her chest was a cavity of broken glass and her eyes were pools of acid. Her head throbbed.

She needed to breathe. She needed this to stop. She needed to escape.

It was all unbearable.

How did she make this stop?

Her body wasn't her own. With fingers like foam, she clawed at the window handle until it turned. Then, with the window open wide, Gabby lunged out and gasped for air, inhaling hard. She needed to breathe. She needed the pain to stop.

But an acid river streamed down her face and the cold air hit damaged lungs with a searing force, and Gabby howled into the abyss.

Two sets of arms folded around her as the howling reverberated in her mind. Her father's aftershave, familiar and secure, soothed the breaks inside her as he kissed her forehead and led her to the bed where they sat.

She was enveloped by the soft warmth of her mother, who cradled her, wiped the acid from her face and stroked her hair. Wrapped in her love, Gabby was reminded that Charlotte Hunt, violinist and global sensation, was also her mother, and that she so desperately needed her.

'The police are here,' her father said, taking hold of her hand. 'They want to talk to you, but we'll tell them you're in no state to see them today.' He bent his head and kissed her hand.

'No,' she croaked quietly. 'I'll . . .' It was like her head was about to explode and only her mother's hands were preventing it from happening. She had to try harder.

'I'll see them.' Pain erupted behind her eyes and Gabby closed them immediately.

Her mother, one arm holding her daughter in place, whispered down to her through the darkness. 'Gabby, you don't have to do this. I know you want to help . . .' Her sentence tripped over Ivy's name. She gently cleared her throat and tried again. 'Ivy would understand if you put this off for another day.'

Ivy *wouldn't* understand because Ivy couldn't understand anything ever again. Gabby pushed herself up. With clenched fists, she rubbed her face dry. 'It's fine. I'll see them.'

Her father towered over her. 'Okay. You can speak to them. But I want you to eat something afterwards, even just a couple of slices of cheese on toast.'

Gabby agreed.

Her mother handed her the oversized cardigan abandoned on the end of the bed. 'I'll make you a hot chocolate.'

With one last stroke of her hair, they clambered off the bed. Her mother wrapped the cardigan around her shoulders and pulled her into a tight hug, kissing the top of her head as Gabby leaned into her shoulder.

Without a word, her father stretched over the bed and pulled the window to.

The pain was crushing, but her parents' presence had a dulling affect. Maybe she could sleep between them, like she had as a child.

Maybe they thought her too old for that, and she had to be an adult now?

'You're sure?' Her mother peered into her face, searching for something.

Gabby didn't know if Charlotte would find what she was looking for, so she nodded, mutely.

Her mother took her hand, like she had when she was a small child — maybe there *was* a possibility of sleeping with them through the night — and they unsteadily made their way downstairs.

'I'll make the drink,' her father said, and veered off to the kitchen.

Her mother stood in front of her and with the pads of her thumbs wiped under Gabby's eyes, before cupping her face in her hands. 'You can still say no.'

They were outside the door to the sitting room.

'I want to do this,' Gabby said. 'For Ivy.'

Once again, her mother smoothed her hair.

Did it really matter what she looked like to the police? Gabby pulled the cardigan closer around herself like a protective shield.

Ivy's cardigan.

As best friends, they swapped clothes so often their mothers never knew which clothes belonged to who anymore. Now Gabby could never return the cardigan.

She would never want to. It was a piece of her best friend.

Her mother took her hand, and before Gabby had a moment to think further, the sitting room door opened and she was led in.

The police officer waiting rose to meet her. She stepped forward and held out her hand. 'Hi, Gabrielle. I've been told you go by Gabby. You tell me which you prefer to go by today.'

Gabby blinked, confused. She didn't know what she expected, but it wasn't this. Time was slowing down around her. Her best friend, dead, police in her living room, her mother clinging to her hand like she might actually be next.

And as the thoughts slipped through her mind, her mum squeezed her hand and Gabby blinked again.

Oh, the police officer's hand was still outstretched.

Gabby took it.

Her whole body was shaking.

Her mum squeezed again. Gentler this time.

'Gabby.' Her voice quiet. 'Gabby's fine.'

The police officer gave a small nod and released her hand. 'I'm Detective Inspector Claudia Nunn. You're more than welcome to call me Claudia. We won't bother with formalities.'

Her mum ushered Gabby to the sofa, where they sat as close together as they'd ever sat before. Her mum was not leaving her side.

Gabby leaned into the familiar softness, warmth and scent of her perfume, the soft rose and delicate fruity undertones. Charlotte Hunt was a classical woman, and didn't do anything over the top. She always told Gabby wealth and class need never be thrown in the face of others. It was something you were, not something you had to try to be. If you had to try, then you had already failed.

A stray strand of her mother's hair tickled Gabby under her chin. She let it be. It was a comfort to be this close for a change. Her teenage years and her mother's career had distanced them. But this feeling of being cared for, especially by her mother, was precious.

The detective returned to her chair. 'Ms Price said you weren't at school. She also said you were Ivy's best friend.'

The area behind Gabby's eyes turned acid hot again. She bowed her head, and her mother's hand tightened its hold on her shoulder. Gabby nodded silently.

'I'm sorry for your loss, Gabby.' The detective lowered her voice. 'I'm sorry this happened to your friend.'

Her throat was closing, and her eyes were burning. Her body was failing her. There was no way to respond. Gabby took hold of the necklace around her throat and gripped hard.

'It's okay; take your time. There are no right or wrong answers. This isn't a test. We want to know who Ivy was, so we can do the best we can for her.'

Her nose was becoming blocked and she was struggling to breathe. Gabby opened her mouth and gasped. Tears fell, blinding her. The room, and the detective gone from view. She gurgled, choked and sniffed. Her mother leaned forward and with a handkerchief dabbed away the tears from her cheeks and patted under her eyes, murmuring sweet words of reassurance as she did. And all the time, one arm rubbed Gabby's back.

Comfort like this from her mother was unusual, but her touch and gentle whispered tenderness, was very much needed.

Gabby slowed her breathing and took the proffered handkerchief, making the most disturbing sound as she blew her nose.

'As you can see, it's not really the best time,' said her mother.

Her father pushed his way through the door with her favourite pink glitter mug and the biggest, wobbliest tower of cream just waiting to fall. She couldn't help but grin as she took the drink from him. He always could make her feel better.

Once relieved of the unstable hot chocolate, he looked from his daughter to his wife to the police detective. 'What have I missed?'

Charlotte stiffened. 'I think Gabby needs her rest.'

Lawrence knelt in front of her. 'What do you want to do, sweet girl?'

Gabby ignored everything but her father. 'I want to help Ivy.'

He clapped his knees as he rose. 'Okay, then. Decision made. It's never going to be easy, but it's what we're doing. Shall we get on with it?'

'Are you okay to continue?' the detective asked.

Gabby nodded as she popped the top of the cream tower into her mouth and closed her eyes.

'What can you tell me about Ivy, Gabby? What was her life like?'

There was a tiny spoon that came with the sparkly pink mug. It dropped into two holes in the handle. Gabby pulled it free and scooped up more cream that was melting into the hot liquid. 'Like mine, I suppose.' She sucked the cream from the spoon.

'In what way?'

Not everyone had the privilege they did. Though what was that privilege worth, if it didn't prevent the horror inflicted at the hands of a male counterpart? Gabby tapped the porcelain spoon on the rim of the mug as her mind recalled the nights spent crying with her best friend and the complete inability to take the pain of it away.

Nothing could take that away.

'Gabby?'

It was her dad's soft voice. The only man in her world she could trust.

'We were friends. We spent time together. She was the kindest person, and she wanted the world to be a safe place. Her plans were to follow her mother into law, but to take a different path.'

Gabby sensed her own mother's surprise at this revelation.

'Ivy wanted to help those who really needed it. She understood her privilege and wanted to use it to educate herself, so she could then offer legal help to those who might otherwise slip through the system.'

The police detective, Claudia, was taking notes and at the same time listening and nodding as Gabby spoke. 'Was Ivy worried about anything recently? I believe you were with her after school that day.'

Gabby remembered Ivy's bedroom that last afternoon. Ivy's determination to stop the strong from causing harm to the weak. She shook her head. 'She wasn't like that.'

'Ms Price said something changed in Ivy a little while ago. Her grades slipped. Do you know why?'

The cream curdled in Gabby's stomach. She put the mug on the carpet. Her mother cleared her throat, but kept the words she'd be itching to say to herself. Gabby didn't care about the carpet. How could her mother even consider it today?

And how could Gabby break Ivy's confidence? If her best friend wanted everyone to know, then she'd have told the authorities at the time, but she hadn't. She'd dealt with it in her own way, and in doing so she'd climbed out of her despair and given herself new life and new purpose. Gabby couldn't destroy that. Her stomach twisted some more.

'Ivy was fine,' she muttered. 'She's a teenager, isn't she?'

'Gabby . . .' Her mother's voice was light in her ear.

The detective shook her head. 'What about anyone she had issues with?'

Gabby's head was spinning. Memories spiralling in and out of focus. It was difficult to hold on to one at any time. All she wanted was to hide under her duvet and shut out the world. To stay there and never see anyone again.

'I won't take up much more of your time . . .' The detective was speaking again. 'I only need to get through a couple more questions, Gabby, if you can stick with me for them?'

She nodded. A gesture she seemed to have on repeat. But this time the motion brought with it the threat of vomit. She ground her teeth together and held her breath.

'Did anyone have an issue with Ivy?'

'No. She was popular.' The words slid out between gritted teeth. The quicker she answered, the faster she could be back in bed, shutting out the world.

The detective scribbled in her notebook. 'And when did you last see Ivy?' Her tone was sympathetic, but the words were a blade through Gabby's insides. Without a moment's notice, she opened her mouth and brought up the tea and toast she'd had for breakfast, with a little added cream.

CHAPTER 19

Claudia

She'd never seen anything like it. The girl heaved up her breakfast in projectile fashion, like a newborn baby throwing milk across a room. Claudia moved her feet rapidly to avoid splatter. Gabby groaned as she sank over her knee and her mother let out a high-pitched squeal. Lawrence Hunt jumped to his feet, circled on the spot for a second or two, then rushed from the room muttering inaudibly under his breath. Claudia followed him out into the kitchen where he filled a bucket with soapy water. It was better to do something productive than flap like Charlotte Hunt.

'I thought Gabby could do with a glass of water,' she said.

Lawrence turned his attention on her. 'Oh, yes, good idea.'

He reached for a tumbler out of the glass-fronted display cupboard and held it under the rushing cold tap until it filled. He handed it to Claudia. His hand was shaking.

'I'm sorry.' Charlotte might have been the one to overtly appear panicked by the turn of events, but Lawrence's face told Claudia how shaken he was. He returned to filling his bucket. 'Do you need to be here?' his voice was weak and shook.

Claudia was on thin ground. They could easily ask her to leave and she'd have to. 'All I need is this one last question answering. It will help with the timeline. Then I can leave your family in peace, Mr Hunt. Gabby is obviously struggling.'

He looked into his bucket. The bubbles high enough to be visible. Lawrence Hunt was lost in a world of his own.

Claudia took his silence as permission to obtain the answer to her last question. She took the water and headed to the living room. Moving toward her were Charlotte with Gabby, a large fluffy blanket wrapped around her shoulders.

'We're moving into the dining room. Gabby will answer your question, and then she's going to bed.'

Claudia couldn't argue with Charlotte. This was her daughter. She followed them into another room, which was again larger than Claudia's entire downstairs space. In the centre was a heavy-looking pale hardwood table with eight duck-egg-blue cushioned seats around it. Charlotte called to Lawrence that they were now in the dining room, then steered Gabby to a chair and the girl sank listlessly. Charlotte pulled the ends of the blanket tighter around her, tucking them into each other so they were secure and Gabby was kept warm.

Claudia had to make this as quick as she could.

A few seconds later, Lawrence appeared. 'I've taken a bucket of soapy water into the sitting room. I shall sort it out when we are done here.' He looked pointedly at Claudia.

'Can we finish this please?' Charlotte's face was drawn.

'Yes. I'll be out of the way soon. Do you mind if I sit?' Claudia indicated the chair at the end of the table so she'd be side-on to Gabby.

Charlotte gave a quick nod and placed herself the other side of her daughter.

Claudia dragged the chair out, which was far heavier than it appeared, and perched facing the young teenager. She had to tread lightly. She was on fragile ground, both with the witness and her parents. If she wanted to get further, she had to be at her best and consider the person in front of her.

'Again, Gabby, I'm so sorry for your loss.' She paused and collected herself. 'They may sound like words police spout and you might believe I'm giving my condolences because it's what I have to do when I turn up to your home, but sudden and violent loss of a much-loved friend is traumatic. I know that from experience.'

The memory of Ruth, the pool of blood left behind, it crowded in on her. How she missed her friend. The good times. The drunken conversations, the laughter, having each other to confide in. It was gone, destroyed, and all because a killer didn't want to be caught.

Muscles contracted throughout her body as Claudia held herself together. This wasn't about her. She'd shared a little of Ruth in the hope of letting this poor girl know it was possible to recover your life after brutality like this.

Gabby was staring at her. Charlotte, too.

'So please do believe me when I say how very sorry I am. Your mum and dad are going to take great care of you, and I won't be here long, just a few minutes, if that's okay with you?'

Gabby, mouth a little ajar, managed to whisper that it was. Her hand on the table gripped firmly by her mother.

Great, she had Gabby's attention again. All she had to do was get her through the next five minutes. 'Take me through when you last saw Ivy and what her mood was like, please.'

It wasn't good practice to ask multiple questions. It could confuse the interviewee, and at a later date they could claim they were responding to one question when police were reacting to the answer as if it were to the other question.

Tears slipped down Gabby's cheeks, and she turned to her mother, who glared at Claudia as she asked her daughter, 'Do you want—'

'No, it's fine.' Gabby's voice was hoarse. Most likely a result of bringing up everything she'd eaten this morning. 'I want to do this.'

Claudia gave her an encouraging but brief smile. 'Go on.'

Gabby picked up the glass Claudia had brought in and sipped at the water before speaking. 'I was at her house after school that day.'

Charlotte's eyes welled and her hand tightened on her daughter's.

This family had a long journey ahead of them. Claudia held her tongue and allowed the silence to naturally ease Gabby into speech.

Gabby retrieved her hand from her mother's protection and cradled the glass under her chin, close to her chest. 'Her parents weren't in, and Theo was in his room with his music blasting out as usual . . .' She dipped her chin on to the glass. 'So me and Ivy drank some of her parents' gin and replaced what we'd drunk with water.'

There was a low gasp, and Claudia just caught the tail end of Gabby's full name being thrown at her. Gabby had the presence to shoot her mother red-hot pokers of a look. Claudia couldn't say she blamed her. This was not the time for recriminations. It was the time for truth and honesty, and Gabby was providing it.

She had to help the girl out. 'That's extremely helpful, Gabby, thank you.'

Gabby's mother shifted uncomfortably in her seat. Not a sound had come from Lawrence. Claudia imagined he'd probably get it in the ear later, after she'd gone and Gabby had returned to the sanctuary of her room.

'How much would you say each of you drank?'

Gabby shrugged. 'Only half a cup each. I suppose you'd call it about three shots. Ivy was doing her homework, and my mum texted me to come home, so I left her . . .' She tipped her face into the top of the glass, hair sliding forward to shield her from view.

Claudia turned her attention to Charlotte Hunt. 'Why did Gabby need to return home?'

Charlotte patted her chest, heat rising in her cheeks.

Why had a simple question made the woman so anxious? 'Was everything okay at home?'

Charlotte patted her chest again, then her daughter's shoulder. 'Oh, yes. Like she said, they had homework to do. You know what they're like at this age. They have exams coming up this year. I was being a pushy mother.'

Theo hadn't seen Ivy leave the house. He hadn't mentioned Gabby being there or leaving. Not a surprise, if he was holed up in his room the majority of the time, or he was too emotionally overwhelmed and didn't think it relevant. That was a problem in homicide inquiries, when witnesses decided what was and wasn't relevant. It had been the judge who had provided the information. 'What time did you leave, Gabby?'

'I . . . I'm not sure. I don't really notice, unless it's getting late.'

'Can you check your phone for when your mum texted you?'

Gabby patted her tracksuit bottoms and raised her palms. 'I've left it upstairs.'

Her mother stood. 'It's okay. My phone is in the kitchen.' She quickly strode from the room.

'The world will be a different place,' said Claudia to the now solitary child. Though her father was in the room, he was not within contact distance of his daughter. 'But you'll learn to live within it, and you will heal. You'll carry Ivy's memory and the pain will lessen.'

Gabby shook, her eyes wide, tears falling. She held her hands together as if letting go would see her slide into a waiting abyss. Claudia understood the shock and distress that came from the murder of a loved one. She could only imagine how frightening it must be for one so young.

'I have it!' Charlotte Hunt re-entered, holding the mobile aloft like a prize.

Lawrence was moving. He was sitting down in her seat. Taking Gabby's clutched hands in his own and whispering in her ear.

'What? What did I miss?' As the woman of the house, the one who held the power, she clearly wasn't happy to have been absent during a conversation that appeared important.

Was she more concerned about missing the conversation and her loss of control of the situation, or was her concern genuine for her daughter? 'Nothing in relation to the inquiry, Mrs Hunt. It was a personal comment to Gabby.'

Charlotte Hunt looked at her daughter leaning into her husband and placed a hand on her hip. 'I asked you a question, Detective Inspector Nunn. As a guest in my home, I'd like the courtesy of an answer.'

Charlotte Hunt really didn't like to be left out of the loop. No matter how small that loop was. Something Claudia would remember.

'As I said, it was a personal comment. I simply told Gabby that life would be different with the loss of her best friend, but that with time, she would adjust to that difference and move forward, with Ivy's memory something she could visit in a healthy way.'

A pulse flicked in the woman's jaw, but she kept her counsel, turning instead to the task at hand, the mobile. She tapped at the screen a few times. 'I texted Gabby at five twenty-six p.m.'

Mustering the gentlest tone she could, Claudia turned her attention to Gabby, who probably needed to be assessed by her doctor. She'd deal with this and leave the family to care for their daughter. 'Gabby.'

The girl lifted her chin. Her skin was pale, as if leached of blood, but blotchy from crying. She wiped her nose, then pulled her cardigan tighter around herself.

'How long after your mum texted did you leave Ivy?'

'A couple of minutes.' Gabby's chin trembled.

'Last question, Gabby. You're doing great. Thank you for talking to me today. I know it's not easy.' Claudia held eye contact a moment, trying to remind the girl she herself had been there and it was possible to get through this. 'When you left the house, did you see anyone outside who was unfamiliar, or who was standing around, that gave you reason to remember them?'

Gabby shook her head. Tears streaming down her face again. 'No one. There was no one there. I was the last one to see Ivy alive.'

CHAPTER 20

Lawrence had returned Gabby to her room. That left Charlotte to grudgingly walk Claudia out, silence following them like a cloud on a stormy day. The weight of it smothering, just waiting for the rain to break through.

Claudia paused in front of the door before Charlotte could open it and push her out. 'I'm sorry for Gabby's pain and distress, Mrs Hunt.'

Charlotte's hand, already outstretched to the door handle, stilled. Her arm relaxed, then dropped to her side. 'Thank you.' Gabby's mother clenched her jaw and blinked several times in an attempt to hold back the emotion, but Claudia could see it welling. The tension in her shoulders and the flush rising up her neck. This was a mother who was attempting to hold everything together for the sake of her daughter.

Claudia was caught off guard, as it yet again dredged up her own memories. Was that what Dominic had done for her? Was that why he never seemed to show her his sadness over the loss of Ruth, because he was protecting her?

At their age? Seriously? She'd have words with him about that. It wasn't like she was a sixteen-year-old child who needed protecting from the pain of grief.

She was an adult, and she still needed help dealing with grief.

'Gabby's going to need a lot of support over the coming months.'

'She will have it. We're here for her.'

'Today was a brief interview to obtain what's called a first account. But we'll need to organise taking an official statement.'

Charlotte took a step back, as though Claudia had physically lashed out. 'Seriously? She didn't witness Ivy's murder — thank goodness. Gabby was in Ivy's home with her. Ivy's own brother and sister were also in the house with her, for heaven's sake.'

It wasn't easy. Charlotte only wanted to protect her daughter and that included preventing her reliving her last moments with her best friend. There was no malice in the pushback. Claudia had to step carefully.

'It's about dotting the i's and crossing the t's. Gabby's *short*—' she emphasised the 'short' — 'statement is part of Ivy's timeline, which is why it's imperative we get it down in an official capacity as soon as we can.'

Charlotte crossed her arms. 'I understand you have a job to do, and heaven forbid it was Gabby in Ivy's place and we were relying on Verity and Ivy to do this. I don't know how I'd cope losing her.'

Claudia recalled Ms Price's words about the girls' mothers also being close.

'Lawrence and I will support Gabby through this, but it's tearing her apart, DI Nunn.'

'I could see her distress, and as I said to Gabby, I've been where she has.'

'Oh, I'm . . .' Charlotte touched her throat as if her words were stuck in there. 'I'm sorry.'

'Thank you. That's not why I told you, though. I want you to know I genuinely understand what Gabby's going through. It's not platitudes in order to get what we need. I'm not pushing her for the sake of it. If she wants justice for her

134

friend, with your support, she has to find that inner bravery for a short period of time, to talk to us.'

Charlotte inclined her head and put her fingers to her lips. 'I will contact my agent and request some compassionate time away, so I can be there for her myself. I'm already away from work, as my son has had his tonsils out.'

It would help Gabby, having her mother close by to lean on. Though teenagers didn't like to own up to the fact they needed their parents at all. She could only hope that an issue like the murder of her best friend would close down that teenage instinct and allow the girl to access the support she needed and deserved.

'Once Gabby's provided her statement, she can access therapy if you think it would help. There are some CPS guidelines, but they have Gabby's best interests at heart.'

'I shall research those guidelines. Thank you, Detective Inspector Nunn.'

It was clear the woman wanted her out of the house now. Her time was up. Claudia had one question she wanted Charlotte Hunt to answer. 'You mentioned Verity earlier. You're friends with Ivy's mother?' Ms Price had said as much, but she wanted Charlotte Hunt's take on the friendship.

Was it a private school thing? Were these types of schools a small world? Were fundraising events and parties at Christmas just an opportunity to network with other parents in the same or higher pay bracket?

Charlotte's skin flushed and she covered her cheeks with her palms. Her bottom lip trembled. 'Verity and I are old friends. We were friends well before the children were born.' Her words were soaked in the pain of decades of love, torn through the centre by an event neither of them could have anticipated.

Claudia didn't have the answers on how they would move on together from this. Her own friends had actively avoided her after Ruth's death, because they didn't know how to be around her. Yes, they'd been there for her those first couple of weeks, but after that, when their lives moved on and hers was still chiefly about mourning, they were in different places. Time helped, simply because Claudia was healing and thus easier to be around. Not through anything her friends had done. Not that she blamed them. She was sure she'd done exactly the same thing to others in the past. It was the way the world moved.

But this, two friends wrapped up in the same violent event. Not equally. One suffering a life-altering loss; the other supporting a child through her own loss and grief. How did the friends unite their heartbreak and hold on to each other?

'I shall be there for Verity, Owen, Theo and Jasmine.' Charlotte shook her head. 'Those poor, poor children. Why did this happen, Detective Inspector Nunn? Why would someone kill a beautiful child such as Ivy?'

'That's what we aim to discover, Mrs Hunt. And Gabby's help in creating Ivy's timeline is a crucial first step.'

Charlotte stiffened, leaned forward and opened the door. Claudia thanked her for her time and stepped away. There was no other choice: they needed to obtain Gabby's taped interview as quickly as possible, before her mother put a stop to it.

CHAPTER 21

Dominic

This was Dominic's first time at the prestigious Wellington-Bell school. On both sides of the driveway as he entered, the gates were loaded with flowers, the likes of which he'd never seen. These were no supermarket eight-quid-a-pack flowers. These were hand-tied bouquets in all the beautiful colours.

A small woman in a black dress and thick black coat was out moving the bundles further back, so they wouldn't be run over by vehicles entering and exiting. It was tradition now for the living to leave these floral tributes to the dead. Not just at gravesides. No, the leaving of flowers had moved on to the place of death or somewhere meaningful to the loved one they lost. And today, that was Wellington-Bell.

Once parked, Dominic entered the building. The descriptions from his colleagues who'd attended yesterday hadn't done it justice.

Wellington-Bell was no magical school for wizards, but the rising domed entry hall alone reminded him of the popular movies.

Dominic had browsed the website last night. When he'd seen the fee, he'd presumed it had been per year, but had nearly fallen off his kitchen stool when he saw it was per term.

But as the *About Wellington-Bell* page declared, the students were provided with excellent pastoral care, along with the expected level of educational excellence and a wide range of extracurricular activities, so the students were well-rounded young people who could enrich the lives of their communities.

That sounded like a lot of expectation to put on the shoulders of both the school and the kids, if you asked Dominic. But no one was asking Dominic. Dominic was the one here to ask the questions.

'Hello,' a friendly voice greeted him. It came from the lady sitting behind the suitably large desk to the side.

This, Dominic had been informed, was Mrs Margaret Honeycutt. Fount of all knowledge at Wellington-Bell. He pulled his ID from his pocket. 'DS Dominic Harrison, Mrs Honeycutt. I believe you're expecting me?'

'That I am.' She tapped the nameplate in front of her. 'I was informed there would be a couple of you today, in order that you could progress through more students and not cause so much upheaval for them by continuing to return.'

The note about how long this was taking was not said with any malice. Dominic studied Margaret Honeycutt and couldn't imagine her being malicious if she tried. Unless there was a deeply dark side she kept well-hidden. With that thought, he had to contain a smile. 'Yes, there will be another officer joining me. He's tied up with something else at the moment, but will be along shortly.'

The receptionist hummed her approval. 'Very well. Let me organise your lanyard and get you on your way.'

With nimble fingers, Margaret Honeycutt completed the paperwork with Dominic's details, sliding the paper into the ID holder on the lanyard before handing it over. 'If you walk through the archway, the first door on your right is the classroom you've been allocated. I shall request the first student be sent in.'

The archway rose ornately high up to the ceiling, and led to a wide corridor beyond. Would Claudia really have done better if he and her mother had paid out for private schooling? As far as they were concerned, she'd turned out pretty well as it was.

'It's a beautiful building,' Mrs Honeycutt said, as he continued to stare.

'Yes, I'm sorry. It is. I was a bit lost there for a minute.'

She smiled at him. 'We are lucky, and we are aware of it. Please don't think the teaching staff or the students, for that matter, forget the blessings around them.' The smile slipped.

Ivy Henthorn hadn't been blessed.

'You are here to finish interviewing the students in Ivy's classes.' Mrs Honeycutt switched back to proficiency mode. 'And you intend to eventually talk to every student in Ivy's year group, to be thorough.' She looked up at him, raising her eyebrows. 'That is a comprehensive investigation, detective.'

He would be here for days.

'Please don't worry,' she rushed on. 'Remember, our classes are small.'

It was as though she could read his mind. He'd have to be careful.

'And with two of you doing this . . .' She trailed off.

It would still take days. Though if a student didn't have anything to offer, he could take a brief first account in his notebook rather than a full statement. It was only if there was anything worth adding to the inquiry that a statement would be required. This was the way of homicide investigations. They weren't the high-excitement jobs people thought they were after watching shows on TV. 'I'd better make a start. Thank you, Mrs Honeycutt.'

'It's such a sad loss. Ivy was a wonderful girl, and would have gone on to do great things with her life. She was gifted, kind, creative . . . she had the world at her feet.'

But someone, possibly inside these walls, didn't think Ivy Henthorn was kind, and definitely didn't want her to have the world at her feet. And Dominic was about to delve into the minds of teenagers, to see what they really thought of the victim.

The first student through the door was Melvin Obasi.

He strutted in with the confidence of a full-grown man. Though with his height of over six foot and the width of someone who went to the gym, it didn't really surprise Dominic. He imagined the knowledge of wealthy and powerful parents added to the persona Obasi presented.

Dominic was at a desk against the far wall where there was natural light streaming in from the windows. His Major Incident Notebook open in front of him, pen resting in the centre crease. 'Melvin?'

The boy gave a single silent nod.

'Have a seat.' Dom indicated the chair opposite. The desks were made for individual students, but unlike the old desks of the same purpose, the chair was not attached. Dominic surmised the purpose for this was to allow for group work to be engaged in.

Melvin slid into the chair. He was well-presented, as Dominic expected all his interviewees would be today. His black curls cut short to his head and faded at the temples, and his uniform neat and well-fitted. Melvin was a young man who was sure of himself. He wrapped an arm lazily around the back of the chair as he sat in it sideways. Did he think Mummy and Daddy would get him out of anything? Not that there was anything to get out of today. Dominic was here to learn more about their victim.

'You have the signed slip from your parents that they're happy for you to talk to us about who Ivy was?' he asked.

Casually Melvin handed a balled-up piece of paper to Dominic.

'Glad to see you took care of it.'

'No one said it had to be pristine.'

Smart arse.

'Okay.' Dominic gently pried open the paper, found the signature he wanted and pushed the note into the back of his book. 'Tell me about Ivy Henthorn.'

Melvin tipped his head back so he was looking up at the ceiling. Dominic mimicked him. There was nothing up there other than the cold glare of the recessed lights that filled schools around the country.

Dominic tapped his fingers on the table. 'Melvin, if you can focus. I've a lot of students to talk to today.'

Melvin sighed. 'We were in a couple of classes together,' he said finally.

'And how did you get on?'

'Ivy was a girl's girl, if you know what I mean.'

Dominic couldn't simply agree with him. What he needed was Melvin's account of either Ivy or their relationship if they had one. 'What did that mean for you and Ivy?'

Melvin jolted upright. His arm flying from the back of the chair and into his lap. 'There was no me and Ivy. Like I said, she was a girl's girl.'

Had he rehearsed this? 'I didn't mean you and Ivy like "girlfriend". I mean, how did you get on?' Dominic had to keep Melvin calm, and he had to remember these kids had probably never interacted with the police in their lives before. They'd definitely never had one of their own killed.

'Ivy kept a tight-knit group of friends. Yeah, she was nice enough, but she wasn't interested in getting more friends. She was happy with her group. I might have been in one of the homework groups once or twice, but it was never an alone-with-Ivy kind of thing.' He paused and tilted his head, clearly thinking about something.

Dominic let him be for a minute.

'You know, she was weird for a beat. Her friends, or should I say, Gabby Hunt, glued herself to her, and then the thing with not wanting to be friends with many people happened. Before that, she was . . .'

The head tilt, the thinking thing happened again.

'She was high-key friendly, if you know what I mean.'

Was it wrong that he didn't? 'High-key?' God, he was old.

Melvin rolled his eyes. 'Intensely. She was all about being friends.'

'You don't know what changed that?'

'Nah. It didn't bother me. I had my own friends, my own stuff. I wasn't paying her much attention.'

The carefree attitude finally muted. The light in Melvin's eyes dulled. 'Maybe I should have been.'

* * *

Next in was Hugo Phipps. Dominic recognised Hugo by name. His dad, Mark Phipps, was a chocolatier who had made his first chocolate creation in his kitchen at home. It had been something he loved and experimented with. The experimentation had gained an early social media following, which had enabled him to open a bricks-and-mortar store in Sheffield. To Mark's surprise, the store had received critical acclaim, and now, not only had he opened more stores across the country, but he'd opened them around the world. He was known to have received requests for his chocolate artwork from A-listers in music and movies.

With Hugo, Dominic had expected a character like Melvin. After all, the success and recognition that came with the Phipps name would put confidence in anyone's step. But the boy seemed nothing like the father, the character Dominic had watched on reality television with Ruth.

His chest tightened as the memory flickered through his mind. He took a breath and welcomed the subdued boy. 'Thanks for coming, Hugo. Do you have the signed slip from home?'

Hugo handed it over. The note was neat and pristine and signed by his mother, Eleanor Phipps.

Eleanor shied away from the spotlight whenever Mark was on reality television or allowed cameras into more private areas. It was clear she didn't want to be involved. Her son, it appeared, was made of his mother's metal.

'Thank you. Have a seat, Hugo.'

The boy placed his rucksack on the floor and sat.

'What can you tell me about Ivy?'

Hugo sat quietly for a moment, as though he hadn't expected the question.

'Were you close?' It could be that Hugo was grieving.

The school had set up the therapist in a room close by so the students could pop in to see him straight after their appointment with the police, in case the interview had stirred up difficult emotions. They were doing all they could in the circumstances. Dominic doubted the murder of a student was something teacher training actually prepared you for.

'I'm not close to many people. I tend to be too quiet for most. There are a lot of large personalities here.'

Dominic surveyed the boy in front of him. He was tall and slim, hair shaved short at the sides, longer at the top and brushed upwards, opening up his face. The style showed the tangle of freckles that lay across his cheeks and nose.

As far as Dominic could tell, Hugo Phipps was a good-looking lad, but what would he know, a man in his fifties? Dominic would not have put this young man as an outsider among his peers, though. Maybe growing up in the long shadow of Mark Phipps was too big an ask. Perhaps Hugo, similar to his mother, shunned the fame his father's name brought, and had shrunk inside himself.

'I can imagine,' Dominic said. And he could. Melvin had been confident in his own skin and in his own space. This was his school, and Dominic the visitor. 'But what about Ivy in particular?'

Hugo shook his head. 'She used to be the life of the school. The one person everyone knew.'

Except Hugo, were the unspoken words.

'Used to be?' There was a clear divide in Ivy's life. The before and the after. But what was the event in between?

Hugo flushed. 'Yeah, I'm sorry. I don't know . . . I *didn't* know . . .' The flush deepened as he corrected his language. 'I didn't know Ivy. I can't speak of who she was. Yes, we were in one class together, but I was at the front, interested in Maths and all it can do in the world. Ivy was at the back somewhere, behind me. I can't say I ever really saw her.'

Dominic thought some more before he approached Hugo with another question. The quiet ones within a forced group, such as a workplace or school environment, tended to gather knowledge of the group as they watched from the outlines. It was possible Hugo knew more than he realised, but how to get him to that place? 'Okay, let's talk about something different for a minute. Would that be good with you?'

Hugo shifted in his chair.

'Hey, Hugo, it's okay, you're not in any trouble. I'm still here to learn what I can about Ivy. It's just there are different ways to do that. As you've said you weren't friends with her and don't have a lot to say, I thought we could try a different approach. I'd like to find out about Ivy's environment. We're all, in part, a small piece of our environment, aren't we?'

Hugo didn't look convinced but agreed anyway. Dominic was certain he'd agree to anything right about now, if it meant he could leave quicker.

'Try to relax, shake your arms out.'

Hugo stared at him.

'Go on, give them a shake.' Dominic shook his own arms. He needed to connect with the kid.

Hugo stared some more, then gradually, as Dominic continued to shake, he raised his arms, dipped his chin so he was no longer looking at Dominic and shook his arms.

'That's great.'

Hugo dropped his arms like he'd been holding lead weights.

'You did good. Okay, if you're ready, think back to around May last year. What was happening within the school that was of significance? Whether inside or outside school, involving students or staff — anything that had everyone talking.'

Hugo returned a blank stare.

'Even if you weren't involved, Hugo. You say you're too quiet to be involved, but you're an intelligent lad. You might not be involved, but my guess is you certainly keep yourself informed. Knowledge is power, isn't it?'

Hugo squirmed in his chair. The heel of his foot bounced on the floor.

'What is it, Hugo?'

He placed a hand on his knee in an attempt to slow the giveaway bounce.

'I can see you want to help.'

'A year ago . . . no, it's not related to Ivy. It's nothing.' The boy leaned further back in his chair.

'Hugo, take a breath.' Dominic needed to calm the kid before he hyperventilated. 'Steady down.'

The bouncing slowed.

'It was a long time ago. You can tell me.' A year was a long time in a kid's life.

It came out in a jumbled rush, and wasn't what Dominic was expecting. Though he had asked the question with an open mind, with little in the way of expectation, Hugo had surprised him.

'Around then, someone from Wellington-Bell created a TikTok account and posted a video that set tongues wagging for weeks. The account blew up. It turned into a tell-all account. The user asked followers, for *girls*, to tell their own stories. The user created an anonymous email account, so they could release their . . .' Hugo paused, thinking of the word he needed.

Dominic tugged at his ear. What did a social media account have to do with the investigation? Still, he had asked the boy to tell him of anything of note. He'd give him the space to tell his story.

'Torment!' Hugo announced the word triumphantly, his hands rising from his lap slightly, like he actually had a trophy to lift. 'Students flocked to the account, and girls emailed as requested. It was carnage. But the girls, they strutted around the school. The TikTok account said they were owning their power.' Hugo lost energy and slumped.

'What was the account? The first video?' How did this link to Ivy?

'The account — it *wasn't* a name. It was a phrase, so the user couldn't be identified,' Hugo mumbled.

'Which was?'

'*ThinkyoucanhideWB.*'

Dominic repeated it back to confirm. 'I take it the WB was meant to signify Wellington-Bell?'

Hugo shrugged. 'Your guess is as good as mine.'

'Really?'

'Yeah, okay. It probably was.'

'And the first video?'

'A dramatic video of kids partying with alcohol—'

'Did you recognise any of the kids?'

Hugo shook his head. 'No, it wasn't like that. It wasn't one of those videos that people make themselves. The account user created the video using stock images.'

'Okay, I got you. Go on.'

'So it was a happy image in full colour, then it faded to black and white and the music changed to dark and moody. A short clip of a glass smashing to the ground, with the sound. Then a hand pushed up against a wall . . .' His voice faltered.

'It's okay, Hugo, you're doing great.' Dominic didn't like the sound of this. The pieces were starting to click into place.

'Then the last clip in the video was the half-face of a girl crying alone in a corner.'

'You did well to remember all that.'

'It's all everyone talked about. Plus, it wasn't just the video. There was text over it.'

Dominic picked his pen up. His forearms tensed. 'What did the video say?'

Hugo scrubbed at his face. He was crumbling. Dominic needed to pull this to a close soon.

'The text was by a girl, who said she'd been sexually assaulted by a boy from Wellington-Bell while she'd been drinking. She carried a deep shame, while the boy carried on with his life oblivious. It said the best she could do was to tell her fellow girls to be aware for their own safety.'

'And the reaction?'

'There was uproar, especially as the boy was named in the video. But no one talked to adults about it, so they were kept in the dark for a long, long time. More and more videos were made telling similar stories, and when those ran out, the account turned to shaming anyone she didn't think was a good person. As long as students emailed with information, she made an anonymous video for it.'

'Who has the skills to make such videos?'

Hugo laughed, then put a hand over his mouth as Dominic gaped at him.

'What?'

'I'm sorry. It would be easier if you asked who *doesn't* have the skills to make the videos. You do know what year it is, don't you, sir?'

'It's Detective,' Dominic snapped.

Hugo's smile vanished and he slipped back in his chair.

'I'm sorry, you're right,' Dominic said. 'I'm an old duffer who is getting lost in the forward momentum of our times. So you're saying it could have been anyone?'

Hugo nodded. The light inside him snuffed out by Dominic's curtness. He was a sodding bad-tempered idiot. Poor kid.

'Thank you. What's been said about Ivy's death?'

'Nothing. The account has been silent since Ivy was murdered.'

CHAPTER 22

Theo

Alek, or whatever his name was, was sitting in the kitchen with his mother, both quiet, both cradling a steaming mug. For the life of him, Theo couldn't understand why they had this stranger in their house.

It was fucking hideous!

Ivy was dead and now what? They'd moved a strange man in to replace her? Seriously?

'Theo, you're up.'

His mother's face was pale. He'd never seen her so washed out. Was that how they all looked?

'Come here, darling.'

Theo scowled at Alek. His too-straight nose and those ridiculous golden tips on his dark hair. Wasn't he supposed to be a cop? Yet he was here looking more like a fashion model. He could get the fuck out.

'Theo?' Her eyes filled.

Pain seared his chest, like a hot blade through a piece of melt-in-your-mouth Wagyu steak. With an inaudible gasp, Theo dipped his chin and moved closer. His mother reached out until the tips of her fingers touched his sweater, curled them around the material and tugged him to her.

Theo jolted the short distance to her. She smelled different. Not like his mother. His mother was fresh and bright, like cut flowers and clean washing dried in a summer field. Her fragrances were never stifling or overpowering. They were never made to enter a room before she did. Her fragrances accentuated who she was as a person.

Today she was warm, creamy and salty, and Theo wanted to pull away, but at the same time he wanted to crawl in closer, to tuck in under her arm and stay there, protected from the world that had crashed down around him. But while she held him close, it was in such a position that she could see him.

And he could see the infiltrator.

'Theo . . .' She kissed his cheek and a damp spot was left where she'd lingered.

'Where's Jasmine?' It came out as a croak.

'She's in her room, switching between reading and watching television. I'm torn whether to send her to Grandma's for a week, but don't want to push her out of the family home when she might need to be here.'

The source of the damp spot was evident as tears flowed. A constant since the police visit yesterday.

Theo's chest tightened, and the pain crippled his voice. He dropped his head to his mother's shoulder. She wrapped an arm around him.

'Owen's gone into the office to organise compassionate leave and complete the handover to his temporary replacement.'

He truly did not give two fucks where Owen was. Though Owen was the better option than Pretty Boy Alex, who had kept his head bowed, staring into his mug, so far.

'Will you spend some time with your sis — with Jasmine today?'

Heat flared through him. 'I'm about to go out.'

His mother's mouth parted. Pretty Boy finally lifted his head, but had the good sense to stay silent.

'Theo . . .'

149

'I'm not a prisoner, am I?'

Her mouth tightened. 'No, you're not a prisoner. It's just, only the day before yesterday Ivy was—'

'I know what happened yesterday!' He yanked himself free of her hold.

She noticed his trainer-shod feet for the first time. 'Oh.'

'I'm not a prisoner—'

'No . . .'

'Theo?' Fucking Pretty Boy spoke.

'*No*. Who are you, anyway? What are you doing here? In our house? Making yourself comfortable. Using our things? Drinking our coffee? Just who the fuck are you?'

His mother launched herself to her feet. 'Theo! I will not have you speak to Alek like that. He is a guest in our home, and he is a part of the inquiry team working to find out who . . .'

Her face reddened. Theo couldn't tell if it was the anger aimed at him or the horror of what she was about to say.

'Stop being chil . . .' She wailed and pushed her face into her hands. 'Theo, please,' she whispered.

'I can't stay in here.' He took a couple more steps back. 'Can't you see? I'm being smothered. Everywhere I turn . . . Ivy is . . .'

There was no way to control the shaking, the pain in his chest. Theo clamped his fists to the sides of his face. 'Her photographs . . .' He shook his head. 'She's staring at me everywhere I go, her stuff is abandoned, waiting for her to pick them back up. But she's never going to tidy up.' His voice hitched. 'And you blame me for that.'

Her gaze lifted slowly. An expression he couldn't recognise directed at him.

Theo had no idea how to deal with every emotion pressing in and suffocating him. He had to escape. Quickly surging round, he put his back to his mother.

'Theo,' she choked out. 'What about Jasmine?'

Jasmine would be better off without him.

They all would.

With his mother's judgement boring into his back, Theo ran through the house and out the door.

CHAPTER 23

Theo needed to use his Uber account to get to Ed's. His house was in the middle of nowhere. Gorgeous as it was, they had no neighbours, so it was perfect for Theo today.

He'd wait here until Ed finished school. His friend wouldn't mind. The pair of them, along with Miles, did everything together. If Ed was aware Theo needed somewhere to hide out, away from his mother, he would have offered this place.

In the rear garden was the shed thing they hung out in, but with multiple windows. More like a miniature house in the garden, really, with double doors, and a sloping roof. Theo quickly pulled together the heavy cream curtains, over the light net stuff with a fancy name. He wouldn't have had to draw the curtains, but the net stuff had been tied in the middle, cinching it in, to allow light into the shed.

With no nosy neighbours within viewing distance and both Ed's mums at work, Theo wasn't likely to be interrupted, but better safe than sorry.

Instead of garden tools as was usual in a shed, the inside also followed the theme of miniature house, or rather one room of a miniature house. There was a sofa, rug, cushions, a throw, three lamps of different heights, floating shelves with books, and a desk bearing a green plant of some description and a laptop that Ed's mum Therese used.

Theo could never figure out why Ed's parents had the thing built. Their house was similar in size to his and had a home office, but here was an outside one.

Ed said Therese liked to work outside with the doors open and the fresh air around her. He also said it was used in the winter, when both his parents wanted to sit outside in the evenings to drink, but the weather wasn't good enough.

Whenever his parents weren't using it though, Ed and his mates were given free range to enjoy it.

Taking that into consideration, Theo didn't think Ed's parents would mind him taking this day off school to hide out here. They were a great couple. Always open to Ed having his friends around.

To cover his bases, and so he didn't scare the shit out of his mate, Theo tapped out a quick text and sent it.

The sofa was perfect for snoozing when a toke hit too hard, so in preparation, Theo slumped down, rolled a joint from the bag he'd brought that night, and lit it. If there was ever a time he needed to lose his memory, then this was it.

He was ready for the last two days to be completely wiped.

As his body relaxed and his mind wandered free, images of Ivy came unbidden.

'*No!*' he roared into the empty space. He would not go there.

Ivy stood, hands on her hips, hair flipped over her shoulder, eyes staring daggers at him.

'*No.*' Theo twisted away from the memory, falling to the floor and the reasonably soft landing of the rug. His hip taking the brunt of the position in which he fell. 'I said fucking no,' he growled.

Desperate, Theo took another pull on the joint, breathing in as deeply as possible. The cannabinoids flowing through his body.

Theo, you're letting yourself down. If I have to, I'll—

He pulled again. Still on the rug, now on his back, looking up at the cream painted ceiling with fairy lights hung across it.

Jas, sweetie, can you go and do your homework while I clear up?

Gabby took Jasmine's hand and led her from the room, away from the two warring siblings.

Theo was unable to get up from the floor. Too doped up to run any further.

Those dark eyes, as Ivy threw daggers at him, like they were piercing his soul. All he wanted was for her to stop and leave it alone.

Theo, you're letting yourself down. If I have to, I'll—

You'll what, Ivy? What will you do? His anger boiled over. Red and raw. He was furious that he actually had nowhere to go in this argument. She was such a fucking priss.

You know I will, Theo. I will, because I love you. Like you love me. She'd used that soft voice on him then. She wanted something from him so she tried to soften him up. But he couldn't give it to her.

You fucking wouldn't. Theo clenched his jaw.

She raised her voice, but not loud enough for Jasmine to hear. *I said I love you and because of that I'm going to tell Mum. I'm telling her tonight. She'll know what to do.*

You're an evil fucking bitch, do you know that? You know I'll never let you tell Mum.

He would never see her again. Theo smoked the joint.

You're an evil fucking bitch, do you know that? You know I'll never let you tell Mum.

He smoked until there was nothing left, of the joint or his mind. And then, finally, he curled into a ball and Theo Henthorn cried.

CHAPTER 24

Dominic

Dominic was writing up his notes from the previous student when Phoebe Samek walked in. She waited by the door, her bag slung over her shoulder, long hair tied messily at the base of her head with long strands loose and falling around her shoulders.

Dominic finished the entry, asked her to join him and give him the permission slip.

She handed him an envelope.

He took it and extracted the paper within. Turning the page in his notebook he scribbled Phoebe's name and date of birth. Her permission slip had been signed twice, two signatures, two names. 'Your parents?'

'Uh-huh.'

Well, she appeared a chatty little thing.

Dominic checked the permission slip again. Did two signatures mean her parents were separated or divorced?

It was an amicable way to go about things, reading the opposite parent into every decision. A pain in the arse, though, if he'd had to do it. He was glad he and Penny hadn't divorced until Claudia was an adult.

'Thanks for coming to talk to me.'

Phoebe was chewing gum. Dominic was already offside. 'I didn't have any choice,' she said.

This was true, but where did kids get their bluntness, their directness with their elders from, nowadays? Dominic would never have dreamed of talking to a cop like that when he was her age. He'd have shit himself, if he was honest. Afraid he'd have received a clip for his trouble, or worse, that his mum would have found out, and that meant no TV for a week.

Kids, they didn't know they . . . Jesus, just how old was he? Get back on track.

'How well did you know Ivy?'

Phoebe wiped under an eye with a finger. Dominic wasn't sure why. There were no tears.

'We knew each other.'

That didn't tell him a lot. 'I'm sorry for your loss.'

She bowed her head.

'Was Ivy upset over anything recently? Having trouble with anyone?'

Phoebe played with the phone in her hand. 'I can have therapy after seeing you, yes?'

'The school are providing it.'

She beamed like she'd been gifted something precious.

'Ivy?' Dominic reiterated.

'Oh, she was weird, if you know what I mean.'

'I really don't. Please explain.' It was a direction. If she was smart, this girl could slip out of a request.

Instead, Phoebe waved a hand in the air. 'She was probably one of *those* girls.'

'What girls would those be?'

The sun had shifted position in the sky now and was glaring into the classroom, turning it into something akin to a greenhouse. He stood, reached up and fiddled with the blinds at the window until they dropped enough to provide some coverage.

Phoebe watched him.

'Go on,' he encouraged.

She lifted her nose in the air.

Dominic had the urge to smell under his arms, but he wouldn't give this child the satisfaction. 'Ivy might have been one of *what* girls?'

'I'm sure you know, doing your job. You'll come in contact with all sorts of people.'

Oh, he could vouch for that.

'There was a miniscule, insignificant "MeToo" kind of thing started on TikTok for girls our age in Sheffield. It's first focus was here, at Wellington-Bell. You should have seen it.' Phoebe shook her head in disbelief. 'The way people were whispering in corners, boys stomping or skulking, girls walking tall like they'd slayed a dragon rather than whispered sweet nothings into an anonymous email account with their own anonymous email account. It was completely and utterly absurd, if you ask me.'

The distaste at Phoebe's snide and arrogant remarks slammed up against the relief she wasn't one of the young girls who'd needed the external release of the anonymous account, because no one wants to be in that club, or wants anyone they love to be in that club. He settled on asking why she thought Ivy was one of those girls.

'It was so obvious. One minute, she was the party girl of our year, and *boy* was she a party girl. I mean, she put me to shame.' Phoebe crossed her legs and tapped her toes in the air. 'The next minute, she was over it, and then this thing erupts and Ivy stands like a monument, stiff and proud, but still no partying. You had to be dumb not to see it.'

She smiled, and Dominic's skin shrivelled like it was too small for his body.

'Do you know what else?'

He really didn't, and he was no longer sure he wanted to know if this heartless show of a human would be telling him. He stayed silent.

Phoebe continued, oblivious. 'Since Ivy's murder, the account has been silent.'

Thank God. He already had that information. 'I'm aware, yes, thank you.'

The smile shifted. It became crooked, a smirk. 'Of course you are.' She leaned forward and picked up her bag. 'But if that means the account belonged to Ivy, what about the people with secrets, those she named and shamed. The ones she exposed after she ran out of boys to target, to fill her "MeToo" chasm?'

CHAPTER 25

Claudia

Claudia strode across the concrete car park, her shoulders bunched up to her ears in an attempt to keep warm.

Smoke rose gently out the front of the allocated smoking shed as she approached. 'You wanted to see me?'

Sharpe inhaled on the cigarette. 'My doctor keeps telling me I need to quit.'

Claudia couldn't argue with Sharpe's doctor. Smoking was a nasty habit, but it wasn't an opinion she would dare to share with her supervisor. Instead, she took cover from the chill air inside the shed but further away from Sharpe.

'Your body language says it all, Claudia.'

'Better my body language than outright offend you.'

Sharpe flicked a length of ash on the ground. 'You're sometimes too smart for your own good, do you know that?'

'Was there a reason you wanted me to freeze my arse off this afternoon?'

'Don't you think it's nice to get out of that sodding building every now and again, and step away from the pressures of who you are in there?'

This didn't sound good. 'What is it?'

Sharpe waved the hand holding the cigarette, the end flaring red. 'Oh, you know exactly what it is with these high-profile cases.' She inhaled and held it a moment.

Claudia watched the pleasure on Sharpe's face. 'The press?'

'If only.'

Claudia looked out across the yard at the parked cars. 'The judge?'

'Judge Verity Henthorn-Kimber has been on the phone direct to Connelly.'

'She has some serious connections. I'm just surprised it wasn't direct to the chief constable.'

Sharpe threw her cigarette end to the ground and stubbed it out with a polished shoe. 'You mock, Claudia, but that specific call is waiting in a back pocket, let me assure you. At the moment, the judge is being extremely restrained, but don't let her fool you.' She pulled a pack of cigarettes out, balanced a fresh cigarette between her lips and lit it.

Claudia waited.

'The judge demanded several things from Connelly — who, I can tell you, was pretty damned stressed after the conversation. Guess who he took that call out on?'

Ah, fair warning, she supposed. Claudia had to walk on eggshells now, because shit only rolled downhill. 'How bad was it?'

'Verity Henthorn-Kimber is a grieving mother, and that grieving mother, with a modicum of influence and power in her pocket, wants, no, she *demands* answers on who killed her daughter. As any of us would.'

There was more to come; Sharpe was making short shift of her second smoke. It was already irritating Claudia's rumbling headache.

'Not only did she demand answers, and an expedient investigation into her daughter's murder, but she insisted on privacy at this difficult time.'

Claudia was confused. 'She's not requesting privacy from us, surely?'

Sharpe blew a smoke ring. Claudia, impressed and disgusted in equal measure, watched it float skyward.

'If only. No.' Sharpe sighed.

Was this the first time she'd seen any sign of fatigue from her boss?

'You were also right with your first presumption. The press. Ivy's mother wants privacy from the press, but the press is who I took a call from while Connelly was talking to Henthorn-Kimber.'

'Shit.'

'Shit, indeed. Because we released the basic information, as a safety precaution, advising young people not to travel alone through Bingham Park during the evening, due to a murder that had occurred there. The press naturally want an ID on the victim.'

'Mum says no?'

'Mum says no and expects a continued blanket embargo. The family needs time alone to grieve.'

'And the press won't let up.'

'No, they won't.'

The task force were between a rock and a hard place, as the press was a necessary medium in requesting information from the public. Information Claudia and her colleagues were very much in need of. The relationship with the media was a two-way street though. If the police were withholding, then the press could make life difficult. Not only for the inquiry, but for Ivy's family — which, in turn, made things hard for the investigation team again, with a judge bearing down on them.

Standing stationary in the cold was chilling Claudia to the bone. Sharpe was close to the end of her second smoke. Well, her second smoke since Claudia had been there. She hoped there wouldn't be a third. 'So this meeting is to tell me to pull our finger out?'

Sharpe inhaled on the cigarette, then threw it on the ground, watching it die a while before putting it out of its misery with her shoe, the bin beside her left unmolested. 'I wanted to check in with you. See how you're doing.'

Claudia rubbed her head. 'I'm fine. I went to see Russ yesterday.'

'Yeah? How is he?'

Claudia laughed. 'He's thinking of not coming back.'

'Give them some time. It wasn't easy, and made especially worse being outside their front door where the kids slept.'

Sharpe spoke sense; that's why Claudia admired her.

'But, Claudia, it was only two days ago we were in court for very personal reasons and you were telling me you're fine. Now we're standing in the middle of a high-profile case. It's okay to take a minute. I'm not a monster.' She looked up to the sky. 'Regardless of what my reputation is.'

She was right. In all the ways. Claudia had bounced from her personal trauma, cancelled her appointment with Robert, and walked straight into this new inquiry because someone didn't take her off the on-call sheet. Plus, Sharpe was also right that she wasn't a monster. Her reputation was of a hard-working DCI who expected results and time and effort, but once you proved your worth, she classed you as one of hers. That meant everything.

'Yeah, there's all that,' Claudia said. 'I'll sort it out once we're done with this.'

Sharpe narrowed her eyes.

Claudia laughed. 'I promise.'

'Okay. One more thing Mum said. Theo went walkabout this morning and she doesn't know where. She's sure he's fine, but is worried because he's grieving.'

'I'd better go.' She moved away.

'Claudia?'

Claudia paused mid-stride. 'Yeah?'

'Talk to me if you need to, and for God's sake, keep me updated. Especially if you don't find the kid.'

Not finding Theo was not an option. Claudia headed straight for the incident room.

* * *

Most of the team were out on inquiries. Claudia entered her office and sent out a global message that Theo had left home that morning and to keep an eye out for him.

Next she made a call to Alek, the family's FLO. Alek told her Theo was angry, but he wasn't overly worried. Mum's anxiety was also natural: as she'd just lost one child, she didn't want to lose another. Alek had every confidence Theo would skulk home later when he'd done what he needed to.

Claudia asked Alek to keep her updated.

As SIO, there was far too much administration work to take care of. She checked her watch. 3.25 p.m. She'd give herself twenty minutes to sort through her emails before she updated the policy log.

Ten minutes later, an email caught her eye. The sender was Hayley Loftus, the woman who had been on her dad's previous team, and the woman he'd had an affair with prior to Ruth's murder.

The title on the email read: *Please can we talk?*

Claudia rubbed the back of her neck. Did she really want to open this? The header of the email didn't make it sound like Hayley was contacting her in a professional capacity.

What could her dad's ex-lover possibly want to talk to her about?

What could she possibly want to *hear* from her dad's ex-lover?

There was nothing Claudia could think of. And yet, she found herself clicking on the email.

Claudia,

I'm sorry for the intrusion. I wouldn't have written this email if it wasn't necessary. It's also extremely private and sensitive.

Would you be willing to meet me? At a place of your choosing.

What I need to say is too important to write here. Also, I apologise, but I need to request you don't tell anyone of this meeting. You'll understand why if you hear me out.

Hayley

Claudia stared at the message. She read and reread it time and again. Forwards and backwards, and still it made no sense. Eventually, she typed out a response agreeing to meet after work. There was no point putting it off. It would completely distract her, trying to work out the Hayley riddle. Better to get it over and done with, so she could put all her focus on the investigation.

What *did* concern her was the request she not tell anyone of the meeting. The questions she asked herself before opening the email circled back in her head. What could her dad's ex-lover possibly want to talk to her about that was so private and sensitive?

She had to shut the questions down and get on with her day.

Next, Claudia moved on to completing the policy log. As she typed, she watched through her office windows as her staff returned. She closed down the log and was about to the head into the incident room when her phone rang. It was Alek.

'Hey, Alek. Any news?'

'Boss, Theo's home. He's pretty stoned, and Owen's putting him to bed. The judge is in a state. She was wound up tight today, and Theo losing his shit and going off-grid didn't help. Jasmine isn't coming out of her room much. It's overwhelming her.'

'Okay. Ask if she's open to a visit tomorrow, please.'

A hand went over the mouthpiece. Alek was clearly walking between rooms. There were mumbled voices before he returned. 'Tomorrow's fine. Do you need anything else this evening?'

'No, thanks, Alek. You're doing a great job.'

*Fin*e. Tomorrow's *fine*. Everything was *fine*. It was a word used so often lately. Claudia had told Sharpe she was *fine*. What did it really mean? It was such a nonentity of a word. One with no real meaning. A word you'd just throw out there to appease someone you didn't really have the energy to bother creating a full sentence for.

Was that all she'd done for Sharpe?

The headache thundered behind Claudia's eyes, and she thought about the meeting with Hayley after the team briefing.

'Okay, let's see what we have today.' Claudia quieted the incident room.

Rhys tapped his computer screen. 'There's another online article in the local rag. It's only short. Want me to read it?'

'Okay, go on.'

'To be honest, it's not really an opinion piece. It's quite reserved still.'

'I wonder how long that'll last,' Dominic said.

'Not long, if we don't work quick enough for them.' Rhys straightened in his chair. '*A Teenage Girl Murdered.*'

'Well, that's not a clickbait header, is it?' Lisa moaned.

Rhys ignored her and read out the article:

'As previously reported, police are investigating the murder of a teenage girl found dead in suspicious circumstances at Bingham Park, Sheffield, late on Monday evening.

When asked for comment, Detective Chief Inspector Sharpe, of the Major Crimes Department, said, "This is a tragic loss of life and our thoughts at this time are very much with the family of the young person. The investigation into her death is up and running, and is led by the task force, within the department, best equipped to deal with her murder.

"The family are understandably devastated and a family liaison officer has been appointed to support and keep them apprised of the investigation.

"They have requested space to grieve at this time and hope that request will be honoured."'

'Good for Sharpe,' said Krish, with a nod. 'Everything is so intrusive during a homicide investigation as it is. Then you add the media frenzy and the public interest. It's crazy. People need to learn that not everything is their business.'

'You want me to carry on?' Rhys looked to Krish. 'You're finished?'

'Yeah, sorry. It just pisses me off.'

'I know. Me too. It's fine.' Rhys looked back at his monitor and continued reading.

'The post-mortem has been conducted. Police refuse to provide precise details on the teenagers death, but said the medical examination revealed a traumatic head injury.

DI Claudia Nunn the officer in charge of the investigation said it is believed her death occurred between the hours of nine and eleven thirty p.m., and, has appealed for anyone with information to contact the helpline listed below or their local police station.

'That's it?' Claudia asked.

'Yeah,' said Rhys. 'It's mostly a regurgitation from Tuesday's online piece, with the extra post-mortem detail. They appear to be sticking with the request to not identify the victim.'

'We can only hope that lasts. In the meantime, we move on. Lisa, you went to the judge's offices and spoke with her assistant. Remind us what he said, in brief, please.'

Lisa tapped her notebook with a pen. 'Her assistant doesn't believe there's a current case in front of the judge that would trigger something like Ivy's murder. There are serious cases pending, but nothing involving an organised element. He did provide me a list of court numbers where the judge has imprisoned an offender in the last five years and where that offender has sent threats to the judge because they lost contact with their children due to their own criminal behaviour.'

'Thanks. That's an interesting line of inquiry we need to explore. How many court numbers or, more specifically, threats, did the judge receive?'

With her pen, Lisa ran down the pad until she found what she needed. 'Thirteen.'

'Thirteen offenders lost contact with children because of the judge's sentences?' It seemed like a high number. Jails were full of kids visiting parents.

The door to the incident room swung open and Dominic strode in, jacket over his arm, hair mussed as though he'd had his hands in it all day. Though if Claudia knew him, which she did, he probably had, after spending his day interviewing public schoolchildren.

'Yeah, sorry I'm late.' He threw up his hands, walked to his desk and sank into his chair. 'Did I miss much?'

Claudia shook her head. 'No. This should be quick then I'm sending you all home.'

There were smiles all round. Dominic draped the jacket over the back of his chair.

Claudia returned her focus to Lisa. 'Sorry, Lisa. You were saying: thirteen offenders lost contact with their children because of the judge's sentences?'

'No. Thirteen who threatened the judge after losing contact with their kids.'

'Shit.' It was clear what offence Acts the behaviour fell under. 'That'll involve a lot of follow-up work.'

The Complex Crimes Task Force had only been allocated a small team, as it was believed only a few cases would fit their criteria, and in turn, the team would have the time to work the inquiries at their own pace.

Typical blue-sky thinking. The higher-ups brainstormed, had an idea- generation meeting, but the idea had no grounding in reality. A complex crime needed the same level of work that a homicide inquiry needed, if not more. The clue was in the term: *complex crime*.

'We follow it up,' Claudia continued. 'But Ivy was laid out carefully after she'd been murdered. If someone wanted to hurt the judge, I don't think they'd take their time to pose Ivy that way. But we can't leave any stone unturned.'

She moved on quickly, aware the team needed to go home and get some rest. 'Taxi companies?'

'None that we could find so far,' said Graham.

Claudia nodded. 'CCTV?'

'Nothing interesting as yet.' Graham again.

'I have something interesting,' Dominic jumped in.

'Go on.'

'We've already hypothesised that Ivy may have been sexually assaulted, which caused a change in her demeanour . . .'

'Yes . . .' Claudia was interested.

'Around the same time a TikTok account was created with the username *ThinkyoucanhideWB*. The understanding that WB stood for Wellington-Bell.'

Everyone was listening. The memory of Claudia saying she'd send them home, long forgotten.

Dominic continued. 'In the first video the creator of the account said a male student of the school assaulted her and walked away, scot-free. The girl's identity was anonymous, but the boy wasn't. All hell broke loose.'

Rhys let out a long low whistle.

Dom hadn't finished. 'The TikTok account grew — in today's terms, it went viral. More girls contacted the user and told their stories with the promise of anonymity, and it started a whole thing that couldn't be stopped.'

'Do we have a name for the boy?'

'Windy.'

'What the hell kind of name is Windy?' Rhys again.

'Windemere Pembroke, or Windy for short,' said Dom.

Pens scribbled these details into notebooks. Dominic himself would type it up later and send the report to Kai Tanaka the HOLMES inputter.

'So we have an anonymous TikTok account and a boy who may—' Claudia emphasised the may — 'have assaulted Ivy a little under a year ago.'

'That's the gist of it,' Dom agreed.

'Okay, good work at the school. It's pulling in results. We put young Mr Pembroke at the top of our list of people we want to locate and speak to.' She turned to Krish. 'Can you add the TikTok account to list of enquiries you're making please?'

Krish smiled. 'Can do. Though TikTok isn't known for passing on its users' details easily.'

Claudia sighed with resignation and nodded.

'I have some news though.'

At last. 'Go on.'

'Ivy's phone provider finally sent over what they had stored.'

'And you kept it until now to tell me?' Claudia gave him a pointed look.

He smiled again. Like he had his own little secret. 'We've been busy. TikTok accounts. Boys assaulting girls.'

'Okay, okay, you made your point. Get on with it.' What she wouldn't do for a hot shower and a good book right about now.

'Someone texted Ivy the night she was killed asking to meet in Bingham Park.'

'Krish!' Claudia jumped from the desk she was balancing on. 'What the hell?'

He held up a hand. 'You've been busy, boss. I submitted a subscriber request. DCI Sharpe signed off on it.'

The fizz of fury that had electrified her off the desk abated. 'Was the number recognised by Ivy's phone and attached to the message list the provider sent?'

'Yeah, it's listed as "donkey".'

Rhys laughed.

'We don't need an illustration,' Dominic said. That only served to make Rhys laugh harder.

Krish waved a wad of paper in Claudia's direction. 'I thought you might want to trawl through it, so I printed the text messages off.'

Claudia walked over and retrieved the paper. 'Thanks. What does the text say? Does it give us any inkling of who "donkey" is?'

Krish flicked through his paperwork. '"Need to talk, urgent. Bingham Park in an hour".'

'There's no mention of where they were meeting. Bingham Park isn't a small place,' said Lisa. 'Whoever this person is, Ivy knew them, and she knew exactly where to go.'

'What about previous texts to and from the number?'

Krish tapped at his keyboard, nose to screen as he searched the Excel document. 'Not many, and the few there are, are in the same vein, this blunt shorthand. You wouldn't understand what they were saying, unless . . .' he leaned back. 'You understood what they were saying.' He raised his palms upwards.

'Kids,' muttered Dominic.

'Great work, Krish. When we get the subscriber check back on that number, we find out who met Ivy the night she died.'

CHAPTER 26

Albie's coffee shop was an easy place to meet, because it was so close to work that no one would expect a private conversation to be held there, and most officers and staff were either walking out the door and heading straight home, or to a bar for a drink with a couple of mates.

Hayley Loftus was already waiting when Claudia entered. She was seated at a small round table facing the door.

Claudia smiled — it was the polite thing to do — and pointed at the serving counter. Hayley shook her head and gestured at the mug on the table in front of her.

A couple of minutes later, with a steaming Earl Grey in one hand and an almond croissant in the other, Claudia sat opposite Hayley, her back to the door and the rest of the customers.

'Thanks for meeting me.' Hayley wiped a palm down her suit trousers. She'd obviously also just come from work.

'I don't understand why I'm here, if I'm honest.' Claudia pulled the small point off the croissant. 'I don't appreciate the cloak-and-dagger approach.'

A flush ran up Hayley's neck and into her cheeks. 'I'm . . . I . . . I'm sorry it had to be done like this.' She patted a hot cheek with a shaking hand. 'It really did feel like the only way I could do it. The only *thing* I could do at all.'

Claudia chewed on the croissant, giving Hayley little in the way of reassurance. That wasn't why she was here. She focused on the croissant. The shell was crisp and the inside soft and buttery. As delightful as she remembered them to be.

Across from her, this woman, this police officer, was nervous as hell. Whatever had wound her into this state, she believed Claudia the person who could help. Claudia needed to get to the bottom of why they were here, because the sooner she found out, the sooner she could leave.

'What is it, Hayley?'

Claudia waited. The tea was warm and florally bitter. Hayley's nose was in her own mug, her head shaking slightly.

'Hayley, talk to me.' Claudia spoke to her like she was a victim. Gentle and calm. She had no idea what had happened, but it was obviously upsetting her. 'You brought me here for a reason.'

A horrific thought struck her. 'Hayley . . .' she lowered her voice further. 'Do we need to go to the station?'

Hayley's eyes widened like a trapped animal. 'No. That's not why I asked you here.'

Claudia tried again. 'You know there's a back entrance for the soft interview suite, so you won't be seen. I'll take care of it all myself, if that's what you need.'

Hayley brought the mug down hard, hot coffee swishing side to side, high up to the rim. She raised her palms. 'No. No. I promise, no. It's not that.' Her eyes were steady on Claudia's.

Claudia sagged. 'Okay.' She pulled another piece of croissant off and shoved it in her mouth, grateful a colleague hadn't been hurt in this way. What a world, that they had to ask this of each other at the first sign of real and impossible trouble in their lives. She spoke through the relief: 'Why are we here, Hayley?'

It was like the wall of fear around the woman had finally been breached. The shared moment of possibility they both lived as women had removed a single brick, and the rest had tumbled down.

Hayley pressed a palm to her chest and blew out a small breath. 'I haven't had a lot of sleep,' she began. 'Coming to see you has been one of the—' She stopped. 'You know how that sentence finishes.'

Claudia did, but what she didn't know was why. Claudia didn't particularly consider herself one of the most fearful bosses to approach with a problem. Claudia was a rule-follower, but it didn't mean she was unapproachable. She considered herself fair and accessible, because in being that way with your team, they did the best for you.

She wasn't about to push Hayley. If the detective wanted to talk, then she'd do so in her own time. Claudia added another piece of almond croissant to her mouth and relaxed in the soft yet crunchy texture and the smooth flavour.

'It's Dominic.'

Claudia leaned forward, trying not to choke on the pastry. She sipped her tea again, hoping she wasn't turning blue.

'I'm sorry.' Hayley's arm lurched across the table. To do what, Claudia wasn't sure.

When she'd managed to get herself under control, Claudia nudged the small plate away. 'Why've you come to me about Dominic?' Her tone cooler now.

'I'm sorry,' Hayley said again. Clearly upset by the whole thing, being here and upsetting Claudia.

Hayley had worked with her father before the task force had been created, Claudia remembered. She couldn't see why any issue would have arisen since. Though hadn't they gone out for drinks after the trial?

Don't say he made a pass at you. Not after it all ended. Claudia would string him up by his balls.

'You've brought me here for a reason,' she said. 'Out of the way of . . . I don't know who you're hiding from. Do you plan on telling me the point of this little rendezvous?'

Her patience was thin, but Claudia attempted to rein in her emotions.

'I saw Dominic the evening of Tyler's verdict. Everyone from the old team was there . . .' Hayley fidgeted with her cup, spinning it slowly on the table. 'There's something Dominic said that night that worried me. I've gone over it in my mind time and again, and I can't make sense of it. I thought you, being closer to it all, could put my mind at rest.'

Claudia didn't want to hear the shit Hayley had to spout about her dad. Jesus, what did this woman think this was? In what world did she think her ex-lover's daughter would hear her out? Claudia rose, bumping the chair back as she did. 'I'm not the person you need.'

'He argued with Ruth the night she died.' The words were out so fast they nearly ran into each other.

Claudia scrunched her face as her brain attempted to process the sentence. Without turning, she asked, 'What do you mean?'

Quieter now, Hayley told her, 'Dominic was drinking. He said he regretted arguing with Ruth the night she was murdered.'

The words were there, out in the space between them, but Claudia couldn't understand them. She turned back to the table. Hayley's eyes were wide, her face pale and her upper body shaking.

Claudia approached the table like she was approaching a wild animal that might, with the slightest provocation, pounce and destroy her. She lowered herself on to the chair, afraid to ask the next question.

The chatter and noises of the coffee shop were gone. All that existed for Claudia now was the bubble of their table and the conversation within it. 'What exactly did he say?' Her throat constricted.

Hayley chewed the inside of her cheek a moment as she continued to spin the half-empty cup.

'You started; you have to continue.'

'He was hammered, the night of the verdict. He hit the booze hard.' Huge eyes rose to meet Claudia's. 'I'm sure you were just as emotional.'

Claudia glared at her. Not wanting to shoot the messenger, but this woman had already impacted her family's life,

173

and now she was about to again. Keeping her emotions in check was not the easiest of tasks.

Hayley chewed at her cheek some more. Then she brought Claudia's unspoken thoughts into the open. 'Right at the end of the night, he brought Ruth up.'

Claudia clenched her teeth.

'I'm not sure how much the guys were taking in, because they were also quite the worse for wear and busy talking among themselves.'

Hayley was clearly putting off the whole disclosure, even though it was what she'd dragged Claudia here for. And even though Claudia had eaten today and had scoffed half the almond croissant, there was now a threat of nausea, as butterflies fluttered under her ribcage.

Hayley's mouth opened slightly and she blinked quickly before she gathered herself. 'Claudia, I didn't ask for this meeting to hurt you. You have to believe me. If I wasn't concerned by what I heard, I'd never have sent that email. I came straight to you and only you, rather than going to anyone else in the command chain, and starting something that could escalate into a drama that might not be necessary. As Dominic's daughter, and also a detective who knows the case inside out, I wanted to give you the information, so you can process it and make a level-headed decision. You're known for doing what's right. Everyone's heard about the Cunningham case and what it did to your team. You never backed down, even when the ACC became involved.'

Claudia had no words. She picked up her cup and sipped the remains of her tea.

Hayley took a deep breath.

They were here. At the point of all this.

'Like I said, Dominic told me he regretted arguing with Ruth the night she was murdered.'

Claudia jumped in and stopped her. 'Are you certain he said the "night" she was murdered, and not the "day" she was murdered? He could have meant the morning before they both went to work.'

Hayley looked at Claudia with pity. 'He said the last time he saw Ruth was that night, after he got home from work, and that their last words were angry words. I am certain of that. Otherwise, I wouldn't have come. The reason I came to you, specifically, was that from my understanding of the inquiry Dominic came home from a day at work and Ruth was already missing, and he phoned it in. If this was the case, then how did he have angry words with her? And the blood was found in the house, yes?'

Claudia went cold, like a stone statue out in the rain in the midst of winter. The bitter temperature breaking her down right to her core. So brittle she might splinter and break. With a voice flat and dead, she pushed back. 'You were having an affair with him. How do I know this isn't a scorned-woman thing?'

Hayley finally put her own cup on the table, thrust her shoulders back and raised her head. 'I didn't want to go further than what I already said, but you leave me no option.'

The frigid core cracked.

'Yes, we had an affair, and it's one I'll regret for the rest of my life. Ruth didn't deserve that.'

Claudia sensed movement around them, customers leaving and customers entering, but the bubble they were in held; the world beyond was a vague blur. The discussion of Ruth so soon after Tyler's verdict was spinning her mind out of control. Whatever happened here today, she needed to remake that appointment with Robert.

Hayley pushed on. 'After the conversation about Ruth, Dominic being so drunk, he made a pass at me.' She made sure their eye contact was maintained. 'I rejected it.'

Claudia didn't move.

'He became annoyed, and the lads can vouch for that,' she rushed on. 'Our affair ending was the best thing that could have happened. My life has been so much better without him in it.'

Claudia studied her.

'I'm sorry.'

Claudia shook her head.

'Like I said, I was concerned, and I didn't want to create a whole train wreck that couldn't be stopped, so I came to you. I trust you'll know what to do, or even if anything needs doing at all.' She rose from her chair. 'I won't be attending any more of his old team get-togethers. I did it for old times' sake. To remember Ruth.'

She had the sense to hang her head.

'I'm sorry, Claudia.' Hayley turned and walked away from the table, away from Claudia, away from the huge bombshell she'd just exploded in Claudia's lap.

Claudia stared down at the table. What the actual hell was she going to do now?

CHAPTER 27

What the hell had Hayley expected of Claudia when she laid that information at her feet? It was like she'd passed it on and washed her hands of it.

In fact, that was exactly what she'd done. Like she had no culpability for what she was saying, that South Yorkshire Police could be employing a potential killer.

That was no small thing.

It was so far from being a small thing you couldn't get further away.

The media as a whole were on the rampage at the moment. The theme being highlighting police officers or staff who had committed criminal offences against members of the public. Most notably women. And here she was, with information that her own father might be one of those very men, and her stepmother and best friend, one of those women. And Hayley Loftus, a detective and female herself, had washed her hands of it all. She'd just thrown it all in the lap of the man's daughter.

So much for women supporting women.

Claudia's impression of Hayley had not improved since meeting her, she could say that for sure.

But what now?

The rental flat was small and dull. It was basic, but basic was all she needed while her home was repaired. Claudia removed a meal from the freezer and popped it in the microwave, then she headed to the shower to clean the day away.

It was too much to hope that the trickle of water this flat called a shower could clean away the horrific day she'd had. The water was as hot as Claudia could bear it, with the aim that the heat might at least tear some strips off her, if the water pressure couldn't. Anything to numb the pain clawing away at her insides.

Eventually she gave up, dried, dressed in soft jersey and collected the unappetising lamb hotpot from the microwave. She tipped it on to a plate, in an attempt to make it more palatable, and took it to bed with a mug of camomile tea. There, she picked over the plate, barely eating a morsel as Hayley's words circled in her mind.

What the hell should she *think*, never mind do?

The first thing was to weigh up the information.

Hayley was right. Dominic had said he'd been at work all day. Personnel had informed the investigation team they'd both been on duty that day. Dominic's account was that when he arrived home, the place was quiet. He presumed Ruth was still tied up with a job, as her undercover team had been involved in the case he'd been running. The horrific investigation that resulted in Tyler's arrest. Women with children being murdered.

When she never arrived home, Dominic made a few calls, including to her office, her colleagues — this had been corroborated — to ask where she was. He'd been told she'd gone home hours earlier. Dominic pleaded for help, believing Ruth had been abducted by the very man their investigation team were hunting — now known as Tyler.

At no stage had he said Ruth had been at home that evening.

A throb deep inside Claudia's head pulsed its first beat of the drum. She scraped the prongs of the fork along the plate as she stared at the cooling food.

At no stage had he mentioned an argument with his wife.

She raised a forkful of lamb and potato to her mouth and sniffed. Her stomach gurgled and she replaced the food on the plate.

They'd interviewed Dominic. As with most cases, police turned to those closest first, and he was no exception. But he had walked away a free man, and Samuel Tyler had been arrested and convicted of Ruth's murder.

Tyler had insisted every day since his arrest that he'd never killed 'the cop', as he called Ruth. He admitted the other women, but had always denied killing Ruth.

Claudia pushed the plate away, on to the bedside table. The smell of cold food was making her ill. In turn, she picked up the camomile tea to calm her frazzled mind.

She had spoken with Tyler and had always wondered about the reason for his insistence on denying Ruth's murder. It hadn't made sense. If he'd killed her, why deny it? Adding Ruth to the count of his other victims wouldn't make any difference to his sentence. So why deny he'd killed her? Claudia had leaned towards believing him, but had no reason or evidence as to why she had.

Could what Hayley said really be true? Had she missed so much of what was right in front of her? Her very own father?

The tea was warm and comforting, but the meal congealed at her side. Claudia took it through to the kitchen, cleared the plate and placed it in the dishwasher before plodding back to bed. There was no energy for reading or watching any episodes of a box set tonight. Instead, she cleaned her teeth and turned off the light.

Her night would not be a settled one, as dreams of Ruth earnestly talking filled the hours. The only problem with Ruth talking to her was that the sound was off.

CHAPTER 28

Claudia was the first in the office the next morning. A full night's sleep had eluded her, and the Ivy Henthorn inquiry needed a lot of work. She walked through the motions of her early work day — making a hot drink, sitting at her desk and logging into her computer — but it was all autopilot.

Her mind was elsewhere. It was with Ruth.

Claudia had made an initial visit of Ruth and Dominic's home the morning after he reported Ruth missing.

Sharpe had requested Claudia's involvement because it would rattle Dominic, and because there was no reason to suspect Ruth had been murdered at that point. No search of the premises had been conducted. As far as the force were concerned, they were searching for a missing undercover officer.

Everything changed with one sweep of the house. Claudia entered the garage through a door in the utility room. Inside was a pool of blood, later identified as Ruth's.

It was at that point Claudia had arrested Dominic.

She'd fought Sharpe on the matter of the interview, but her DCI had been firm. There was nothing in writing that prohibited officers from interviewing family. The police were not the same as doctors in that regard. But still, Claudia had resisted it.

Sharpe had pushed, using the possibility that Ruth could be alive and fighting for her life, and if Dominic was responsible, then Claudia would be the person to unsettle him.

It had been a rock and a hard place, as the phrase went. Finally, Ruth's body was located in a shallow grave. All evidence pointed to Samuel Tyler.

But Claudia returned to Tyler's denial. His denial on arrest, and his denial when she visited him in prison and his denial at court. He persistently denied abducting or murdering Ruth Harrison.

Claudia opened her policy log and began updating the team comments from the last briefing yesterday. Her plan was to speak to Verity, Owen and Theo, to find out why Theo was so unsettled last year and if he'd provide any light on his sister's issues.

As she typed, her fingers slowed and her mind wandered off topic again. To the recent past, now. To Hayley's revelation.

Ruth didn't deserve for her to ignore the information. Ruth, the woman who sat and laughed hysterically with Claudia, and who would never laugh again. That woman deserved real peace. A peace that came from the truth being brought into the light.

That was Claudia's job.

And she had a way to do it. A potential line of inquiry that might shed some of that light and find the answers she was looking for.

That first day, when she'd walked through Ruth and Dominic's home and found the pool of blood, she found something else, and she'd had it recovered and exhibited. A broken glass tumbler in the kitchen rubbish bin.

Dominic, in his distress over his missing wife, couldn't say when the breakage had occurred.

It could have been placed in the bin days before Ruth's murder. Drinking glasses broke all the time, and the bin would be where you dropped the pieces. But it was the only piece of evidence they could test now that specifically related to both Ruth and Dominic and their home.

Could she do this to her father?

Nausea swept through her and she rested her head on the edge of her desk.

It wasn't about Dominic. She had to think of it as being for Ruth. It was the only way she'd cope with what she was considering.

A decision had to be made, so she could focus on the Henthorn case. The policy log only had a few sentences typed out from this morning. With such a high-profile investigation, she should be much further along.

Finally Claudia made the choice: she'd submit the tumbler and have it examined. It would quiet the confusion in her head.

She opened the required document, typed in her request, then opened Tyler's case file and searched out the exhibit number of the tumbler and typed that into the form.

The tumbler hadn't been examined because it had been deemed unimportant to the inquiry once Ruth's body had been found and Tyler put in the frame.

Members of the public presumed everything collected during a homicide inquiry was forensically tested, but the truth was that money drove all decisions; that included the exhibit list. Exhibits were assessed and items put in a priority order. Only the exhibits that were judged to be evidentially necessary were forensically examined. Those not tested were held in storage. Like the tumbler.

All paperwork and evidence collected and created during an investigation was securely stored for a number of years, even after a conviction. It was how cold cases could be run and old convictions could be overturned, as science progressed. The main example being the advancement of DNA testing. So the tumbler was available.

This was a huge decision she was making, though.

How would she face her father while she waited for the results, knowing what she'd done?

Claudia's finger hovered over the *enter* key, ready to send the request. Nerves shaking her to the core.

Did she really believe her father capable of murder?

He was a grumpy old twat at times, who hated his placement on her team.

He'd had a brief affair, which he'd admitted to when Ruth was missing. Well, people had affairs; it didn't make killers of them. This was all so far-fetched. It had driven her crazy through the night. And Claudia had run through all this when Ruth was missing. She wasn't sure she could go through it again as she waited for the forensic test to come back.

The not-knowing was unbearable, but Hayley had opened up Pandora's box. Claudia tapped the *enter* key, and with a quiet swoosh, the email was gone.

She had reopened Ruth's murder inquiry.

CHAPTER 29

Gabby

Her mother slid from Gabby's bed. The warmth and comfort and the scent Gabby remembered from her childhood left with her. Instead, she was alone in a cold and barren land. Here she lay, as if on a slab.

Emotion caught in her throat.

She kept her eyes closed as her mother leaned over and kissed her head. Then the door clicked, the temperature in the room dropped to freezer levels, and Gabby was abandoned.

The early morning light fought its way in through the crack where the blackout curtains met; she hadn't closed them properly. It danced tauntingly across the bed, her floor, to the desk where she and Ivy had been working on an assignment for school together.

Gabby stared with dry eyes.

How? How did anyone do this?

Day in and day out?

It was utterly impossible.

Her body was too small. Her head too small.

Her head. A place that Gabby, no, Ivy, had always thought huge. Huge enough to change the world, Ivy told her. It had shrunk in a few days, and Gabby hadn't known that was possible. She hadn't known grief was capable of physically making your body smaller. Because, she, Gabby Hunt, was far too small to contain the width and breadth of the emotions she was feeling.

She turned her face into the pillow, still damp from the night, and she screamed, and she roared, and she screamed some more. But it wasn't enough.

Her door opened a crack and dark ruffled hair over a slim pale face poked through the gap. 'Gabby?' Her brother's voice was cracked and hoarse from the operation.

She had forgotten he was even in the house, if she was honest. He'd kept to his room and out of the way. Gabby scrubbed a hand across her face.

'Are you okay?'

'Go away, Tobes.' She sounded nearly as bad as he did.

'Do you want some biscuits? I have some in my room I can't eat.'

If only biscuits could make this better. 'You keep them. You'll be able to eat them soon.'

'Okay.' His voice was weak, but kind. He backed away and the door closed.

Gabby's heart splintered a little more.

A soft knock at the door roused Gabby again and she lifted her head. If it was Toby she might just throw her laptop at him.

The door opened and her mother entered, wrapped in her long silk dressing gown of blues and lilacs, with a cup in her hand. 'Camomile.'

Gabby eased her head back down.

Her mother placed the drink on the bedside table and sat on the bed. 'I might take you to see Dr Harris today, Gabby.'

'It hurts so much.' How was she supposed to live like this?

'I know it does. I'll make that appointment.'

Gabby didn't have it in her to argue, so she just shook her head.

'Drink your tea.' Her mother kissed her and left again.

The tea cooled untouched. Gabby lay on her side, motionless, continuing to watch the line of light dance across the room to the assignment she'd been working on with Ivy, when an idea came to her.

That's what she'd do. It was, at least, something active.

* * *

Gabby banged on the door with the heel of her fist, unable to stop the tears. It wasn't what she'd wanted, to arrive in full emotional turmoil. This wasn't what they needed. Her intention had been to spend time with Ivy's family. With those who loved her.

'Hello?'

Gabby took a step back. 'You're not Mr Kimber.'

'No, I'm not. I'm Alek. Can I help you?' His face was soft and kind, and Gabby cried some more.

'I . . . I . . . Ivy . . .'

Alek took a step towards her. 'I'm sorry. I don't think the family are up to visitors yet. Maybe you can leave a message on Ivy's Facebook wall. I've heard that's what all her friends are doing.'

'I'm not just her friend. I'm her *best* friend.' She lifted her chin and shouted. 'Theo! Theo!'

'Hey. You can't do that.' Alek wasn't happy now.

Owen and Verity arrived behind Alek.

'What's going on, Alek?' Owen saw her first. 'Oh, Gabby . . .'

Verity took his hand and shook her head.

'I'm sorry, Gabby.' Owen used that soft tone that everyone was using on her.

'Theo!' she yelled into the air.

Theo was at the doorstep. His eyebrows rose. 'Gabby? What are you doing here?'

'I loved Ivy,' she sobbed.

'I'll call Charlotte.' Theo's mother turned, abandoning Gabby on the doorstep.

'I loved Ivy like you loved her.' The words were out of her mouth before she could stop them.

Owen put his arm around her. 'Come on. You can wait in the kitchen until your mum collects you.'

Why didn't her body fit her anymore? Why didn't she understand what everyone was saying to her or why they said it? Had Ivy been the glue holding the world together? Had her death made everything come unstuck?

'Everything's broken because Ivy's dead,' she wailed.

'I have to see if Verity is okay,' Owen said to Alek.

Alek nodded.

Theo and Alek watched her like she was a wild animal that might pounce at one of them any moment.

'I just want Ivy back, Theo. You can understand that, can't you?' she pleaded. Desperate to . . . What was it she wanted from him? Why had she come to Ivy's home?

Ivy was no longer there.

Theo's face contorted in a manner she was no longer able to read.

'I can't do this, Gabby.' He left.

All that was left was Alek. A stranger.

Gabby slid off the stool and backed away into a corner, where she crumpled into a heap on the floor. Muffled voices in the distance spoke her name, and then a face she recognised hovered over her.

'Oh, Gabby, love.' Hands reached down and raised her up. 'Gabby. Come home, love. Doctor Harris has said he'll come out to see you.'

Gabby allowed herself to be shepherded out of the house Ivy had lived in, that was now empty of Ivy, empty of feeling and empty of love.

CHAPTER 30

Claudia

'This is a quick recap briefing, as nothing came in on the overnight line.' Claudia couldn't look Dominic in the face. It scared her what would show on her own.

Would she give herself away? No. It wasn't possible. Your face couldn't say, *By the way, I think you might have murdered your wife, my best friend.* But what *could* give away the thoughts tumbling around inside her head would be her demeanour. He'd definitely pick up that she wasn't comfortable around him anymore.

It would be an idiot that missed it.

Her head ached. 'I think we cut the briefing short yesterday after Krish found the text to Ivy, so let's see what else we have.' She thought back. 'The TikTok account. Last night we made the presumption it was Ivy's, because of our previous hypothesis about her assault. Has anyone looked at the account to see what, if anything, it's had to say about her murder?'

Dominic looked like he didn't have a care in the world, and she didn't know how he did that. 'I stayed on a while after everyone left, just to write up my notes.'

She nodded. There were no words.

'While here I checked the account. Or rather I checked the accounts I'd been given by two of the students and they were correct.'

Her head was thundering. She couldn't make sense of what Dominic was saying. 'How does this relate to Ivy?'

'Two kids said the account had been silent since Ivy's murder.'

'Okay.' Claudia rubbed her forehead with her fists.

Dominic hadn't finished. 'One of them brought up a good point.'

She wished he'd get to *his* point. 'Which is?'

'If the account was Ivy's, what about all the people she has demonised using it? We're not just looking at Windermere.' Dom frowned. 'Windy. Can I just say Windy? It's much less of a mouthful.'

'Jesus.'

'Were you pissed last night, boss?' Rhys was the only one idiotic enough to outright ask her.

'Headache.'

Lisa shot Rhys a hard glance. He shrugged in response.

'You want to go home, boss?' Krish asked. 'We can cover you.'

'No, it's fine. I'm due to speak to Ivy's family today. I was thinking maybe Theo can shed some light on his and Ivy's history, in the timeframe we're talking about. That's if I can get him alone. He's old enough. I could maybe broach this TikTok thing.'

'Good luck with that,' Dominic said, his voice strained.

She needed to focus. 'You're going back to the school today?'

'Yeah. I thought instead of people who knew Ivy, I'd talk to those the account targeted, so I made a couple of lists yesterday evening. One was of those who attend Wellington-Bell, and the other are people the account targeted who don't. They include other young lads, some low-level weed dealers . . . and, bizarrely, Charlotte Hunt is on there being accused of not loving her daughter enough. I think Ivy must have run out of things to make videos of that day, or her best mate had just been crying on her shoulder about her mum.'

Claudia shook her head.

'The lists were easy enough to create. TikTok's in the public domain.'

'And someone's working the TikTok account to confirm Ivy was behind it? I don't want us to do all this work, only for it to have nothing to do with our investigation. Also, if it is Ivy's account, we need to work the non-Wellington-Bell targets and not just assume it's someone close to her.'

'Though "donkey" does give that impression,' said Krish.

'Yeah. We need to cover our bases, though.'

'I'm going to have a look at it today, boss.' Rhys said.

He enjoyed the more technical side of things, but even with open-source research, he'd still have to submit a request to identify who was behind the account *ThinkyoucanhideWB*, and that could take a lot longer than a homicide investigation generally allowed.

'TikTok's a Chinese-owned company,' he reminded her. 'So don't expect us to officially find out who the user of the account is. They're not going to comply with a British police request for help in a criminal investigation.'

'Even if it is murder,' Claudia muttered.

'Even then.'

'Everyone's busy. Do your best and don't forget to eat, and keep me updated, please.' She turned to Lisa. 'Sorry, Lisa. Do you have any more of those painkillers? I haven't had chance to pick up my own.'

Lisa rummaged through her bag and threw a strip across to Claudia. 'Keep them, boss. You need them more than me at the moment.'

Claudia thanked her and headed out, checking her emails from her phone before starting the car. Alek was at the Henthorn-Kimbers', and everyone was up. Theo was in better shape than when he'd arrived home the previous day. Though Alek couldn't promise the boy would talk to her.

There was also an email from the forensic lab, which had responded to her submission already. Claudia's heart jumped into her throat. She swallowed. It was thick and awkward, like there was something stuck in there.

She had to get a grip. Find out what they'd said and go from there.

The email was short and to the point.

DI Nunn,

Our records show this case has been finalised at court, therefore a rush cannot be put on your submission. It will go in the queue with all other submissions.

If you were lucky, you could get exhibits from a homicide inquiry examined urgently. Being in the queue with the rest of the force means that your submission will processed in approximately eight to twelve weeks.

Forensic submissions

Claudia only had to wait eight to twelve weeks to find out if her dad was a killer or not.

CHAPTER 31

Theo

The trying-too-hard Pretty Boy cop was still in the kitchen, where he appeared to live. Theo couldn't remember him leaving last night.

He couldn't remember much about last night. There were snatches of images. Mostly of Ivy. But interspersed between them were Ed, Ed's most wonderful parents, overhead lights at crazy speeds . . . Then this morning there was Gabby, and now Pretty Boy was offering to make him a drink.

In his own kitchen.

Maybe Pretty Boy had moved in.

'If I want a drink, I'll make it myself,' Theo growled.

'You must be thirsty.' His mother hovered over him.

'Why?' The truth was, he was gasping, but he wouldn't admit that to Pretty Boy, or even while Pretty Boy was in the room.

His mother's face was thinner, if that were possible. Paler and bony. And her eyes darker. It made her look less human, more feral.

'It's okay, Theo. We're all hurting. I'm not angry. We're not angry.'

We?

Just then, Owen appeared behind his mother.

Oh, that we.

At least she didn't mean Pretty Boy.

'Angry?' Shit, his throat was like a cat litter tray after a desert had blown across it. He coughed feebly.

Pretty Boy placed a glass of water on the counter in front of him, cold condensation slipping down the side of the tumbler.

Rage swept up inside him, raw and overwhelming. Too huge for him to contain. Theo, shaking with fury, swept his arm out wide, along the countertop, sliding the tumbler off the granite on to the tiled floor with a splintering crash. His mother shrieked.

'Theo, what are you doing? What is . . . ? Oh, Theo.' She sagged on to a counter stool, not even making a move for the shards on the floor.

'It's okay, I'll do it. Just tell me where your dustpan and brush are.'

The energy had gone from Theo to be angry at Pretty Boy now.

Owen had his arms around his mother and pointed to the far lower cupboard. Pretty Boy got to clearing up. His mother was sobbing again.

'I'm sorry,' Theo whispered, drawing close to her shaking shoulder. 'I'm sorry, Mum.'

From under her hunched shoulder, she reached out a pasty white hand and he took it. The hand he held was slimmer than it used to be, the bones protruding, the skin drier and cooler.

'I'm so sorry, Mum. I'm sorry.' Theo collapsed on to her shoulder, and the weight of Owen's hand pressed down on his back.

His mother twisted in her seat and took him in her arms and they sobbed, Owen a silent presence beside them.

Quietly something was placed on the counter. Theo wiped his eyes with the back of his hands. Another glass of water waited for him.

He scrubbed at his face with the sleeve of his sweater, then reached out and drank. The water was gone in only five gulps.

'Better?' asked Owen.

'Yeah.'

'We don't have long.' His mother's voice was cracked and broken. 'Detective Inspector Nunn will be with us shortly, Theo. She would like to speak to us all, and she's requested to speak to you alone.'

'What? Why?'

She rose from her stool and rubbed the top of his head before walking around to the sink for her own glass of water. 'Because she's investigating your sister's murder, Theo, and she thinks as you're Ivy's brother and of similar age, you might be able to provide her some insight that we can't. It's all very normal.'

'Why don't you go and wash your face?' Owen said gently.

Theo didn't have an argument in him. He left the kitchen and skulked up to his room, where he scooped off his sweater and threw it to the floor.

In the en-suite bathroom, he was surprised by his reflection. He couldn't even remember when he'd last showered. How disgusting was that?

The shiny chrome of the showerhead sparkled at him in a way that taunted. The showerhead was clean and bright; Theo was dirty and all things dark.

In the distance, the doorbell chimed. Theo's stomach lurched.

Turning his back on the shower, Theo washed his face and brushed his teeth.

Tired of the too spotless bathroom, Theo returned to his room, pulled a sweater from his drawer and yanked it over his head, before sinking down on to his bed. How was he supposed to talk to the detective about his sister? What was he supposed to say? It all seemed far too impossible, a leap too huge to make.

Then Owen shouted up the stairs for him to join them. He couldn't put this off any longer.

It was the blonde-haired cop from the night they'd come to tell them Ivy was dead. She must be the inspector. He had not been capable of absorbing details that night. He wasn't sure he could absorb them any better today. Pretty Boy was standing kind of out of the way, at the side of the room. The inspector must be important. His mum and Owen were together on one of the sofas.

'—mother came and picked her up, and took her home. Poor girl, she—' Owen was talking about Gabby. He was telling the cop. Why would he do that?

Theo's mother saw him at the door and reached out her hand to him. Owen, no longer rattling on about things that didn't concern him, shifted so there was room for Theo between them. It wasn't that Theo wanted to sit between them, but he did want to be close to his mother.

'Hi, Theo.' The detective greeted him. 'I've been telling your parents that I've come to see how everyone's doing and to update you all on the investigation so far.'

Parents, plural. He wished people wouldn't use that word. He had a father. It's just that he was no longer here.

The detective continued: 'It's only early days—' she directed this to his mother and Owen — 'but I believe it's important you are kept aware of what we're doing.'

His mother's face was tense. That face she had when if you didn't do as she said there would soon be shouting. Would she really shout at the detective running Ivy's investigation? Theo sank further into the sofa.

'The post-mortem and witness evidence tells us Ivy was drinking before she was killed.'

Go Ivy.

'Is this relevant?'

'We're not sure what is and what isn't relevant at this time. In the first few days, we collect all the information we can.'

His mother clamped her jaw shut.

'We're interviewing everyone at Wellington-Bell to build a picture of Ivy. Judge Henthorn-Kimber, we've talked to your assistant, and he's helping us work through your caseload over the last year, and anyone who may have been released over the last six months. Can I ask, do any of your cases, any of the defendants, stand out to you?'

His mother's hand tightened around his own. Her mouth thinned into a fine line. She shook her head. 'I can't think straight; I'm sorry. I'll have to leave it to Neil and your team.'

'That's fine.' The detective made a note. 'It's part of our job.'

'You took Ivy's things . . .' That break in his mother's voice was a permanent fixture now, cracked at the end of the half-unasked sentence.

'We're working through them. Thank you for releasing them. As you know, you will get them back.'

His mother, the strong one in the family, sagged against him. Immediately Owen's arm came around him to reach her. Theo felt in the way. Like he shouldn't be there. A regular feeling, if he was honest.

'It's part of the reason I've come today. It's important to build up a complete as possible picture of Ivy, to better know who might have done this to her. And while we wait for the digital department to examine her laptop and phone, I'd like to ask you, as a family, a few more personal details about her.'

'Shall I make some more drinks?' Pretty Boy finally spoke.

His mother went to rise from the sofa, pushing her hands down to lift herself. 'That's my job, Alek.'

Owen must have applied pressure, because she didn't get very far.

Pretty Boy held up his hand. 'No. It's fine. I can do it while you're talking.'

His mother's eyes closed.

'I understand this is the most difficult thing you've ever gone through,' the detective said. 'There's no rush. We can sit and have our tea and have a chat at your pace. I have all the time in the world for you. And if you have any questions as we go, I'll answer them the best way I can.'

'You sound extremely capable, and you are very kind, Detective,' his mother whispered, 'but that capability and kindness will not bring my daughter back, will it?'

* * *

Pretty Boy brought the large tray in with an array of teas, coffees, milks and sugars. He placed it on the coffee table and returned to his spot at the side of the room as unobtrusively as he could.

Theo's mind was still spinning at the frank exchange between his mother and the detective. It hadn't been unkind, but his mother's grief had made her more forthright than he'd ever seen her.

He imagined it was similar to her work head. The one he'd heard about. Apparently, she had a bit of a reputation for not putting up with shit in her court.

The detective had taken it all in her stride. If she worked this kind of case all the time, she was probably used to grief and people striking out. He'd know more about it if he studied a more socially centred A level, but Theo was all about science: physics, chemistry and maths. He was going to take the science world by storm. Or he'd been going to.

That was until . . . Ivy.

'Would you like a little time alone?' the detective asked. 'I can have a chat with Theo, if that's okay?'

His stomach twisted so hard he winced.

'Do you really need to?' his mother asked.

The detective shared a look with Pretty Boy, who shook his head. No, Pretty Boy had not been able to talk to him, because Pretty Boy was an invader in his home.

'Theo?' His mother put her palm to his cheek, her skin cool and dry.

'I'm okay.'

She brought up her other palm and held his face between her hands. The freshness and familiarity of her shower gel cut deep in his heart. 'You can do this. Yesterday was tough.

Today is tough. Tomorrow will be tough. But we are family, and we love you and we are always here.'

Theo swallowed the threatening tears and nodded. He couldn't say no when his mother was doing the very best she could. It would look like he had something to hide.

He *did* have something to hide.

CHAPTER 32

Claudia

Claudia followed Theo to the kitchen. He was silent, his shoulders hunched, his hands in his tracksuit pockets. Socked feet padding silently through the house.

He didn't look like he'd cleaned himself since the night she'd delivered the death message. His hair was limp and lacklustre, and his skin dull and grey. While his mother was pale from grief and lack of food, she was cleaning herself. Claudia hoped Theo would take personal care of himself soon.

Alek's reports said he was difficult to connect with. That he seemed to take it as a personal affront that Alek was in his home when Ivy was not.

Detective constables often wanted to work on a homicide team, but they rarely understood what the emotional toll, the reality of working closely with the family, meant.

It was this hostility Claudia could sense vibrating from Theo now as she walked through his home, his back to her as they moved forward.

But the murder inquiry wasn't just a case. It was about real people. Those left behind picking up the pieces of their own lives after a loved one had been removed without

199

warning and without a chance to say goodbye. It was violent, and the emotions were brutal. They swung from one extreme to another, from one moment to the next, and being a DC on that team meant more than investigation. It meant connecting on a level with a person going through real traumatic grief. If a detective wasn't willing to reach out to the person, if all they wanted was the glory of an arrest in a murder case, if the chase was all they had, then Claudia's team was not for them.

And this boy in front of her, he was giving off all the anger, all the fury and all the grieving turmoil she'd ever seen. Her mind snapped back to her conversation with Nadira and Smithy during the post-mortem: at eighteen, his brain was still developing. It was no wonder he didn't have a clue how to process what had happened.

Finally they reached the kitchen and Theo dumped himself on to a high chair. Claudia matched him, sitting side-on to him. She'd brought her Earl Grey and Theo had a glass of water, both now sitting on the island.

Somehow she had to reach this boy. She had to break through the solid wall he'd erected and talk to him about Ivy.

'Thanks for coming to talk to me,' she said. 'When I said it's hard, I know how hard.'

Theo glared at her. She wouldn't share her personal stuff with this kid. He had enough on his plate without her dumping more, and he wouldn't thank her for it.

'How are you doing?'

It might sound like a stupid question to some, like a waste of a question, because how the hell would anyone think he was doing? But if Claudia understood anything about teenagers, it was that they didn't feel heard. If Theo here was one of those teenagers, then he might see everyone ask his parents how they were, or some version of the question, but no one ask him. So that was where she'd begin.

He picked up his glass and stared into the bottom of it.

'It's a pretty unanswerable question right now, isn't it? Take one day at a time. We're doing everything we can to find out who killed your sister, Theo.'

'Her name was Ivy.'

He was talking. That was a start. 'Yes, Ivy. We're doing everything we can to find out who killed Ivy.'

The silence echoed in the cavernous kitchen.

'I'd love to know more about Ivy. Would you tell me what she was like?'

He glared again. Claudia could see the fire burning in his soul.

'School tell me that you two were close. They said Ivy kept you on the straight and narrow, and she could be seen ticking you off.' She put a small laugh in her voice.

Theo's head jerked to look at her again. 'Who said that?'

'I think it's lovely that you were so close. Can you tell me about it? I think it might really help.'

It made her itch using the past tense word 'were' when talking to a murdered child's brother, who was not much more than a child himself.

'They're all talk at that place.'

Something passed through his mind. Claudia saw the thought in his eyes, and then he closed it down. What was that? Why, when he said they all talked there, did he shut himself down?

The anonymous account! Was it really Ivy?

She had to tiptoe around this.

'Theo, both you and Ivy had some trouble about a year ago. Can you tell me what it was about? Why you were so angry?' She held up a hand before he could react. 'You're not in trouble today. I'm here for Ivy. I don't care what you did a year ago at school. Unless you killed someone there a year ago, but I'm going to presume the school wouldn't have kept that quiet.'

'You'd be surprised,' he muttered.

'They like to keep their own dirty laundry to themselves?' she asked.

'Oh yeah. It's not the done thing to have word spread that there's trouble at Wellington-Bell. Too many rich donors who might withdraw their funding.' He was opening up.

She'd caught him on the school hook. 'I thought with a private school it was funded through the extortionate fees.'

'You'd think so.' He took another gulp of water. 'But they rely on wealthy donors to pad the coffers.'

Wow, money did flow to money. But that didn't take her any closer to understanding Ivy or what occurred a year ago. 'Once again, you're not in trouble. It would really help if we understood what happened last year. That way we can figure out if it impacted on Ivy.'

Theo shook his head. 'It was Ivy's story to tell.'

Claudia considered this. The comment made sense if what they'd hypothesised about a sexual assault was actually what had occurred. 'And your story?' How had Theo become involved?

He finished the water, whereas Claudia hadn't even picked her tea up. 'You know everything. I wasn't happy. I got into some trouble. The school dealt with it quietly, and Ivy, being Ivy, tried to keep me on the straight and narrow.'

He looked wiped. She didn't want to push him much further but she had to try. For his sister, for him and for his family. 'What do you know about the TikTok account?'

Theo picked up his empty glass. It was his excuse to fiddle, the tumbler a way to hide his face, but he'd used the evasion tactic up too quickly.

'Theo, please.'

'I don't use social media.'

The team hadn't found anything for him online. It didn't mean he didn't have an online account, though. Kids were sneaky about their internet lives. They had dummy accounts so their parents didn't know about their real accounts. 'Was it talked about at school?'

'Like I said, I'm not interested in social media.'

'Not even if it's your sister running it? The account is pretty damning, Theo.'

His jaw clenched, the pulse throbbed and his eyes darkened.

'How did you feel about her running that account? Was that why you were so angry back then? Do your parents know?' There was one chance with Theo, which was why she'd asked multiple questions.

Theo flew off his stool. It skittered across the floor behind him before toppling with a metallic crash from the legs and dull thud from the seat. Theo was already out of the door before the stool hit the floor.

Claudia bent to collect it and brought it up to standing.

The judge ran in, her face wild with concern.

'He's obviously struggling,' Claudia said quietly.

'You pushed too hard.'

A door slammed overhead.

'You were here to help us, and this is what you've done.'

Claudia remained calm. There was already too much high emotion; she wouldn't add more. 'I am here to help.'

'But Theo . . .'

How did a parent grieve when she still had two children to care for?

'You didn't tell us that Theo had problems last year at the same time as Ivy. I wanted to know what had caused them. That was all.' She kept her tone level.

'How do Theo's issues relate to Ivy's murder?' The judge was nearly screeching.

If she were not grieving and were in her own courtroom, she would assess the situation calmly and see the sense in Claudia's explanation. But as the mother of a murder victim, for her, the world was upside down.

'Until we know the details, we're pulling information together as best we can,' Claudia admitted. 'All we know at this point is that it's unlikely someone killed her because of your work. Ivy was laid out peacefully and with some thought. I'd suggest a person who wanted to cause you hurt would not kill your daughter and then make her comfortable. I'm sorry to say, I wouldn't have thought they'd care. So, we need to review Ivy's life — not just her recent life but her recent past, and as I said on the phone, Theo can help with that. Teenagers tend not to tell parents everything, much as parents would like to believe they're close. There are still secrets being held tight to the chest. Theo walking out the way he did leads me to believe I was right about that.'

CHAPTER 33

Dominic

The day was bright. A blue sky overhead deceived the people below into thinking spring had arrived. The cold soon snapped that wishful thinking in the bud. March was unpredictable.

Dominic walked towards the entrance of Wellington-Bell for his second day there. Concern for his daughter foremost in his thoughts. She'd been off-kilter at the briefing, and he wasn't sure when her next appointment with Robert was.

Sharpe had been good to the pair of them, but her support couldn't last for ever. They had to buckle down and get on with their jobs. Claudia had been through so much the thought of it terrified him. The abduction, the fire, Russ. How much could she take before crumbling and finally breaking?

Robert appeared to help, but she had to go for him to work his magic.

The large wooden doors of Wellington-Bell towered over him.

Time to put his work head on. He'd worry about Claudia later. The best thing he could do for her now was get as much information on Ivy and Theo as possible.

He was about to step over the school threshold when his phone vibrated in his pocket. Dominic turned and walked back down the steps as he pulled the phone out.

The number flashing across his screen was Adrian Cox. Dominic had played football with Ade in the force team many years ago, when they were both much younger men. Now they were both counting down the last few years to retirement.

Dominic answered. 'Hey, Ade. This is a surprise. It's been a bloody long time, mate. I hope you're not attempting to recruit me for a new team. We're dinosaurs now, you know.' He laughed.

'Hey, Dom. I thought I'd check in with you, see how you're doing, after the Tyler stuff.'

Dominic frowned. He'd heard from a lot of people after Ruth had died. Mates had come out of the woodwork to offer their sympathies and support, mates he'd not spoken with for many years, but the police was seen as a big family when tragedy struck; they were there for him. Ade hadn't been one of those mates, though. So why now, when it was all over?

'Yeah, it's been a tough one, as I'm sure you can imagine. Getting a guilty verdict helps with closure, though.' He needed to get off topic. 'Fancy a beer some time? Catch up?'

'Yeah, course. We'll sort that out. Email your availability, I'll check my rota and we'll sort it.'

The sentences used when there was no intention of meeting. Dominic scratched his head. 'I'll do that.' He hoped that was the end of the call. 'Great to hear from you, mate.'

'Erm, that's not all, Dom.'

Obviously. Ade had not called from thin air because he suddenly needed to catch up. 'What's up?'

Where was he working now? Dominic had to admit he was as guilty as Ade for not keeping in touch. He had no idea where his mate had landed. There was always a lot of movement within the police service. So many departments and ranks; people could regularly change where they were. It kept officers and staff from becoming bored, and it was how people stayed in one career, yet felt like they'd had many and varied ones.

'I'm seeing out my years in forensics . . .'

That was an odd choice, but Dominic supposed it kept Ade away from the front line, so he could keep his nose clean and retire easily, without an idiot putting in a complaint about him. 'Cushy.'

'Yeah, it's not bad. The thing is . . .'

He was dragging this out. Dominic tried to trawl through his mind and check for the cases he might have running now. He'd been involved in the Cunningham inquiry, but hadn't thought his name was on any of the exhibits. As the task force sergeant, he could clearly be the place to touch base. 'Spit it out, Ade. Some of us are working.'

'Yeah, sorry, mate. The thing is, we just received a new submission with Ruth's case number on. I was a little surprised to be honest, bearing in mind Tyler's just been convicted of her murder.' His voice lowered on the last two words.

What the actual . . . ? What was happening? Dominic's mind was spinning. Had he heard this idiot right? 'Say that again, mate.'

'A tumbler from your kitchen, Claudia submitted it for examination. It confused me a little, and being mates, I thought I'd ask you rather than Claudia. I don't want her to snap my head off, if you know what I mean?'

Dominic did, and he was holding himself back from doing the same. If it wasn't for Ade's complete nosiness, Dominic would know none of this, so he had to hold it together. 'Yeah, definitely.'

'You worried there's another suspect? Or Tyler was working with someone else?'

'Nothing so serious, mate.' He forced a laugh. It was like trying to breathe through a mouthful of the desert. 'Like you said, you know what Claudia's like. She's tying up loose ends. Dotting Is, crossing Ts. Doesn't want the bastard to walk at any point in the future, even if it means making the force pay up for more testing, even if they don't realise she's doing it.'

What the hell had got into her head? The tumbler hadn't been submitted, as it hadn't been deemed important.

He'd completely lost his mind leaving it in his own rubbish bin in the first place, but come on, killing his wife in their house, leaving her blood at the scene and trusting he could get away with his plan, disposing of her body, washing his tyres to remove evidence from the dump site and changing them as soon as possible, dumping his own clothes and washing furiously — in bleach — was it any wonder a small thing like the tumbler had slipped his utterly fucked-up mind? *No.* No, it fucking wasn't.

Dominic went on: 'She could get kicked up the arse for this though. You know how it is. Too many in the know and it gets leaked.'

'Yeah, I get it. I'm glad I called. Good catching up with you, Dom. I hope you're both doing as well as you can. Give me a call when you're up for a drink some time, yeah?'

'Absolutely, I will. Remind me how long for the results?'

'Oh, as I emailed Claudia, it can no longer be classed as urgent, as Tyler's been convicted. So unfortunately you're looking at eight to twelve weeks.'

Ade was about to end the call, but Dominic needed something from him now. He needed to control the shitshow that had slipped out from under him unawares. 'Just one thing, Ade.'

'Yeah, what's that?'

'Let me know the results before you send them to Claudia, yeah?' He had no idea what they'd say, how damning they'd be. If blood was found, it was easily explainable as shed when the glass was broken. But Ruth hadn't any cuts other than the ones he'd inflicted. It was still a long way from prosecuting him.

Dominic had no idea how he'd deal with this. No matter what he had on Ade, the man wouldn't destroy evidence for him. The best he could hope for was that he be pre-warned.

Silence slithered down the line.

'Ade?'

'I . . . I'm not sure . . . It's not professional. I could lose my job. I know what you've—'

'Ade!'

'Dom, it's my job.'

'And this was my wife.'

Silence again.

Dominic pushed further. 'Remember your wife, Ade? You still with her?'

'Yeah . . . What's she—'

'And your mate Tim?'

The silence was brittle now.

'And I know you remember Tim's wife. What was her name, Ade? Go on, you remember. What was her name?'

'Fuck you, Dom.' It was a low, hard hiss.

Dominic smiled. 'Your lovely wife had just given birth to your eldest, as I remember. All happy homes and knitted booties. I suppose there's a choice to be had here. Your job or your marriage.'

'You're dead to me now.'

'That's better. So I expect to kept informed of the results of the examination. Before Claudia.'

'Fuck. You.'

The memory slid into his mind's eye. 'Oh, and if you consider calling my bluff, I have photographic evidence of that evening.'

If it were at all possible, the phone line crackled with Adrian's fury. This made Dominic laugh, and with ease this time. 'I'll speak to you soon, Ade. Mate.'

The line went dead.

CHAPTER 34

It would have been easy to say he'd been expecting it, but after Tyler's guilty verdict, he'd begun to believe he'd got away with killing Ruth. No one would think he'd killed her if her killer was already in prison.

Mrs Honeycutt was as charming as she'd been the previous day, but Dominic had difficulty connecting to her; he was afraid he'd probably insulted the receptionist with his aloofness today. She was a kind woman, but all he was worried about was spending the rest of his life behind bars.

That couldn't happen. Ade had promised to alert him before updating Claudia. That would provide him with a head start, should he need one. A head start from his own daughter.

What a pile of shit he'd landed in.

How the holy fuck had this happened?

Why the fucking hell had she submitted the glass in the first place?

Samuel Tyler had just been found guilty. Regardless of Claudia's reservations — because the murderous bastard refused to take responsibility for the crime he didn't do — Dominic believed she'd moved past it, and certainly since the verdict had been delivered.

None of it made sense.

His life was about to fall apart, and Dominic didn't understand why.

He was directed to the same classroom as the previous day and inside he walked over to the desk he'd used before.

His list of interviewees differed slightly today. The alteration made, with Claudia's authorisation, after talking to the students yesterday.

Today, it comprised students and staff named in the TikTok videos, if that's what you called the cut-throat pieces on the anonymous account that may or may not have been created by Ivy.

They were still trying to pin that one down.

It would be an interesting day, one that had the potential to take his mind off the other issue.

First in was Mr Miles Gillingham.

Mr Gillingham knocked, five minutes early, and strode right in with confidence and assuredness. This was his school, his ground. Dominic, his stride said, was a visitor.

Gillingham didn't wait to be asked. He took the chair, seated himself opposite Dominic and held out his hand. 'Miles Gillingham, chemistry. Pleased to meet you.' This man was saying he had nothing to be concerned about. He was here in his school to help Dominic, the visitor.

'Detective Sergeant Dominic Harrison.' Dominic couldn't help it; he held Gillingham's hand a little harder and for a little longer than necessary. He wasn't in the mood for games.

When he released the hold, Gillingham plastered a warm smile on his face, placed his hands in his lap and crossed one leg over the other. For all intents and purposes, he was here for a friendly chat. 'What can I do to help, Detective?'

Dominic studied his notes, making Gillingham wait. The phone call from Ade lingered in his mind, and this man had irritated him, simply by the way he'd walked into the room. Finally, he pulled himself together. 'Did you see the TikTok account the day Ivy was killed?'

Gillingham's eye twitched. 'I have a Facebook account to keep in touch with family in America, but that's all I use it for, and it's the only social media account I have. It's against school policy to connect with the children's social media accounts.'

'I didn't say the account belonged to a student of the school.'

His face paled, but a flush crept into his cheeks. 'Oh . . . I . . . Well . . . as you're here . . . I presumed . . .'

The confident, what-can-I-do-to-help teacher had suddenly disappeared and in his place was a bumbling idiot. How the hell did these people get paid so much in these schools to be left in charge of children with mouldable minds? 'Shall we start again?'

Gillingham cleared his throat. 'Thank you. I'm sorry. Yes, can we?'

So today would be interesting.

* * *

The second person through the door was a student from Theo's year. Alistair Fox, a short blond boy with a red face that screamed permanent embarrassment.

'You have the signed acceptance form from your parents?' Dominic asked.

Alistair produced the crinkled form and Dominic directed him to the chair recently vacated by Mr Gillingham.

'I'm not sure why you want to see me,' Alistair mumbled, face down. 'I didn't really know Ivy. We weren't in the same year. I was more likely to know Theo than his sister. But even me and Theo weren't friends.'

Dominic paused. He was about to make this perpetually embarrassed-looking boy actually embarrassed. It didn't give him enjoyment. All they wanted was to find out the truth behind the account, rather than running up the wrong tree. 'Alistair, you're not here because of a personal relationship with Ivy, but because of an online account you may know something about.'

Dominic was surprised to find Alistair's cheeks could actually deepen in shade. It at least told Dominic they were going in the right direction.

'I had nothing to do with that,' he spluttered.

'I don't imagine you did.' Alistair's video hadn't been particularly complimentary. 'What I want to ask is if you know who was behind it? Who would have known the information that made it online?'

Neither of them had named the account, and yet they were both aware of which account they were speaking.

The colour deepened further and Dominic worried Alistair might actually combust. A lot of people had heard of spontaneous human combustion, but Dominic didn't want to be the cause of such an event. 'Are you unwell? Do I need to call you a doctor?'

'No. No, I don't need one.'

Did he trust the boy and continue, or request help? 'This, uh, *complexion* is usual for you?'

Alistair nodded.

'Okay.' Dominic waited as the colour faded a little. 'So the account?'

Alistair sucked in a breath.

'It called you a cheater, said you'd copied someone's answers. You can't have been happy about that.'

Alistair pushed the chair back. 'It didn't mean I wanted to kill her.' He held up his hands. 'I didn't kill Ivy.'

'So it was Ivy's account? How do you know?'

Alistair looked at him like he was stupid. 'You really don't know?'

'Would I be here, talking to you, if I did?'

'It was obvious.' Alistair's voice was strong. 'When the account opened, the first post was about Windy.'

'It was about Windy?'

'Yeah, he doesn't go to Wellington-Bell anymore. Not after what happened.'

'What did happen?' And why hadn't the head told Claudia?

'The account said Windy had sexually assaulted her, well, not her, but the account holder, and the next thing is Theo is beating the living shit . . .' Alistair bit his lip.

'It's fine, go on.'

212

'Theo beat the living shit out of Windy, and Windy leaves with no further notice, and Theo stays with little to no repercussions for his actions. You had to be deaf, dumb or blind to not put two and two together. But I suppose some were, because the TikTok account took off pretty quickly after that, with other girls contacting the provided anonymous email to tell their own stories. If you were a boy who didn't know how to treat a girl correctly, then you were surely shitting yourself last year. Windy's parents were so disgusted by his behaviour they upped sticks and fled the country. Said his dad got a promotion in Dubai, but everyone knew it was to get Windy away from possible real trouble.'

'Did anyone ask Ivy outright about it?'

Alistair flushed some more, but reached down into his rucksack and pulled out a water bottle. He drank from the bottle and took some breaths.

Dominic waited.

'Not that I was aware. They might have done, but it wasn't common knowledge. I think people were more than happy with their own conclusions. They weren't interested in the truth as long as they weren't involved.' He sucked nervously on his water bottle again. 'Which was why half of the boys ended up being named and shamed on there, I suppose. The girls loved it.'

Dominic leaned back in his chair and thought it through. From what he'd heard, there was a lot of student drama last year. 'What about the teaching staff?'

Alistair shook his head. 'Hell no. They were mostly oblivious. The TikTok account was talked about behind closed doors, never loud enough for them to pick up. Even if they knew about an account naming boys from the school, there was absolutely nothing they could do. It was so completely closed off. An anonymous name and an anonymous email address for people to contact with juicy stories the account could share. Someone eventually squealed to one of the teachers.'

The flush reappeared.

'Who reported the account to the teachers and why?'

Alistair shrugged. 'It was bound to happen. That account terrified people. But you could only be terrified if you had something to hide.'

The flush deepened. He'd made his own admission, but that wasn't why Dominic was there.

'Because the school had no control and couldn't gain control, they sent a letter home asking parents to be aware of the account. That was all they could do. It was brushed under the carpet. As far as I could see, that TikTok account kept people accountable, and that's what most of the girls will tell you if you ask them.'

Dominic made notes. 'Let's say Ivy *was* the user of this TikTok account, Alistair . . .'

The boy nodded furiously.

'Who wanted Ivy Henthorn dead?'

CHAPTER 35

Claudia

Claudia walked through the incident room and into her office. There was a Post-it note stuck to her desk in Krish's handwriting, telling her Sharpe had called wanting an update. Claudia sighed, screwed the yellow square of paper into a ball and threw it into the bin beside her desk. Before Sharpe, a welfare check on Gabby Hunt was necessary.

Dropping into her chair, which swivelled slightly beneath her weight, she opened the top drawer of her desk and picked out the pack of paracetamol Lisa had given her. She popped two of the pills out and took them with the days-old water on the corner of her desk, which was warm as it dribbled down her throat.

Claudia screwed up her face, slammed the drawer shut and picked up the landline phone as she scrolled through her notebook for the number she required.

'Charlotte, it's Claudia Nunn, from the Complex Crimes Task Force.'

'You've heard,' Charlotte said quietly.

'Yes. I've been round to see the family this morning.'

'Look, I'm sorry if we upset them. Truly, I am. Gabby is only sixteen. How does someone at that age deal with such enormous emotions, Detective?'

'Charlotte?' Claudia rubbed her forehead and watched her team working, through the glass walls of her office.

Rhys was poking fun at Lisa who was pointing at Krish, who in turn was giving Rhys the finger. Dominic was still out. She'd be interested to hear what he came back with. The TikTok account thing was an interesting line of inquiry. It was Dominic himself she'd grown anxious around. She'd be glad when the results came back and she could get back on with her life.

'You don't want to speak to Gabby about this, do you? Please, Detective, you must have better things to do right now than admonish a child for grieving.'

'Charlotte . . .' She took a sip of the warm water and grimaced. It needed refreshing. 'I'm not calling to point the finger or reprimand anyone.'

'Oh,' Charlotte's voice rose slightly. 'You're not?'

'No. I'm calling to see how Gabby is and to see how you all are. Ivy's murder is having a massive detrimental effect on everyone.'

'Oh.' It was more of a squeak this time.

'Charlotte?'

'Yes. Yes, I'm sorry.'

'Please stop apologising. How is Gabby? How are you holding up? It can't be easy seeing your daughter so traumatised.'

The invisible line between them went quiet. Claudia gave her time to process the fact that this was a compassionate call, and nothing to do with the inquiry itself.

Finally Charlotte spoke. It was low and whisper-like. 'She is not doing well at all. As each day passes since Ivy's murder, Gabby deteriorates further, and I have no idea how to help her. There is no parenting handbook for a situation such as this.' There was a puppy-sized bark of laughter. 'There are so many parenting handbooks out there, but none of them cover what happens when your teenage child loses a best friend to murder. You'd think that book might exist by now, in today's world, wouldn't you, Detective?'

She was rambling a little now. There was no way to interrupt this woman, this mother. Her daughter was breaking with grief, and she was breaking with the inability to protect her daughter from that heartache. The only thing Claudia could do for Charlotte was listen to her until she ran out of steam.

'You would hope the book wasn't necessary, but it very clearly is.' There was a hitch of breath at the end of the sentence.

'I am sorry.'

'No need.'

Tears clogged the words in Charlotte's throat. 'She's my baby, you know? I would do anything to protect her. No matter what that vile video said about me. I am her mother. It's what we do.'

Oh yes, Charlotte had been on that list. Was she aware the video was possibly created by Ivy? Her fragile daughter's best friend. It was a question that had to be asked, but this didn't feel like the time. Claudia was calling to check in on the family.

'I understand that. Is she getting support?'

'Yes. Yes, she is. She's seen our doctor and he's prescribed anti-anxiety medication. When she's less volatile, we will make sure she talks to a therapist.'

'That sounds like a good plan.' Claudia needed to rearrange the appointment she'd cancelled with Robert. The support he offered had helped her deal with a lot of trauma, and in turn, kept her actively at work. 'Don't forget to take care of yourself as well as Gabby. You can't look after your daughter if you're not in a fit state yourself.'

'I will. Thank you, Detective.'

'If there's anything I can do to help, Charlotte, please let me know. I can direct you to some support services.'

'Thank you, Detective.'

Claudia ended the call, drained of all energy. The last four weeks had sucked the life out of her. Maybe she would take some well-earned time off. Robert had suggested the very thing a couple of times and she'd always made an excuse, as if South Yorkshire Police couldn't possibly run without her.

But the reality was Claudia was only a small cog in a huge machine. If she took leave, the machine would continue to turn without noticing her absence. Yes, a beach holiday could even be on the cards. With a book. Or two! Real time away.

All she had to do was close this investigation and wait for forensics to come back with nothing of evidential value on the tumbler, and she'd be gone. Policing in her rear view. Two weeks of sun, sand and . . . wow, how long had it been since she'd had any—

Dominic pushed his way into the incident room, a take-away coffee cup in one hand, his leather work folder hooked in the other and held against his side.

She'd tell Robert at their next session — which she still needed to rebook.

'Anything interesting?' Graham asked.

Claudia rose and walked to her door so she could hear what Dominic had to say.

Dominic threw the folder on his desk, which landed with a thump, and dropped into his chair, making sure to keep the takeaway cup level. 'Let's just say Ivy Henthorn divided people. She was a champion to some, giving voice where they may not otherwise have had one, and to others, she was the villain. They saw her as the trouble-causer. The one who could bring your world to its knees. But—' he supped on his coffee — 'as those who adored her pointed out, you only feared Ivy and the anonymous TikTok account if you had something to hide in the first place.'

'I say good for Ivy,' said Lisa.

'I see your point.' Dominic stared at the ceiling a moment. 'But it's the whole online thing I can't get behind, but maybe that's because I'm old.'

'Yeah, you are,' said Graham with a smirk.

'That I may be,' said Dominic, 'but I've learned today that kids rarely text. They use WhatsApp. Apparently texting is . . . well, old.' He laughed at himself.

Claudia cleared her throat, and the team turned their attention to her. 'I spoke to Theo Henthorn earlier. I wanted to know what happened to set him off last year, around the time the TikTok account went live, as there was nothing about him on there. But if it was Ivy's account, as is being suggested, then it's unlikely she'd reveal secrets about her brother. I'd hoped finding out the truth around events last year, and how Theo fits into that picture, might provide more insight. Unfortunately, he wasn't in a good place and he walked out. Gabby Hunt also had an emotional episode this morning, turning up at the family's home, crying about Ivy. Her mother collected her. I've just finished a call with Charlotte Hunt and Gabby's been prescribed anti-anxiety medication by their family doctor. We need to resolve this as quickly as possible. There are some extremely vulnerable kids involved in this.'

'One of the kids today said Theo assaulted Windy after the first TikTok video went live.' The original victim, Dominic meant. 'Theo was defending his sister.'

'And he wasn't kicked out of school?' Lisa's voice rose in surprise.

'Not only was he not kicked out of school, but he was the one who disappeared.' He quickly cleared up his meaning. 'He left the school and then his parents left the country for a job opportunity in Dubai.'

'This was what Mrs Honeycutt, the receptionist, was hinting at the other day,' said Claudia. 'And if what that kid told you is true, then it's another nail in the coffin of Ivy being *ThinkyoucanhideWB*. Which makes it more and more likely her killer was one of the people the TikTok account annihilated. Just not, Windy.'

'So we work our way through the list of people who were targeted on the account,' said Dominic. 'We speak to them and we find out where they were the night Ivy was murdered. I talked to a couple today, but I've warned the school it will be a lengthy process.'

'We do some more this evening, in front of parents,' said Claudia. 'With potential suspects, we need to approach it differently. We've narrowed down who we want to speak to and why. These are no longer witnesses; one of these kids could be our killer. They deserve to have legal representation or a parent present.'

Dominic rolled his eyes.

Sometimes Claudia despaired of his disregard of procedure. He wanted to skip to the end, where he could obtain the best result the quickest way possible. She ignored the eye-roll.

Krish jumped up from his chair, startling Claudia.

'I just received the contact information on the number that texted Ivy asking to meet.'

Now he had everyone's attention.

'The one she had listed as "donkey"?' Rhys laughed again at the name.

'That's the one. In fact, you've reminded me . . .' Krish's mouth twisted in something akin to a grin. 'I meant to change the identification in my own phone on your name . . .'

Lisa stopped typing and laughed at the pair of them. Rhys screwed a piece of paper into a ball and threw it across the room at Krish. It missed.

'Go on,' Claudia said, trying to get Krish back on track.

'It's registered to Charlotte Hunt.'

'It's what?'

'Yeah. The number that texted Ivy that night is registered to Charlotte Hunt.'

'That doesn't make sense. Why would Charlotte kill her daughter's best friend?' Rhys asked the obvious question.

'We don't know that the sender of the message killed Ivy,' Claudia said, trying to keep the team on the right track. Charlotte Hunt was a globally known name and the task force were not in the practice of making rushed arrests. 'The sender asked Ivy if they could meet. We have no idea what they wanted to talk about, if the meeting actually took place and, if it did, if the sender left Ivy alive.'

'But it's looking increasingly safe to assume that Ivy ran the anonymous TikTok account, and three weeks ago, there was a piece on there about Charlotte spending more time in the US nurturing her career than at home nurturing her kids. That had to piss Charlotte off.' Rhys pushed. 'Plus, weren't we just talking about putting some focus on those targeted by the TikTok account as people who might have wanted to kill Ivy?'

'Is that really enough for a grown woman to murder a teenage girl? To be pissed at her, yes. But to kill her?' Graham was incredulous.

'Remind me what the text said?' Lisa asked.

Krish flicked through multiple piles of paper in front of him until he found what he needed. '"Need to talk, urgent. Bingham Park in an hour".'

'There's no location,' Lisa noted. 'To me, that says Ivy knows where in Bingham Park the sender wants her to go. So she has a relationship with them already. We think she has some kind of relationship with Charlotte?'

Before anyone could respond, she jumped back in. 'I don't mean as the parent of her best friend, because that's not this. I mean, do we really think she has a *personal* relationship with Charlotte Hunt, that they have a shorthand language and can arrange meets this way? Also, would she put her best friend's mother down in her contacts as "donkey"?'

It was a sensible question, but again with the sniggering. Seriously, the boys were like children at times.

Lisa continued. 'And didn't we say when Krish found the text initially that there were very few messages from or to this number? How do we account for that?'

Krish shrugged. 'Having done all the phone work, I can tell you Ivy didn't text much. It was mostly to her parents. Kids tend to use messaging apps nowadays. So maybe this makes sense that it's Charlotte, with it being a text. As for "donkey", if her best friend was moaning about her mum so much, that could explain the name in the phone. It's not as if Charlotte Hunt could see it.'

'None of it makes sense,' Lisa finished. 'Do the other texts to and from this number sound like it's an adult conversation?'

With his finger, Krish ran down a sheet of paper high-lighted in different colours. One he'd read through multiple times. 'They're like the one we're working on. Blunt short-hand. Not easy to say.'

It didn't make sense, but they had the text and they had a name. It was a line of inquiry they had to follow up. 'As we have no CCTV at the park, and no forensic evidence on Ivy's body other than the dirt in the wound from the rock, which is no help at all, we have to follow up on the text. Now we have a name — which we discussed already. The text message alone isn't enough to make an arrest, but I suggest we talk to Charlotte and ask her to account for her whereabouts on Monday night.'

'That'll be interesting,' Rhys was grinning. He now had the violinist pegged as Ivy's killer.

'Even if it's all innocent and above board,' Claudia contin-ued, 'Charlotte may provide information that she might have been previously holding back for some reason. She may be able to tell us if Ivy was worried about anything, or what mood she was in. We need to know why Charlotte wanted to see her and also if Charlotte attended the park, and left Ivy alive . . .'

Rhys huffed.

Claudia eyeballed him and he nodded his agreement to shut up. 'Seeing Ivy and leaving her alive might be the rea-son she didn't disclose the meeting. As we know, fear makes people take the most unusual action.'

The comment drew her to Dominic. Looking at him you wouldn't think . . .

She had to keep on track. 'It would be easy for Charlotte to believe that informing us she saw Ivy moments before her death would put her in the spotlight in more ways than one. She's a mother and an international musician. In her mind, she has a lot to lose.'

'More than Ivy?'

'Mate?' Graham jumped in before Claudia blew her lid.

Rhys could be unfiltered when he spoke. It was always worse in the office. He reined it in when out in public and in front of higher rank, but there were times when it was too much for her, no matter how good at his job he was.

He held his palms up in submission.

Claudia shook her head. Rhys knew, as a fairly new unit, the Complex Crimes Task Force had to keep an open mind and assess all information, follow up leads, push at closed doors and turn over all stones. Jumping to conclusions was not their remit. 'I'll give Charlotte a call and let her know we're coming to have a chat. That way, if she feels she needs a legal representative there, she can organise one. As we're short-staffed and you're all tied up, I'll go and have that conversation. Graham, are you able to attend with me?'

'Yes, course, boss.'

Claudia headed to her office to make the call. Behind her, Rhys lowered his voice, but not enough that she'd miss it. 'She killed her daughter's best mate. Brutal.'

CHAPTER 36

Gabby

Gabby was sitting on the bench in the garden. The day was mild, and spring hinted at a possible early arrival. This was just a tease.

March was often a cold, bitter month. It was a month her mother often spent away, working. She hated the cold and preferred not to have the threat of rain or even snow ruin her day. The West Coast of the US was her favourite place to play at this time of year; it had become an annual ritual.

The only reason her mother was home was that Toby had his tonsils out. Her parents had paid for private surgery, rather than years on the NHS waiting list. Toby was doing well and eating better. Her mother would have returned to the US by now, had it not been for Ivy's murder.

Gabby pulled her knees up to her chest and remembered her best friend's laugh. The way her face crinkled because the laugh came from her belly and her whole body reacted. She was so funny to watch.

Gabby's stomach ached at the thought she would never see Ivy laugh ever again. They would never steal their parents' gin or watch dumb programmes over and over just because the guy was cute.

She hugged her knees to hold in the pain that might very possibly tear her apart.

'Gabrielle?' Her mother silently crept up behind her and wrapped her arms around Gabby's shoulders. 'You understand how much I love you, right?' Her mother rested her head on Gabby's, and Gabby leaned into the touch. Her own head tucking into the soft space between head and shoulder.

'Gabby?'

'Yeah, Mum?'

'Tell me,' Charlotte whispered.

'You love me.'

'I love you more than I have ever loved myself, Gabby.'

Gabby's heart tightened. What was wrong with her mum? Was she ill? Was she dying, too?

Clouds, some a deep grey, drifted across the open blue sky above them.

'I have to go away, Gab.'

A slight breeze fluttered the leaves on the lawn and up Gabby's bare legs as she sat in her short pyjamas. Goosebumps prickled as her skin reacted to the chill. She leaned further into the warmth of her mother. 'Okay.' Her own voice as low and quiet as her mum's had been.

Her mother stroked Gabby's head.

'You have to be brave when I'm gone, Gabby.'

This was very much not like her mother. Did she have the wrong child? Was she giving Toby's speech to Gabby? 'Mummm, you know it's me, Gabby?'

Charlotte moved round to face Gabby and lifted Gabby's face to her own with two fingers under her chin. 'I know who you are, Gabby.' She bent forward and kissed her forehead.

Gabby was seriously worried. 'What's going on?'

'I'm saying goodbye, Gabby, and I need you to be brave. Can you do that?'

'I'm fine when you go to work.' Gabby stared at her feet. Bright pink polish chipped at the edges. 'You're great at what you do.' Did she not tell her mum that enough?

'Gabby, when I'm gone, I need you to take care of yourself. To do that, I need you to shush and live your own life and let me go, okay?'

'Mum?' Her voice trembled.

Her mother continued to stroke her head. 'It's okay, sweet girl. I was never the mother you deserved, always too hung up on my career. I need you to know how much I love you.'

'But, Mum . . .' Tears, never far away, filled her eyes once again.

'It's time for you to fly, Gab.' Her mother cupped her face in her hands. 'I'm so very, very proud of the young woman you have become. I won't allow one mistake to take your future away.'

Gabby's throat thickened and her jaw tightened as she tried to hold back the tears.

'Hey.' The pad of her mum's thumb drew a line under her eye. 'No tears for me. This is exactly what I'm meant to do. You know that. You're a strong, bright girl. I wouldn't do it if I didn't think you could handle it. But I have complete faith in you and the future ahead of you. Promise me you'll reach out for it with both hands.'

The wind blew through again, and Gabby shivered. Her mum pulled her closer, as though at any moment she might slip through her arms. Gabby had never felt so warm or so loved. Especially by her mother.

'Gabby?' Her mum kissed the top of her head. 'You have to promise you'll be okay when I go.' She lowered her voice to a whisper. 'I'm doing this for you, because you are my heart and you are my soul. More than you will ever know.'

A deep unease quivered in the pit of Gabby's stomach. 'Please, Mum, tell me, are you ill? Please, you have to tell me.' She didn't think she could take it if her mother was ill. Not after Ivy. 'I can take it. I'm an adult.'

She couldn't. She really couldn't. If her mother was ill, Gabby would break into the smallest of pieces.

Her mother leaned in even closer still and lingered over her cheek as she kissed it. 'I'm not ill, Gabby. It's just extremely important you understand what I'm saying to you.'

'You're worrying me.' Gabby was terrified.

Gabby had been terrified all week.

The distant sound of the doorbell was nothing but a muted, low-toned chime in the garden. Gabby's mother flinched. 'You've taken your medication you were given earlier, haven't you?'

Gabby grabbed hold of her mother now. 'What? I don't understand.' The air crackled around her. A stampede of horses clattered through her chest, causing her to gasp for air.

'Dad is getting the door. Don't worry. Tell me, Gabby, did you take your medication today?'

Sweat trickled down her neck. 'Yes.'

Her mother pulled Gabby's head to her chest and dipped her own face down to kiss her and to whisper, 'Gabby, you are a strong, beautiful young woman. You are a part of me. The world, as they say, is your oyster. Take care of yourself now. Talk to no one but your father, and know the love I have for you is everything I could have imagined and more.'

Her father stepped outside. His face was pale and drawn. 'Charlotte.'

She kissed Gabby again. 'Go and get some rest, baby, everything will be fine.' She rose.

Gabby leapt to her feet. The lawn spun beneath her.

Her mother took hold of her elbow. 'Go, rest,' she whispered. 'It's better this way.' She kissed her cheek once more before walking back into the house.

CHAPTER 37

Gabby didn't know how long it took before the lawn stopped spinning, but she found her mother and father in the dining room.

Their visitor was the female detective investigating Ivy's murder. With her was a guy in a suit, with his hair cut too short and plain to have any real style. The female detective was doing all the talking and hadn't noticed Gabby walk in. She was quiet and respectful. Gabby had liked that about her when she'd talked to her before.

Why, though, was she here?

Her mother was standing, and her father was pacing beside her, shaking his head like they were being given bad news. Gabby tried to tune in. What the hell was happening? She'd thought her mother was dying — and her dad had that look about him, like he thought that, too — but now the cops were here, and her mother stood tall and proud, like she was about to go on stage.

'. . . her at Bingham Park, and I killed her.' Her voice was low and quiet. Respectful. Like she'd said a prayer for Ivy.

The female detective didn't say anything. She just watched her mother.

Gabby's head was spinning. Sweat poured out of her body. The room was closing in on her. What had her mother said?

As if Gabby had said the words aloud, her mother repeated herself. 'I texted Ivy and met her at Bingham Park, and I killed her.'

'*No.*' It was out of her mouth before the thought even entered her head.

All faces turned her way.

'*No.*'

'Gabby . . .' Her father was by her side in an instant. Where her mother's arms had only moments ago wrapped her in safety, now her father enveloped her. 'You shouldn't be here. I thought your mother told you to go and get some rest.'

'Mum?'

Her mother's face was calm, but Gabby saw the fear in her mother's eyes. 'Mum, no.'

Her mother inhaled deeply, closing her eyes as though to meditate. Gabby's thoughts were a howling racket in her head, detonating against each other so no sense was possible. She didn't understand what was happening, nor what her mother had said.

A moment passed, and then her mother opened her eyes and slowly released the breath. 'Gabby, remember what I told you in the garden.'

The female detective rose now. The man remained seated. The room was closing in on her. 'No, Mum . . .'

'Gabby, I love you. Live your life, sweet girl. Your father's got you.'

And on command, he squeezed her shoulders.

Where was Toby while their mother was admitting to killing Ivy? Where was he? 'Toby?'

'He's asleep,' whispered her father.

Asleep. He was *a-fucking-sleep*. Their mother . . . Gabby's breath tightened.

The female officer moved towards her mother and talked quietly and directly to her. It was too low for Gabby to hear, but her mother nodded along, and her father's hold on Gabby tightened even further.

The room grew hotter, her chest grew smaller and the air grew thicker. Soon everything was all too impossible, and Gabby was a heaving mess on the carpet.

She couldn't see anything. Not even the carpet. It was all grey and fuzzy. A buzzing sound filled her head. Thundering hooves pervaded her chest, and nothing was the right way up.

'Gabby, baby.' Her mother's gentle voice broke through the buzzing. The soft touch of her palms on Gabby's cheeks cleared some of the grey fuzz and slowed the thundering hooves. 'Slow breaths, sweet. One at a time. That's how you get through this. One breath at a time. One step at a time.'

Her mother took her hand. 'I have to go, Gab.'

Hot tears flushed the last of the fuzz out; in turn, everything was a blur. 'I don't understand, Mum,' she cried out. The pain so visceral.

'One day,' her mother said. 'One day you will, Gabby. You'll understand it all so very well, and I will be so proud of you the day that happens.'

Gabby sobbed as her mother released her and she tumbled into her father's arms.

Both detectives were standing now. There was none of the dramatic action they show on TV. They'd waited patiently as her mother reassured her. Now though, with more quietly spoken words and a short glance back at Gabby on the floor, they walked out of the room with her mother, then finally out of the house.

What had her mother done?

CHAPTER 38

Claudia

Claudia watched the screen in the viewing room. Four and a half hours had passed since the completely unexpected confession from Charlotte Hunt.

Lisa placed hot drinks on the battered table. 'I know it's bad, but it's all we have. They even make us drink it.'

She smiled at Charlotte, who was stiff as a board. Her skin was absent of colour and her posture was rigid. She offered no response to the provided refreshment.

Claudia rubbed her forehead as Graham put new discs in for the recording. During the first half of the interview, as Lisa drew out the initial account, Charlotte had been devoid of emotion.

How could a woman kill a child and be so flat about it? Especially considering they were talking about her daughter's best friend.

Maybe the aloofness was an artist thing. Not just an artist, but the prima donna of artists. The top tier of artist who put their art before family.

The team had done their research. Charlotte Hunt *had* spent more time in America than she had at home with her children. The TikTok video from Ivy's account had been correct about that at least. But was that video really worth murdering a child over? Surely a message that told the world how important her career was wouldn't affect said career?

It was possible Charlotte would worry about how people perceived the person behind the artist. They were in a world where the internet could cancel a creative for a slight, no matter how small. If there was enough noise made, the employer of the creative stepped back, away from all the noise, leaving the artist alone and abandoned.

Claudia continued to watch.

Lisa ran through the second set of official introductions, for the new disc: entitlement to legal advice, Charlotte's right to stop the interview at any time for further advice, and the caution again.

Charlotte's solicitor was Steph Maxwell from Maxwell, Clarke and Russell. Claudia had worked with Steph for a number of years. The solicitor was pleasant, but she didn't suffer fools gladly.

If you interviewed a client of Steph's, she expected you to know your way around the offence, the crime and the evidence.

Steph had been in law three decades, and yet she was aware of every change and update to each law as it was made. And if she was able to keep up, she saw no reason why the cops working the case couldn't. Steph was someone you wanted on your side; if Claudia ever needed legal representation, she'd . . .

Claudia forced that thought down.

Lisa was still speaking '. . . you've given us an account of what happened Monday night. What we want to do now is go a little deeper and obtain some detail.'

It was in the detail that they'd make their case rock solid.

'I've explained what happened, and I told you everything. I don't know what else you expect of me.' Charlotte's voice was like glass shards rubbing up against each other.

With a kind expression, Steph put her hand on her client's arm. She had explained the process, but Charlotte Hunt had not only never been arrested before, she'd never had any dealings with the police in any capacity. It was natural that some confusion lingered.

The whole undertaking was an ordeal. The team understood this and would walk her through it as gently as they could. It was always the best way to get all parties through.

'We need a full version of events,' said Graham.

'There is no "version". I killed Ivy.'

Claudia picked up her tea and winced as she peered into its shiny surface. With only powdered milk in Shepcote Lane custody block, the drink had no substance. She replaced the too hot cardboard cup on the table, untouched.

Lisa, unfazed by the bluntness of the admission, continued with her planned interview. 'Tell me why Ivy agreed to meet you.'

Charlotte picked at a highly polished but short fingernail.

'My client can't speak for another person's thoughts and decisions, Detective.'

Steph was correct. It was a question that usually wouldn't have been in there, but it would be the crux of the case. Why had Ivy, a sixteen-year-old teenager, gone out in the dark to meet her best friend's mother?

'Let me ask it another way. Why did *you* want to meet Ivy?'

Charlotte picked at her nails some more.

Lisa waited. Graham, pen in hand, was ready to take notes even though the interview was being recorded. It was easier to refer back to the written notes than the recording when it came to typing up the main points for a prosecution file.

If there was to be one.

Quietly, Charlotte spoke about being at home, taking care of Toby and receiving a call from her agent. That call, she said, had turned her world upside down. It might only be kid stuff, but it was her career. She called Gabby home to look after Toby while she sorted it out. Once home, Gabby recognised the account as Ivy's.

Charlotte had mulled over that information for hours. When Gabby went to her room, Charlotte sent the text to

Ivy. Her only reason was to request Ivy take the video down, but Ivy refused: *I told you this already.*

Claudia stood and paced around the small viewing room. She had gone through this, and the second statement matched the first, but something about it still didn't ring true.

Her work phone vibrated on the table next to the now cooling tea. Claudia checked it. Krish had sent a link to a Sheffield news site with a short message: *It's out.*

Claudia clicked the link.

ARREST MADE IN THE IVY HENTHORN INVESTIGATION

Shit. Someone had leaked the arrest. She had faith in her team. This custody block alone was teeming with staff and officers either working here or coming through with their own prisoners. It could be any number of people. Shit. Shit. Shit. They hadn't even contacted Ivy's mother — Judge Henthorn-Kimber — yet.

Fuck.

She read down the article.

News just coming in.

After three days police have made an arrest in relation to the murder of Ivy Henthorn.

Jesus. The judge would be furious.

South Yorkshire Police have not yet provided a statement or released the name of the suspect but it's believed they may be someone close to the family.

This article will update as further information becomes available.

'Fuck!' It took all Claudia's willpower to not throw the phone at the wall. Instead she closed the web browser, turned the volume down on the monitor, opened the contacts list and called Ivy's mother.

The judge picked up before Claudia even heard the phone ring out. 'You're a little late, Detective Inspector.'

Gone were the small pieces of a broken and left-behind mother. In her place was the lioness protector of her family, who was more than a little pissed at the intrusion into the home she was guarding.

Fuck, some more. She was too late. It was time for her to fall on her sword and not make excuses. 'I'm sorry, Your Honour. It all moved extremely quickly. A confession was made unexpectedly, and I'm sitting in the viewing room as we speak. The interview is currently ongoing.

'I wanted to call you when I had firm information to provide, and not with half-measure bits and pieces. We obviously have a leak in the premises, for which I can, again, only apologise. I'm sorry you had to find out that way, rather than hearing direct from either myself or Alek.'

The judge didn't say a word. Claudia imagined she was taking it in and considering her next words. It was how she worked in court. She was careful and direct.

In the corner of her eyeline, Lisa was talking and Charlotte was as still and upright as she'd been all along.

'Can I ask who made the unexpected confession?'

Claudia hadn't wanted to do this over the phone. She wanted to be there with the judge. To see her face when she passed the information. A person's expression gave a multitude of emotions away — their 'tells', as card players said — no matter how hard they tried to stay passive. Seeing the judge when she was informed her daughter's best friend's mother admitted to murdering her daughter could fill in some of the pieces they were missing. Because none of this made sense yet and Claudia didn't like it when an inquiry didn't make sense.

It was one thing to have it wrapped up in a neat bow, but it had to have meaning. 'Is Alek with you?'

'Alek is always here. Owen is here and Theo is here. Jasmine has a friend in her room. Do you have enough information to tell me who confessed to killing my daughter now?'

She still didn't want to, but there was no choice. She couldn't withhold it. Claudia could throttle whoever had leaked Charlotte's arrest. Not that the paper would release that particular detail. She'd put in a complaint to Professional Standards, though, and they could trawl their way through everyone in the custody block. Normally she wasn't one for making referrals to Professional Standards, but this had seriously hacked her off.

'Detective Inspector?'

'Yes, sorry again. I was thinking about how this had been leaked. I'm not happy. I wanted to be there to talk to you in person.'

The judge mellowed. The hard edge to her voice smoothed. 'It's fine. Don't worry. You're busy doing what I asked you to do. What your job asks you to do.'

In the background, Theo was pushing his mother for the same details she was pushing Claudia for. His mother shushed him and he backed down. If only Claudia could shush the judge.

That image at least made her smile.

She looked to the screen again. Charlotte was talking. 'Charlotte Hunt confessed to killing Ivy, Your Honour.'

There was a huff of air like a balloon rapidly deflating, a rush of voices, a thud as though the handset had been dropped. 'Your Honour?'

'DI Nunn?'

'Alek? What happened?'

'Judge Henthorn-Kimber stumbled into the wall. She's fine. Owen and Theo have taken her to sit down.'

Shit. She hadn't even checked if the judge was sitting. 'Who was it?'

'Charlotte Hunt confessed. She's currently being interviewed. I'm in the viewing room. I have to go.'

'Okay.'

'Alek . . .'

'Boss?'

'Take care of them. Don't release anything to the press when they come knocking, and let me know if anything changes.'

'Yes, boss.'

Claudia turned the volume back up on the monitor.

'. . . was the rock in?' Lisa asked.

Charlotte shook her head. Not that she didn't know, but in a way that said she was frustrated with the questions.

Had she expected to confess and be processed for court with nothing in between? This didn't add up.

'We need the details,' Lisa reminded her.

'It was in my right hand. I'm right-handed.'

This was all correct so far. There was nothing unusual about her confession. Claudia didn't know why she was so uneasy.

'Where was Ivy standing in relation to you?'

The nail polish that had been chipped was now chewed down. Charlotte bit at her nails some more. 'As I said, we were talking and Ivy was in front of me.'

'What happened next?'

'I hit her head with the rock in my hand.'

Lisa looked to Graham. A silent move between inter-viewers that said they could jump in on the questions. It prevented them talking over each other or one jumping in and causing the other to lose their train of thought.

'How tall are you, Charlotte?'

Charlotte checked with Steph, who nodded. 'I'm five foot eleven.'

Graham made a note of her response. 'Where did you hit her with the rock?'

'On the head.' Charlotte had changed from frustrated to the flat tone she'd used when she was first brought in.

'Where exactly on the head?' Graham was persistent.

'It was dark. I was killing a child, Detective. I was scared of what I was doing. I wasn't exactly paying attention to where I placed the rock. My hand came down and made contact with her head.'

It was like she was telling a story or reading a script. A music sheet, even. Charlotte had used evocative phrases like *killing a child* and that she *was scared*, but Claudia couldn't see any of it in the woman.

'Your hand came down?'

'Yes.'

'Can you show us what you mean by your hand coming down, and describe what you're doing for the recording, please?'

Charlotte turned to Steph. 'Seriously? I told them I killed her.'

In a voice so low Claudia barely heard it, Steph replied, 'They're tying everything down. It's fine. You can show them.'

Charlotte huffed and did as was requested. 'I raised my hand with the rock in—' she looked to where her hand was raised as she acted it out, her elbow bent at shoulder height — 'to just above my shoulder, and I brought the rock down in a straight motion.' Her hand in a fist, presenting as the rock, dropped forward.

'Then what happened?' asked Lisa.

Charlotte stared at her.

There were two cameras in the interview room, providing two angles. The narrow end of the table was pushed up to the middle of the long wall on the right as you walked through the door. Officers sat on the side between the table and the door; detainees and solicitors sat on the far side of the table.

Camera one was situated at the ceiling point behind Graham, opposite the door, facing Charlotte, and camera two was secured, again at the ceiling point, in the middle of the second long wall. This provided a view down the centre of the interview table and all present.

On Claudia's monitor, the cameras split the screen in two so she could see both at once. She could see that Charlotte did not like Lisa's question. Her lips puckered like she'd eaten something sour and wasn't allowed to spit it out because she was in polite company.

If she'd killed a child, though, Charlotte would have to get used to not being in polite company for an extremely long time. Even once she was released, it was unlikely her family or peers would take her back. Not after a crime like this.

'Charlotte?' Lisa pushed.

'I heard you.'

It was the first time Claudia had seen Charlotte rattled.

'She collapsed and I left her. I left her for dead without checking. I have no idea if she died instantly or a short time, or even a long time later. I don't know if there was time to save her. I was shocked at what I'd done. I was scared.'

That word again.

'So I left before anyone could see me.'

Ivy collapsed from the blow, and Charlotte was scared and left her for dead. Interesting.

'And you did it because of what she'd written about you?'

'No!'

The polished Charlotte Hunt sheen was thinning. 'I did it because she refused to take it down after I gave her the opportunity.'

Claudia's phone rang. 'Alek?'

'I'm sorry, boss. We've had a little drama at the house, not long after your call.'

'Tell me.'

'Theo ran upstairs. Owen thought it best we left him to process the information alone until he was ready to accept his parents into his space.'

Claudia watched the monitor. Graham was talking. 'Alek, I'm in the middle of the interview.'

'Yeah, sorry.' He picked up pace. 'It suddenly sounded like the ceiling was coming down. Theo stormed out of the house. He's destroyed his room. His parents are frantic. He's taken his phone, but won't pick up or respond to texts. His mum has checked what's left of his room and she's distraught . . .' There was a brief pause as Alek caught himself on his use of the word 'distraught'. For Alek, it would have been the judge's main demeanour since he arrived. 'Theo's taken his cricket bat.'

CHAPTER 39

Theo

Why the fuck had Gabby's mum confessed to killing Ivy?

Who in their right mind would believe that woman would, or could, kill anyone?

Gabby's mum was too clean and too dispassionate to kill. For starters, she'd be terrified of chipping one of those perfectly polished nails. Everything was a show for Charlotte Hunt. She was a mannequin made to perform, and perform was all she knew how to do. There was no emotion of any kind.

As far as Theo was aware, Gabby's mum did nothing when she came home from working in the States. Ivy would tell him — the slow-burning ball of rage curled up in the centre of his chest flashed at the mere thought of Ivy and he swung the bat at the curb with an echoing thwack. The sound reverberating made Theo wince and crouch in pain. His whole body no longer his own.

Oh, Ivy.

Theo straightened, gently put a hand over one ear to ease the discomfort, then continued.

Charlotte Hunt. Ivy told him she'd waft about the house like a queen bee — which was the exact turn of phrase she'd used in her TikTok video — pretending to be a parent, all the while ordering food in and throwing money at any problem that arose.

She never got her hands dirty doing anything herself.

Gabby's mum didn't kill Ivy.

He'd thought that cop with the blonde hair was more intelligent than to believe someone like Charlotte Hunt, but like the TV cop shows, it appeared they had their suspect and could put the crime to bed.

Theo's phone rang for the umpteenth time. Owen's name flashed across the screen. Why did his mother think he'd pick up to Owen if he wasn't picking up to her? At least she hadn't asked Pretty Boy to call him. Maybe that was the next call. What could Pretty Boy say to him that his mother couldn't? He could threaten to arrest him for destroying his room, but Theo's mother would never do that to him. She might have done in the past. But that was before Ivy.

It didn't matter who called. He didn't have the time for any of them, and he'd have left his phone at home if he didn't need it. But he did.

Not long after he left the house, he sent his own text message.

The walk to Bingham Park was about a mile and left him with plenty of time to think.

How hadn't he seen it sooner?

After Ivy's murder, he'd wandered through life blinkered. Like a show horse to prevent it being distracted. Only Theo's blinkers were created by raw grief, regret, guilt and rage.

He was ready to let go of the guilt from lying to his mother.

He'd lied about events that evening, completely failing to repeat the accusations Ivy threw at him.

Guilt that had eaten away at him.

His sister had left the safety of their home and walked to her death, while he was out sourcing weed.

And he lied to protect himself. To buy weed of all things. Because he was furious with Ivy.

But this wasn't about him.

He wasn't distracted anymore. He'd pulled the blinkers off and he'd seen it all.

Everything was as clear as day.

And by the end of this day, everyone would see what he did and then they would feel his rage.

CHAPTER 40

Claudia

'As I see it, we have two problems,' Claudia said.

She was in the report-writing room of the custody block with Lisa and Graham.

Charlotte was in her cell and would remain there until they'd made a decision to charge or release her.

'And they are?' Graham asked, sticking his hand in a packet of cheese and onion crisps he'd bought from the vending machine they'd walked past.

'Charlotte didn't kill Ivy,' said Lisa.

'That's one.' Claudia decided she couldn't wait for real food and walked into the corridor as she talked. Lisa and Graham followed her.

'What's the other?' Graham asked through his mouthful of crisps.

Claudia stared through the glass front of the vending machine. It was said cops only lived five years after retirement. This was no surprise, with the long hours and the crap diet that was necessitated by that schedule. Even if officers brought food into work, you weren't always in the right place to eat it. 'Theo Henthorn has destroyed his bedroom at home and run off.'

'So a missing kid?' Graham grumbled, stuffing more crisps in his mouth, totally uninterested.

Claudia punched in the alphanumeric buttons for her items. 'He's taken the cricket bat he used to destroy his room with him.'

'That's more concerning.' Lisa peered over Claudia's shoulder as the machine whirred and dropped a bottle of water and an oat bar.

'I've called the office, as well as the duty inspector, to make uniform officers aware.' Claudia collected her winnings.

Lisa punched in the same buttons, then crossed her arms as she waited. 'What's he want the bat for?'

A couple of uniform officers walked past with folders in their arms and headed for the report-writing room, discussing the merits of some football manager Claudia had never heard of.

'Alek said his mum doesn't know. They learned we arrested Charlotte, then all hell broke loose. They never had a chance to talk to Theo.'

'And no one in the house has discussed other possible scenarios of who might have killed Ivy before today?' Graham folded the crisp pack along the length until it was a narrow strip, then twisted it into a knot.

They walked back into the report-writing room and he binned his neatly tied pack.

'No. Alek said the family have been grieving.'

'So what's Theo doing?' Graham sat in a chair at the opposite side of the room to the uniform officers who, though logged on to a computer, were still talking football.

'That's what we need to figure out, and quickly,' said Claudia, opening the oat bar.

'What did you make of Charlotte's interview?' asked Lisa.

'The same as you, I imagine, going by your questions.'

'She had no idea Ivy had even been laid on a bench, never mind posed, because none of that information had been released to the press.'

'Also, she's far too tall to have inflicted the head wound at the angle the PM observed — plus she was unable to specify the location of the wound,' said Graham. 'If Charlotte had killed Ivy, and she'd taken an emotional swing as she suggested, the swing would have come downwards as she showed us, hitting Ivy nearer the top of the head, not at the front of her head where it actually was.'

'But Theo doesn't know the post-mortem details,' said Lisa. 'Why's he left the house with a cricket bat and where's he going with it? What does he know that we don't?'

Claudia put the half-eaten oat bar down. 'Charlotte's confessed to a murder she hasn't committed. We need to know why. Is Steph still about?'

'We asked if she could wait, as there might be more questions,' said Lisa.

'Great.'

They initially had twenty-four hours to hold Charlotte, and they had to find out why she'd confessed to a murder she hadn't committed.

CHAPTER 41

Gabby

Gabby charged down the street as best she could with her legs numb below her and the houses but a blur.

Prior to leaving home, she'd rummaged in her mother's medicine cabinet. Her mother bagged herself all kinds of drugs, mostly bought and used in the US, and she had no qualms about keeping them easily accessible. Her mother claimed she suffered with her nerves prior to a big performance. She presumed — well, Gabby didn't know what her mother presumed anymore. This latest action of hers was completely out of the blue, and Gabby's world was gradually imploding.

Her father had lost his mind. It was clear he'd gone along with some ridiculous plan of her mother's as he always did. But once she'd been arrested and taken away, the scale of what she'd done hit him. He'd crumbled, forgetting he had kids, and he'd opened a full bottle of brandy, taken a glass from the cupboard and that had been the last of him.

Gabby hadn't even known where he was in the house.

He hadn't been in front of the medicine cabinet, protecting it from his teenage daughter. And he hadn't been upstairs explaining events to his young son. No, her father had checked out.

The medicine cabinet had provided something to curb the nausea rampaging through Gabby's body. It said so on the sticker attached. She took three of those.

The cabinet also provided something that could have been for anxiety, but it could have been for sleep. Gabby couldn't figure it out. But the way the electricity fizzed through her limbs and fired through her chest, she took just a couple. Better safe than sorry.

Then there were a couple of painkillers she didn't recognise. If she didn't have a serious headache after the week from hell, then she probably wasn't human. Which was likely up for debate, anyway.

The concoction she'd taken helped make her feel less like a coiled spring about to explode into tiny baby coiled springs, so she'd obviously picked the right ones. She'd already taken the doctor-prescribed ones after her outburst at Ivy's this morning.

Gabby thought that leaving the house — leaving Toby without their mother and with their father now checked out for the rest of the day — wouldn't be too bad. He was quite capable at twelve. He'd feed himself and watch a streaming service.

She couldn't remember if anyone had told him what had happened. Did Tobes know where their mother was?

She'd sleep in his room tonight. Not just for Tobes but, she'd admit, because she didn't want to be alone.

What the hell was that screeching noise?

Gabby's legs, jelly beneath her, wobbled some more. She turned, searching for the sound. A car swerved around her, blaring the horn again.

Shit.

She stumbled back up on to the pavement and continued on.

CHAPTER 42

Claudia

Claudia was in the viewing room again.

The half-eaten oat bar and half-drunk bottle of water on the desk beside the monitor.

She trusted her team. They were excellent interviewers. Her task was to oversee and control the whole operation.

In the viewing room, it was possible to hear Charlotte's explanation and reasoning, to view the running incident log on Theo Henthorn, and to take calls when they came in.

Krish, who had done the phone work during the whole investigation, was working with the phone provider to pinpoint Theo's location.

Just where was he taking that cricket bat?

'We don't believe you,' said Graham, taking lead this time. 'Why are you admitting to killing a girl you clearly didn't?'

'No comment.' Even through the monitor, Charlotte's stare was ice.

Shit. This woman was sticking to her story and was determined to go to prison whether she'd done the crime or not.

The murder investigation was still in its infancy, and with little in the way of evidence or information to go on.

They'd learned that Ivy had trouble nearly a year ago and had jumped on that bandwagon, but what if the trouble was closer to home? Not enough evidence had been accumulated to provide an answer either way. Any evidence they'd gathered would take time to be processed.

They had little time before Charlotte had to either be charged or released. All Claudia had right now was her mind. She thought through the conversations she'd had with Charlotte Hunt.

Right at the beginning of the investigation, Charlotte told Claudia that she was best friends with the judge. Was there a purpose behind that comment? Did the woman know this moment would come and it was her way of telling Claudia in advance? Would she be prepared to go to prison for her best friend?

Had a parent killed her own daughter and left her on a bench?

It felt absurd to even consider it, but no more absurd than watching Charlotte Hunt admit to killing Ivy. There had to be another reason.

Claudia dialled Krish. He picked up immediately. 'Boss?'

'The number that texted Ivy . . .'

'Yeah, it came back to Charlotte Hunt.'

'I want you to go back to the provider and find out how many phones are on Charlotte Hunt's account, and I want that answer ten minutes ago.'

CHAPTER 43

Theo

Darkness wrapped Theo's simmering fury like a blanket as he waited.

He held it like a treasured gift.

A gift was to be handed to another and it was in that sentiment he was here.

Time stretched and it slowed. He had no concept of its passing, until it stopped and she was standing in front of him. Her body swaying lightly. A twisted half-smile on her face, like her mouth had forgotten how to form the shape, but softened by her cheeks and the slightest shrug of her shoulders. The night painted shadows in curves and grooves, distorting her expression.

A hand played with the necklace around her throat.

'I didn't think you'd come,' he said.

She looked around, her eyes narrowing to see through the gloom.

'There's nothing,' Theo said. That slow-burning ball of rage simmering hotter. 'Nothing to say Ivy was here.'

She shifted on her feet. Not a word spoken yet.

Sparks flew.

'There's nothing here, Gabby. Nothing here to say Ivy lived. There's nothing to say Ivy died here.' Spit flew from his mouth. 'There's absolutely fuck all. None of that tape stuff. None of them little markers. All the TV crap we see. Nothing. It's like she was never here. Like what happened here didn't happen. Or didn't matter.' He pulled the cricket bat from the bench behind him and rested the end on the ground and his palm on the handle.

'You robbed me of my sister, Gabby. You robbed me of Ivy, and she died thinking I was mad at her. She died thinking I was a junkie, and she died with her last words to me being that she was telling Mum. You took away our time to make it right, like we always did. You took it all away! She was everything. We had each other's back. Always.'

A sob broke from him. 'But not this time, eh, Gabby? Not this time. Because you took her.' He screamed as pain engulfed him. It was impossible to say where it came from. His whole body was at once in agony and a hollowed-out void without her.

Gabby mumbled, her words an undecipherable mess.

'What, Gabby? What? What about Ivy?'

CHAPTER 44

Claudia

Charlotte would not answer a single other question that challenged her original account. The only response was the solicitor-advised 'No comment.'

Ivy's mother had called five times, knowing with each call that Claudia was overseeing everything and that both detectives and uniformed officers were involved in both interviewing Charlotte and trying to locate Theo.

Having a murdered child was enough. Claudia did not want to have to tell the judge she'd arrested one of her remaining children for a major assault.

Sharpe was next to call: 'You're lucky it's me and not Connelly.'

Claudia sighed. 'You're lucky I'm too busy to remember I have a headache.'

Sharpe actually laughed.

'Who'd she phone?'

'The chief constable.'

'Of course she did. To be honest, if my life was that messed up . . .'

'Claudia?'

'Yeah, sorry. If it was, I'd probably pull in the highest favours I could. That pressure doesn't help us on the ground, though.'

'No, which is why I said I'd make the call.'

'Thanks.'

'Don't think the pressure's not there, though.'

'Received, loud and clear.'

'Where are we?'

On the monitor, Steph leaned in and spoke to Charlotte.

'Charlotte isn't talking anymore. Uniform are on the lookout for Theo. Krish is making two different inquiries with phone providers. Both will probably give us the answers we need. Actually, that's him. I have to go.' She ended the call without waiting to hear Sharpe's response.

'Go, Krish.'

'There are four phones on Charlotte's account.'

'She's the main account holder for the family's phones.'

'Looks that way, unless she has more phones than she has hands.'

'Carry on.' She picked up the water and drank as she listened. Custody suites were not only the most disgustingly smelly police buildings, but for some reason, they were the driest. Claudia was permanently thirsty when working in one.

'Well, the number we initially submitted, turns out it never went—'

'To the US,' Claudia finished.

'Exactly.'

'So Charlotte's protecting someone she loves, who isn't a violinist in America.'

'She's not saying who?'

'She's going down with the ship. Anything on Theo?'

'Ah, yes. Young Theo's at Bingham Park.'

'He's what?'

'He's at Bingham Park. You don't think he's gone to hurt himself, do you, boss?'

'I don't know, Krish, but Charlotte put herself here, so she can wait in a cell while we figure all this out. Theo's our priority. That family don't deserve any more pain, and that's nothing to do with who Verity is. It's about the loss of one child already. I don't want lights and sirens frightening Theo. According to Alek, he's in a pretty dark place. We'll travel out and pick him up, if you can stick with the phones for me.'

With Krish still on the phone, Claudia walked out of the viewing room, across the corridor to the interview room, knocked, poked her head in, stated her name and rank, and asked Graham to wrap it up right now.

'Krish?'

'Yeah, boss.'

'The phones. I know we've only got access to the number that texted Ivy. It might take a while and a lot of work, but I want you to figure out who that phone belongs to. Also check GPS data, and see if it was in the vicinity of Bingham Park the night Ivy was murdered.'

'You know I'm on it. Good luck with Theo.'

CHAPTER 45

Gabby

Gabby wasn't quite sure which way was up. She certainly wasn't sure how she'd managed to make it there in one piece.

Theo was little more than a greyed vignette. And what was he holding?

Those drugs she'd taken before setting out, wow, her mother took some serious shit.

Her mother . . .

'Ivy, Gabby,' Theo said. 'Concentrate. What the fuck is wrong with you? She was your best friend. My sister. Ivy!' he roared. He finally rose from the bench. 'You know Ivy, don't you? You recognise where we are, don't you, Gabby?'

Gabby spun, trying to place herself. The world wobbled. She threw out her arms to stop from falling. There was a flash of movement in her peripheral vision and a brighter flash of pain, then her arm dropped.

'You didn't give her that chance, did you, *Gabby*?'

What?

Why?

'Ivy?' she whispered.

'You think Ivy can help you now?' Theo was roaring.

Gabby was on her knees, her left arm limp by her side. Luckily there was no pain. She was in a deep fuzz.

'All Ivy wanted to do was help people. Help *you*. But you, you monster, you killed her.'

It was like someone had stuck those plastic googly eye things over where Theo's real eyes should have been, and he held something in each hand. One hand held out towards her like an offering.

Gabby clenched her teeth together so as to not laugh at his googly-eyed face, but it was too late. He'd seen her.

She was slammed sideways to the ground as something solid collided with her left shoulder. Her mouth tasted of green and soil and something metallic and damp. She spat, but couldn't see what she'd ejected through the blur of tears. 'Ivy . . .' She rested her forehead on the ground for a minute as the tears flowed. 'I'm so sorry, Ivy.'

Theo was ranting. 'They came to my house, Gabby. Do you know that? They came to my house, and they told me my sister was dead. They told me that Ivy — your Ivy, my Ivy, *Ivy* — she was *dead*. We wouldn't see her again, Gabby. Why? Not because she was a teenager and had done something stupid, but because someone else had done something evil. They had killed my sister, my beautiful — irritating, but beautiful — sister.'

'Theo . . .'

Gabby scrunched up her face, but didn't move. Was someone here? Were they here to help her? Or were they here to help Theo? Please let this be over quickly. 'I didn't mean it, Theo,' she whispered. 'It was an accident.'

'How do you accidentally fucking murder your best friend?' His rage was all-encompassing. It was like he was a black hole, sucking the entire world into his event horizon.

She could do nothing but submit and beg his forgiveness, and beg Ivy's forgiveness. It was all she'd wanted since that night. For Ivy to forgive her.

'My mum, Theo. It was my mum.' She sobbed into the dirt. 'She blamed me for the video. She said it would be my fault if she lost her job and we lost our house. Ivy wouldn't listen. She said if she took it down people would know it was her and then that the first girl was her.'

Tears mingled with the ground beneath her, and salt was mixed with grit and snot, but Gabby no longer cared. 'It was my mum, Theo. I just wanted Ivy to listen.' Gabby cried harder. The metallic taste of grass clogged her mouth and nose as her head became stuffier and woozier. 'She just wouldn't listen to me. I didn't mean . . .'

'Theo!' The voice was louder this time, and closer. 'Theo, you have to stop. You have to listen to me. I need you to put the bat and the phone down.'

Oh God, they were here to help her. She didn't care if she died. All she needed was for the pain in her heart to stop. Maybe it would have been better if Theo were left to finish what he'd started.

'*She killed Ivy.*'

CHAPTER 46

Theo

'We know, Theo, and she'll go to court and answer for it. But what will it do to your mum if you go to court for hurting her?'

Theo roared into the night. The deep cavity inside consuming him had been taken over by the rage. 'I don't know if there's anything left of me for my mother to love.'

The detective stayed where she was. Two others were a few steps behind her but widening their distance — to circle him, he imagined. One was on his phone, requesting an ambulance, but telling them to keep its distance until safe to enter.

Between them, Gabby lay face down on the ground where he'd put her, her left arm at an unnatural angle. 'It was only once,' she cried. 'I just hit her once. I thought she passed out, so I made her comfortable on the bench, so she'd be okay when she woke up and could go home.' She wailed some more. 'It was just once. She was my best friend.'

The detective stayed focused on Theo. 'It doesn't matter what you do, Theo, your mum loves you and will always love you. She needs you right now, as I imagine you need her.

You don't need this. This—' she looked at Gabby, sobbing uncontrollably — 'won't bring Ivy back, and it won't help heal the pain or move you or your family forward. It's not even any kind of justice. I won't pretend to know what Ivy would want you to do—'

Theo crashed the bat into the grass with a heaving grunt. The male detective put one foot forward but stayed where he was.

'But I *will* ask if she'd want you to ruin your life over her death. If she'd want you to leave your little sister alone with no siblings to look out for her? From what I've learned of Ivy during the investigation, she cared about people deeply.'

'I read her diary.' Theo moved backwards until he bumped back into the bench Ivy had died on, and sank on to it.

'Her diary?' The detective was confused.

'That night you came to the house . . .'

'I remember.'

'I left and went to Ivy's room to cry on her bed. I found it under her pillow and took it with me to my own room, as it was so personal to her, I didn't want strangers reading it.'

'Was that how you figured out it was Gabby?'

'The time she did the TikTok video about Gabby's mum, she wrote that she expected Gabby to be furious, but she was doing it because she hoped to bring some change to her friend's home life. All she wanted was love for her friend. She wrote that Gabby was a beautiful soul who deserved the world, and even though she was breaking Gabby's confidence, it was done from her heart, so she might have the love that we had at home.'

The bat and his phone were on the floor, and the detective by his side. The other two were with Gabby and blue lights were in the distance. Paramedics would arrive soon.

Theo continued. 'She wrote again that Gabby hadn't said anything after the video went live, and she realised Gabby had stopped following the account. Or at least stopped checking in. It didn't alter her love for Gabby. The account was just an online thing she did. Gabby was her flesh and blood.'

He glared at the girl being supported into a sitting position, wobbling on her bottom. 'When Charlotte was arrested, I knew she hadn't done it. She never gets her own hands dirty, she just throws money at the problem, and Ivy wasn't killed by anyone taking her money. The only alternative was Gabby.'

The detective placed her hand on his arm. We'll take you home to your mum, Theo.'

Gabby wailed. 'Aren't I being arrested?'

'Not tonight. We'll take the clothes you're wearing once you get home. There's a lot for us to wade through. If we need to interview you, I'll let your mum know, but for now, I think you both need to spend some time together.'

Paramedics trotted into view with loaded bags. They eyed Theo as they moved to Gabby.

'He's fine,' the detective said.

CHAPTER 47

Claudia

Five days later, the Complex Crimes Task Force returned to the office for their first morning briefing after two rest days.

'I hope you're all suitably rested and revived.' Claudia held the Earl Grey close. Her time off had been far from relaxing, as she'd tossed and turned during nightmares where she arrested her father again. Only this time with evidence of his participation in Ruth's murder.

'I ate my way through two tubs of ice cream,' said Lisa, grinning. 'If that counts?'

Rhys applauded her.

'Oh, I think ice cream most definitely counts.' She surveyed her team. 'I want to thank you all again for the stellar work you put in on the Ivy Henthorn inquiry, especially the last three days, when the phone information came in and Charlotte Hunt confessed. It went a little haywire from there, but you pulled together admirably and stayed professional. I've even received an email from Detective Superintendent Connelly to say Judge Henthorn-Kimber contacted him and requested he pass on her family's gratitude for the way we handled the investigation. Connelly also sends his personal thanks for—'

'Not making him look shit,' laughed Rhys.

He was definitely back on form. 'Something like that.' Claudia smiled.

'The judge'll be happy that Gabby didn't want to make a complaint against Theo,' said Dominic, looking exactly like she felt, with dark circles under his eyes.

Was it possible he knew about the forensic submission of the glass tumbler? Claudia had avoided him during their rest days, claiming massive fatigue and the need for time to do absolutely nothing.

'I don't think "happy" is a word we can use for the judge. We just investigated her teenage daughter's murder. She might be relieved her family can grieve together in peace.'

'Do we know how the Hunts are doing? Or specifically, Charlotte?' asked Krish. 'It was brave of her to risk a life sentence by coming forward. After you said you were coming for her following phone tracing, she understood why Gabby had been as distressed as she had.'

'Steph is one of the best lawyers I know. Gabby's in good hands. Her account, in interview, that she didn't realise what she was doing, that she just wanted Ivy to listen, is likely to lower her sentence. So is the psychological report they'll have conducted. After Charlotte's fury died down, she said she was taking time away from music to stay by her daughter's side.'

'Shame she hadn't thought about that before her daughter killed someone.' Dominic was not in a good mood, but Claudia had no intention of finding out why.

'There are no urgent jobs needing our input at the moment, so use this time as an opportunity to complete the paperwork for the full court file. Steph Maxwell is a real stickler. She won't miss anything, and she won't let anything slide.'

'Two families destroyed,' said Lisa, 'Lives in tatters. It's heartbreaking.'

'It's down to the fact teenagers can't control their emotions that we resolved this so quickly,' said Rhys.

'That and Gabby sent a text instead of a WhatsApp message,' said Dominic, pointing to the evidence.

'Because she was already in an emotional place,' Rhys pointed out.

Graham jumped in with a deep question. 'You think Gabby deserves to be punished, boss?'

It took Claudia all she had not to look at Dominic. 'She killed her best friend. It's the reason that will be on trial, and we don't get involved in that. All we can do is gather the evidence. What happens next is in the hands of the criminal justice system. It's the families left behind to pick up the pieces I feel the most sorry for.'

Dominic rose from his chair and walked from the room.

CHAPTER 48

Claudia — mid-May

The criminal justice system was slow. Not just slow, but glacial.

Everyone involved needed time to gather and process the relevant paperwork.

It infuriated police officers who were front-facing to the demanding public, and to Judge Henthorn-Kimber, who as a judge worked within the process, but as a mother, was in such a vortex of grief and disbelief it was difficult for her to grasp the realities she once understood so well.

The kettle clicked off and Claudia poured boiling water into her mug and stirred.

The press was still all over the story, even two months later. A prominent judge's daughter murdered by her teenage best friend; the headlines sold papers and attracted clicks.

Claudia unscrewed the lid from the milk, stuck her nose to the opening and sniffed. It'd do. She tipped a splash into her tea and stirred again.

As for Judge Henthorn-Kimber, she'd attempted to return to work but had lasted only the day before submitting another sick note. Her priority, she'd informed Alek, was Theo and Jasmine. They needed time and love to bring them through the events of their sister's murder.

Claudia returned the milk to the fridge, picked up her drink and made her way to her office. She just wished the family could work through their grief and pain in peace, without the country watching and speculating. It was the unsolicited opinions that hurt. They were savage. Keyboard warriors who watched too many cop shows, be they documentary style or dramas, and thought they knew how the system worked. They wouldn't shut up about police incompetence, both families causing harm one way or another and a damaging school environment. There were many varying viewpoints; the internet had room for them all.

The mid-May sun streamed through the office windows. It was glorious outside, and Claudia was eager for her next rest days.

She tapped on the leg of the desk for luck. Not that she was particularly superstitious, but in policing circles, if you spoke or thought about the day being quiet, the total opposite usually happened. The wooden desk leg was a little precaution, that was all.

Claudia woke her computer and logged in, heading straight for her emails. She was so behind with her inbox. With a little peace this afternoon, she could make a dent in it.

Her mobile rang.

It was Russ.

'Hey.' She smiled.

'Hey, yourself.'

'Enjoying your time in the sun?'

'It's not going to be for much longer.'

The top email was from Sharpe, and the header was simply *Russ Kane*.

Shit. 'What have you done, Russ?'

He laughed. It was bright, like the sun streaming into her office. 'Why do you make it sound like I've boiled your rabbit?'

Claudia clicked open the email and tried to read while at the same time talk to Russ, but it wasn't easy to focus on both. Sharpe said that Russ had called her.

'Are you listening to me?'

'Erm, yeah.'

'What're you doing, Claudia?'

'Nothing.'

'Stop reading that email and let me tell you.'

Claudia leaned back in the chair and grinned down the phone. 'You know me so well. I wish you were here. That last case was a tough one.'

There was silence. Claudia checked her phone screen to see if they were still connected. 'Russ?'

'I'll see you tomorrow.'

Claudia jumped from her chair so quickly she slammed her hip into the edge of her desk. 'You'll what?'

Shit, that hurt. She rubbed at the low-level throb she'd self-inflicted.

'Yeah. I talked it through with Maura and my doctors, and I'm coming back to work.'

'Oh, Russ!' The smile split her face and the injury was forgotten. If he were in front of her now she would throw herself at him and not let him go, she was so pleased with his news. 'You're sure?'

'It's too late to change my mind now. It's a done deed.' He laughed some more, clearly happy with her response. 'But please don't get me run over again. It's really not the best experience I've had.'

'You've had your physical?'

'I've been physically fit for a while now—'

'I'm not letting you out of the office on your own,' Claudia said the words without thinking. Russ had been hit in his own street, on his way home from work.

'I don't think I'll need an escort home.'

Claudia could hear his smile. Russ was trying to ease the tension she'd caused. Always the one to placate and calm

266

a situation. 'The team will be so pleased to see you. *I'll* be pleased to see you.'

'Yeah, it was touch and go with the decision there for a while, but I'm ready.'

Maisy shouted incoherently in the background.

'Look, I have to go. My attention is being demanded, and as I'm there tomorrow, I should really be present here for the rest of today.'

Claudia said her goodbyes and told Russ not to expect any special treatment when he returned.

The truth was, she'd watch him like a hawk. As someone who'd been through job-related trauma, she was well aware of the ability of its effects to sneak up when you least expected it.

Occupational health had signed him off, so he was officially good to go. She was thrilled, as the rest of the team would be.

The office had warmed considerably with the sun shining directly in. Claudia pushed a sash window up to allow air to circulate, then walked into the incident room. Graham was at a meeting in the CPS offices, but everyone else was there. 'Hey.'

Heads turned her way.

'Russ called.'

They waited.

'He's coming back tomorrow.' The grin was still firmly in place.

'Fuck, yeah!' Rhys pumped his arm in the air. His face matched her own.

'Seriously?' Lisa leaned back, a little stunned. 'Oh, thank God.'

Krish nodded quietly.

Russ was well thought of. Tomorrow would be an emotional day.

'He'd better bring the cakes in.' Krish rubbed his stomach.

'Oh God, yeah.' Lisa practically drooled.

'I thought you were on a diet again.' Rhys never knew when to keep his mouth shut.

Lisa glared. 'Not when Russ is bringing return-to-work cakes in.'

Dominic walked through the door, saw the lack of work activity, and the excited chatter. 'What did I miss?'

Rhys, still grinning, jumped straight in, not waiting for Claudia to offer up the news. 'Russ is back tomorrow.'

Dominic paused and considered the information. 'That's great. I'm glad he's doing okay. It'll be good to see him.'

Claudia let his tepid response slide. Dominic felt threatened by Russ, and it often came through in the occasional comment, though of course they'd stopped while Russ was absent. The issue was Dominic's insecurity. When the Complex Crimes Task Force had been created, Claudia had the pick of officers, with one condition: Dominic was included as one of the detective sergeants. That hadn't been negotiable. What she *had* done was bring her own detective sergeant to the task force. That sergeant was Russ. Dominic believed she favoured him.

Dominic was her father and she loved him. Russ had been her second-in-command for a while, and she trusted him. Maybe she did rely on him more. It was something she actively tried to work on, separating the work out evenly.

'Okay, then. I'll get back on with trying to wade through my emails.' She turned her back on the team.

'You could delete any that don't look important, or any that are over a month old,' Rhys suggested, to laughter from Lisa and Krish.

'So that's why you never respond to the urgent emails I send out,' she shouted over her shoulder as she strolled into her office.

This time, Lisa and Krish laughed, with an undertone of Rhys mumbling. Claudia couldn't help but join in. Nothing could ruin her mood now.

She sat at her desk, picked up her tea and sipped. The drink had cooled. She quickly glugged a few mouthfuls down before getting on with the task at hand.

In the office, Dominic's mobile rang. Claudia watched him answer. His face changed, and he spun his chair around, rose and stalked out of the incident room.

The powers that be had their reasons for making her supervise her own father. It wasn't easy. For either of them. Even Dominic couldn't ruin her day, though. Russ was healthy and was returning.

Claudia woke the laptop again. The email from Sharpe about Russ, open on screen. She quickly skimmed the report. Russ had been cleared to return. Claudia leaned back in her chair and, with her hands behind her head, looked to the ceiling, unable to wipe the ridiculous grin off her face. Russ would get sick of seeing it from all of them tomorrow. She had to pull herself together.

Okay, back to work. Emails to clear. Claudia moved Sharpe's email to the team admin folder and returned to the inbox.

A new email landed. It was from Adrian Cox at the forensics lab. The header read: *re: glass tumbler.*

Claudia's stomach lurched.

The joy leached slowly away.

It was fine. Everything was great. This was a good day. Nothing would spoil this day.

Claudia clicked the email open.

DI Nunn,

In reference to exhibit number TMR6, glass tumbler pieces, retrieved from the kitchen bin at Green Lane, Wharncliffe Side.

These pieces have been examined and microscopic drops of blood were identified.

Her stomach twisted.

The pattern of these blood droplets suggests a minor injury.

This made sense. Ruth's post-mortem report was imprinted in Claudia's memory, and the report included

269

cuts to her right arm and the right side of her face, including under her right eye. The pathologist had noted they could have been created by the point of a sharp knife. The wounds were a diversion from the MO of the killer they'd been hunting, but there was also a suggestion the knife wounds were a cover for a smaller unknown wound beneath it.

We tested the blood and ran it against the UK DNA database and the police database as requested. The blood matched the victim, DC Ruth Harrison.

Nausea swelled. The blood could have been caused if Ruth dropped the glass in an accident and cleaned it up. That would account for Dominic's lack of knowledge when questioned about it. Claudia clung on to calm with sloth-like claws.

Fingerprints, both partial and full, were recovered from a couple of pieces. These were run against public and police databases. A match was identified.

Not a surprise.

Both Ruth and Dominic Harrison's prints matched.

Okay. That was fine. There was nothing evidential there. The tumblers in the house belonged to the couple. But Adrian's email continued. His last sentence reporting his findings was, as the whole report had been, professional and factual. There was no emotion and no conclusion drawn.

One clear print identified as Dominic Harrison's overlaid one of the blood droplets.

Claudia's world shattered, like the tumbler, on the floor around her feet.

CHAPTER 49

Dominic

A call from a withheld number flashed across Dominic's screen.

'Yeah?'

'You told me this was nothing!' Adrian was furious. 'You told me Claudia was simply tying up loose ends before Tyler was sentenced. What the actual fuck, Dom?'

Dominic was out of the incident room and halfway down the stairs by the time Ade had finished speaking. Speed was of the essence. 'Ade . . .'

This was a call he'd never wanted to receive. That Ade had made it was not good. He wouldn't have bothered if there was nothing to say. Ade had made his feelings on the subject quite clear when they'd talked last time.

'What the fuck did you get me involved in?'

Dominic was moving at speed, and he lost his balance and stumbled down the last steps, his shoulder colliding with a uniformed officer about to make her way up. He didn't even pause to acknowledge her, never mind apologise. There was far more on his mind, far more for him to do, than stop and chat. Especially in here, in this building.

'Dick,' she muttered to his retreating back.

Dominic ran to the back entrance, to the rear door that would take him to his car.

'Dominic!'

Shit. Ade was still on the phone.

'What did you do?'

'Nothing. I did nothing, Ade. Tyler was sentenced for Ruth's murder, along with all the others he did, in court two weeks ago. You know, the court of law, where a panel of his peers decided on his guilt?'

'I know what a fucking court is, you prick! What I don't know is what the fuck you've got me involved in.'

The sun hit Dominic straight in the face as he slammed his way out of South Yorkshire Police headquarters into the small yard where he'd parked. With his hand up to his eyebrows, he jogged across the concrete. 'Nothing, Ade, I told you.'

Sharpe was at the smoking shed, cigarette in hand. She watched him without acknowledgement and Dominic attempted to pretend he hadn't seen her. Sweat poured down his spine and gathered in the waistband of his trousers.

'Your fingerprints were on the glass.'

'Obviously. It was our glass.' He clicked open the car, climbed in and switched the phone to hands-free.

'Dom, you've screwed me. You've really fucking screwed me, you motherfucking bastard. This is the only call you'll receive from me, and I had to use a VOIP service to make it. The other issue is closed. I never want to hear from you again.'

There was no room for manoeuvre. That was clear. Ade was furious, his tone hard and brittle.

Dominic needed to know what he was up against, though. He needed to know how bad this was. If it was that his fingerprints were present he could shrug it off. But Ade was a professional. There was more. 'Okay. I hear you. Tell me.'

A short, deep growl told Dominic that Ade had everything. 'There were trace spots of Ruth's blood on the glass.'

Dominic cleared police grounds. It was time to put his foot down. It no longer mattered if he triggered any speed cameras. What did matter was if he caught the attention of a marked vehicle that could pull him over. He'd pick up his speed but drive sensibly. 'She probably cut herself when she broke it.'

Ade's angry silence thundered down the car handset system.

Dominic forged onwards.

'You're well aware if she did it on the tumbler itself, there would have been more than trace blood. I'd describe this as spatter from a small wound and from a distance.'

Dominic had to get home, pick up his emergency bag and leave. A horn blared as he drove through a red light but he didn't care.

'Your fingerprint was *over* the blood.' An audible sigh. 'Jesus, Dom.' Frustration, fear, terror. Something was thrown, a deadening thudding came through the car's speakers as it tumbled and fell. 'You killed her?'

Dominic ignored the question, asking instead, 'What have you done?' His only consideration now was how long he had to execute his escape.

'You fucking killed Ruth!'

'Ade. Focus. Tell me. What have you done?'

'Fuck you, Dom. Fuck you.'

Ade was gone.

At least he'd given Dominic the heads up. How much of one, he didn't know. The fury in Ade's voice implied it wasn't likely to be much, if any.

The only positive would be that Claudia had to process the information, then she'd run it up the flagpole — because if she was anything, Claudia was a stickler for rules. She wouldn't go all vigilante on him. A rapid meeting would occur to discuss how to approach the situation, then officers would be deployed to arrest him.

It gave him just enough time to grab his emergency escape bag and leave before they arrived.

CHAPTER 50

Claudia

The white of the email screen blazed brightly at Claudia as she ossified in her chair. Her mind congealing in the glare of the screen . . . or was it the message?

The message . . .

Adrian Cox had sent an email.

She'd read it.

The message . . .

Ruth.

A synapse clicked at the back of her brain.

Ruth.

It clicked again. This time sending a flare up.

Ruth.

The message.

Ruth. The message.

Adrian Cox. The message. Ruth. *Fuck!*

Claudia leapt from the chair. 'Fuck.'

Heads in the incident room turned her way. The door opened and Graham strolled in carrying a bag filled with sandwiches. He'd collected the lunch orders on his way back.

'Fuck.' She stormed out of her office. 'Where's Dominic?'

'He took a call and left for some privacy.' Lisa pointed towards the door.

'Boss?' Graham placed the bag on his desk, confusion sweeping across his features.

'Dominic killed Ruth.' She ran out of the room. They had to get on this immediately. Behind her, voices rose in unison.

It was quicker to use the stairs. She ran up two at a time, pulling her phone from her pocket as she ran.

Maxine, Sharpe's PA, was coming out of Sharpe's office, a bundle of folders in hand.

'I have to see her, right now. It's urgent.' Claudia was blunt, bordering on rude, but her brain was scrambling.

Maxine sat behind her desk and dropped the folders in a tray. 'She went for a smoke. She should be back any time.'

The phone grew hot and heavy in her hand. He'd left the office only minutes earlier. A head start, but not much of one. Should she call him? Would she give herself away? A lot depended on the call he'd just received and why he was no longer here.

Sharpe strode in. 'Claudia?'

'Dominic killed Ruth.' The breath caught in her chest and the blood drained from her face. Her body chilled.

'He just left the premises,' Sharpe said, without missing a beat. She took Claudia's arm and guided her into her office. 'Maxine, get Phil. Ask him to wait out here and for no one to disturb us.' She closed the door behind them and lowered Claudia to a chair.

This was her father. It wasn't possible.

But it was. Obviously.

'Tell me.' Sharpe was calm.

The phone, hot in her hands, now rested in her lap. Her body had never felt so cold. 'Hayley Loftus.'

'Go on.'

'She . . .' Claudia needed to gather herself. Gather the sequence of events. She licked her lips. They were dry and coarse.

Events spanned all the way back to Ruth's murder, or earlier. To her father's affair with . . .

'After the guilty verdict, Hayley came to me. Dominic was drunk the night of the verdict. He told her . . .' She swallowed, attempting to create saliva, to wet a now desert-dry mouth.

Sharpe picked up her phone. 'A glass of water, please.'

Claudia swallowed and licked her lips again. What felt like pebbles caught under her eyelids as she blinked. Where had all the fluid in her body gone? She scrubbed at her eyes, then licked her lips again.

Maxine knocked and entered, carrying the requested drink.

'For Claudia.' Sharpe gestured across her desk.

Maxine handed Claudia the tumbler with one of those sympathetic smiles promising everything would be okay.

Claudia couldn't imagine anything being okay ever again. Her father had killed Ruth, his wife and her best friend.

Claudia's stomach contracted at speed and she clamped her jaw shut. Unable to offer the verbal thanks Sharpe's PA deserved, she gave the quick, grateful nod. The glass was cold, slippery with condensation. So much that it nearly glided straight from her hand. Claudia caught it and, with both hands, brought the glass to her mouth and drank. The cool water brought immediate release from the panicked inability to talk.

'I don't want to rush you, Claudia, but . . .' Sharpe tapped her watch. 'He's already gone. Please, we need to do this.'

'You don't seem surprised.'

Sharpe leaned forward, hands folded together on the desk. 'I trust you, Claudia. If you tell me Dominic Harrison killed Ruth, I believe you, because . . .' She shrugged. 'Well, other than trust, you're the last person who'd come to me with that accusation if it had no substance.'

Because this was her dad they were talking about. She was about to send the entire police force after her own father. There was no getting away from it. She'd already set that ball rolling.

'So if we can get on with it?'

She sipped on the water again, returned it to the desk and took a quiet deep breath. 'Hayley came to me after the verdict . . .'

Sharpe opened her notebook and picked up her pen. Her short nails polished in a beige shine. She made a note of the date and time and started to write.

'Dominic's old team went out the night of Tyler's guilty verdict.' Claudia rubbed her forehead. 'Now I think about it, I can vouch for his getting drunk that night. It was the night Ivy Henthorn was murdered. Dominic came into work the following morning with a raging hangover.'

Sharpe nodded as she wrote.

'Hayley said he was completely slaughtered, and it was at the point he'd lost all inhibitions—'

Sharpe held up her pen. 'You're not telling me you've come to this conclusion on hearsay?'

Claudia jumped out of her seat. No longer able to sit still. Stress made her body twitchy and the best way to relieve it was to run, but during a working day there was no running to be had, so pacing was the only response. She moved around the room as she talked. 'You just finished telling me how much you trusted me. How can you then ask me that?'

Sharpe held up a palm. 'Okay. But if this is Dominic, it's a major problem for us—'

Claudia glared, unworried at the moment that this was her supervisor.

'And a huge shock for us all, Claudia. You especially.' She tapped the pen against the edge of her desk in a slow rhythm. 'When Ruth was missing and I requested you interview Dominic, you were on task. This appears to have spun you for a loop.'

The question missing from the end of the sentence didn't need asking. It was still present.

'Ruth was *missing*. There was a possibility we'd find her alive and well. And if my involvement brought her home in one piece, then that's what I was prepared to do.' Claudia paced around the back of the chair. Arms and legs itching to let loose and run it out. 'Once the pool of blood was found, it became more difficult, but I hadn't given up hope. This time, Ruth is gone. There's no hope to cling to.'

'And Dominic?' Sharpe's voice was quieter.

Claudia paced back and forward again. 'He told Hayley he regretted the fight he had with Ruth the night she was murdered. He hated that the last words they said to each other were angry words.'

'And when interviewed, he said he arrived home from work to find Ruth already missing.'

'Yes.'

Sharpe tapped the pen on the notebook this time. 'It's suspicion. You know that's not enough. We can open up an investigation.'

'No!' There was no more pacing.

Sharpe put the pen down. 'Claudia?'

'He saved my life. In the woods that time? Dominic saved my life. If he hadn't traced me, I wouldn't have made it out. And again with the house fire. It was his voice I heard. His voice I followed to the window. This is my *dad* we're talking about.' She scraped her hands through her hair. 'But he killed Ruth.'

Sharpe leaned back.

'There was a broken glass tumbler in the kitchen bin. On walking through the crime scene that day, I asked officers to seize it. I wasn't sure why; call it a hunch, a feeling. The crime scene was in the garage and nothing was out of place in the rest of the house.' She shook her head. They'd been so, so stupid. He'd fooled every single one of them. 'We're not going to come out of this smelling of roses.'

'Never mind that now. First we have to deal with what's in front of us. That means you tell me what we have.' Sharpe put a finger to her watch again.

'It was decided it wasn't relevant, so was way down the exhibit list. Then when Ruth was found and Tyler identified, there were more pressing exhibits to be forensically examined and deemed worthy of the cost.'

Sharpe held her tongue. Not examining every item recovered during a homicide investigation because of cost would not go down well with the public once this came out. Regardless of the fact it was policy in every force area to prioritise exhibits, to go down the list only examining the important and relevant items until a case was proved either way.

'After the conversation with Hayley, I submitted a request for the pieces to be examined, and agreed for the cost to come from our budget.'

Sharpe waited her out. It was clear where this was going.

Claudia's pacing slowed. She grabbed the back of the chair she'd been sitting in with both hands and leaned on it, the strain of the words she was about to utter taking the strength right out of her. 'I've come straight from reading an email that states both Ruth and Dominic's prints are on those pieces. That though blood wasn't visible, there were miniscule droplets. It was identified as Ruth's.'

The air was thick and breathing became difficult. The final sentence she needed lodged in her throat. Claudia stepped forward, picked up the water and drank half the contents before she dropped, exhausted, into the chair. 'Dominic's fingerprint was lifted from above the blood.'

Sharpe was no longer taking notes; she was tapping at her keyboard. 'Let me check Ruth's post-mortem report. We can't go into this half-cocked, Claudia.'

This time, it was Claudia's turn to wait.

Ruth's post-mortem details were seared into her mind.

Yes, her murder was identical to the women attributed to Samuel Tyler, except with Ruth there had been extra cuts on her body. Not just the usual MO of strangulation and a following cut across the throat. Ruth also had very small but, according to the pathologist, quite precise cuts elsewhere. There were several on her right arm and some on the right-hand side of her face, one of which was quite pronounced under one eye.

Claudia clenched her jaw, closed her eyes and breathed deeply as she thought of her friend's savage murder. And that it could have been perpetrated by her own husband, Claudia's father, was close to unbearable.

'I have it.'

Claudia opened her eyes. Sharpe's office had two huge windows, so that the sun Claudia had been enjoying not that much earlier now blinded her. Claudia squinted and put her hand to her eyebrow. 'Can I?' She pointed with her other hand to the window.

'Oh, yes,' Sharpe said distractedly.

Claudia rose again and went to the end of window, where the beads to control the blinds hung. She looked down at the street below. The building was on an incline. It was a busy road, in and out of Sheffield, and cars moved steadily in both directions, the sun glinting off metallic bodywork and shining windows, reflecting back at her. She spun the beads and the blinds closed, blocking the day out.

If only it were that easy to block her own day out.

Sharpe used her pen as a pointer and tapped at the laptop screen. 'Here. The pathologist said on visual examination of Ruth's body . . .' She paused. 'You okay to do this?'

'I know what it says. Ruth's wounds were different to the other victims. She had extra cuts, that, though small, were not simple. They were widened by the knife. Nothing came from the swabs, because he'd washed out the wounds with bleach.'

Sharpe tapped her screen again. 'As if he'd been digging out glass debris.'

Claudia's stomach curled in on itself at the thought of what her friend had gone through. The man she loved and trusted had betrayed her in the most savage way.

'The knife was never found, though, Claudia, and evidence has just convicted Samuel Tyler.'

With emotions swirling, Claudia finally let go. 'You don't think Dominic was in a position to pin his own wife's murder on the man he was hunting himself?' If this was a cartoon, she'd have exploded into thin air at that point. But this wasn't a cartoon; this was real life, her life. She had to pull herself together.

'Sit.' Sharpe picked up her phone and tapped out an internal extension.

'I'm sorry. I'm fine. We need to bring him in. The fact that he's run tells us a lot.'

'Hold, please.' Sharpe covered the handset with her hand. 'Claudia, sit, please. The evidence you've brought is enough to bring him in and to tear his life apart. Take a few breaths. We'll get this rolling.' She uncovered the handset. 'Can you come to my office, please? Yes, right now. It's urgent. We need to act fast.'

CHAPTER 51

There was a quick rap at the door and DCI Adam Blackwood from the intelligence unit strode in. Claudia hadn't seen Adam for some time, even though they worked in the same building, and imagined she mirrored the surprise she saw on his face now, as he slowed mid-stride.

'Come in then, and bring Phil with you.' Sharpe wasn't wasting time now the decision had been made. 'And close that door behind you.'

Adam clicked back into work mode, spun on his heels, popped his head out the door, and quietly spoke to someone. Then DI Phil Carlyle, from one of the Major Crime teams, followed him in.

Of course her team couldn't deal with this. She hadn't thought that far ahead, but it was obvious.

The two men strode to the spare seats in front of Sharpe. Adam offered Claudia a quick half-smile before Sharpe got down to business.

It was then Claudia remembered Adam couldn't smile straight. It was crooked, and the half-smile even more so. Last time she'd seen him, she remembered his teeth fitting his mouth incorrectly. Even in these circumstances, she couldn't help but respond to his gesture in kind.

Without knowing it, the warmth he offered with his wonky smile lifted her, supported her, and boosted her to continue through what was to come.

'Are we ready?' This time, there was no pressure or curtness. Sharpe wasn't stupid. She could see the toll this discovery was having on Claudia and had clearly picked up on the slight release in tension.

'What do we have?' Adam opened his notepad, ready to work. Phil followed suit. Both about to be hit by a bombshell.

The whole force was.

One of their own had betrayed them. This was catastrophic. Never mind the external furore and disgust, first the police officers and staff had to wrap their heads around the fact Detective Sergeant Dominic Harrison had not only murdered his wife, but he'd gone on to put her murder at the feet of another man. Another man who was serving jail time for her death.

Sharpe asked Claudia again. 'Are we ready?'

Adam frowned.

Claudia gave a barely perceptible nod.

Sharpe closed her laptop and folded her hands on the desk. 'Claudia's come to me with both information and evidence that her father, DS Dominic Harrison, killed his wife, DC Ruth Harrison. It wasn't the man who has just been convicted and sentenced for her murder, Samuel Tyler.'

'She . . . he . . . he did what?' Adam looked from Claudia to Sharpe to Phil.

'Adam,' Sharpe's tone was pointed. She wanted his full attention.

He straightened in his chair. 'Yeah, okay, I'm here.'

'While intoxicated, Dominic let slip that he argued with Ruth the night she went missing. We have it on record when he reported her missing that she was already gone when he arrived home.'

Adam and Phil, like Sharpe before them, were recording the meeting now.

Sharpe went through what they had.

Pens moved over notepads as information was laid. Adam nodded all the way through. Not a look was spared for Claudia. They were working.

'Dominic received a call about the time Claudia received the email. He immediately left the premises — I witnessed that myself. He may have been tipped off, so we have no time to waste. We need to work quickly. Adam, your team needs to pull Dominic's life apart. Leave nothing untouched. The priority is his financials. If he's running, where's he running to, how's he getting there and how's he funding it? Locate him and bring him in first. But we also prove beyond a shadow of a doubt that he did this.'

Her tone was hard and unforgiving. 'We're in for a world of pain, and we deserve every moment of it. Ruth's family will demand answers, and we have to be in a position to provide them. Turn him inside out. Everything. The weeks and months leading up to Ruth's murder. Was this premeditated? And the time since. Has he been unravelling in any way? If there's anything to find, we find it. I even want to know what he eats at night, understood?'

'You got it.' There was no argument.

Claudia peered into Adam's notepad. There was a list of bullet points. The list Sharpe had reeled off.

'Phil, you're leading the manhunt.' Sharpe faced Claudia as she spoke. Her expression soft, though her voice was hard.

Claudia inclined her head.

'Grab a team, including uniform, and head straight to his house. Lock it down tight. Create a perimeter. Brief everyone on the way. I'll speak to the uniform inspector and put her in the picture. I think Trina McGregor's on today. She knows her stuff. If Dom's not at home, secure the premises and bring CSIs in. Something in that house will tell us where he is.' She sighed and rubbed her face.

This was no small feat. It was obviously going to take its toll on everyone, not just Claudia.

'Any idea where he'll go?' Sharpe asked her. 'A holiday caravan he bought, a favourite area of the country?'

284

'He works hard, and he likes to chill out at home.' What an inadequate response. 'I can't think straight right now. I'm sorry.'

'It's okay. Don't worry.'

Phil and Adam got to their feet.

Sharpe jumped up to meet them. 'I don't want any leaks, do you hear me? You tell your people if I hear they've told anyone, even their mum, I will pull their tongue straight out of their mouths with my bare hands.'

'Ma'am?' Adam pursed his lips.

Sharpe shooed him away with a hand. 'Don't "ma'am" me, Adam. This is not to leak before I've taken it higher and we've talked to Ruth's family. Have I made myself clear?'

Phil tucked his pen into his shirt pocket and kept his head down.

Adam sighed. 'Crystal.'

The two detectives headed towards the door.

'I want to go to the house with Phil. If my dad's there . . .' It was no longer Dominic, the professional she worked with. This was personal. He was her dad, and her dad had murdered a woman. His own wife.

It was because of the personal aspect that Sharpe should say no to her.

'If he's there, I could be the only person to bring him in quietly and without fuss.'

'Claudia, he's your father. You're too—'

'It's because I'm his daughter and this is personal that I stand a chance of getting through to him. He's been there for me when I've desperately needed him.'

She remembered the night in the woods. The utter terror that raged through her veins that her life would end in the dark and the dirt. 'His natural desire to protect his child is still there . . .'

Had that terror run through Ruth as, horrified, she stared into her husband's eyes? Claudia's scalp prickled and tightened across her skull like it was too small a fit.

She pushed on. She'd do this for Ruth.

For Ruth's family.

It was the least she could do, after being the one to support him when Ruth's body was found. Her stomach roiled and she clenched her fists. 'He still wants to protect me, even though I'm an adult and his supervisor. He's protected me. For instance, that time in the woods.'

Finally, tears pricked hot behind her eyes. There was no getting away from the emotional toll of the situation. The tangled mess she was standing in.

Phil hovered by the door. Adam had left.

Sharpe shook her head. 'Connelly won't like this. We're already in the shit up to our necks.'

Claudia railed at her: 'What about last time? You and Connelly had no issues with me arresting my father when Ruth was missing!'

Phil slipped from the room and quietly closed the door behind him.

'Claudia, this is entirely different.' Sharpe came around the desk to face her, perching on the corner at a safe enough distance to not overcrowd her. 'You were deemed the best and fastest way of getting Dominic to talk so we could find Ruth. Here and now, we're way past that. You have to see that?' Her voice softened. 'One of our own killed. His daughter was allowed to investigate, and he slipped through the net. You can see how that looks.'

'Yes,' Claudia growled. 'But it was me who finally identified him.'

'Because of his own slip-up and Hayley Loftus coming to you with the information.'

Claudia flung her arms up. 'Yes! But if I hadn't taken the glass tumbler from the kitchen bin in the first place, we wouldn't be here now.'

Sharpe thought for a moment. Claudia held her breath and clenched her fists to keep herself still. She didn't dare move for fear of stopping Sharpe's train of thought, hoping it was going her way.

Sharpe pulled her phone from her pocket and tapped on the screen. 'We have a major incident,' she said, 'and it's one of our own making. I'll be there in two minutes.' She ended the call.

She turned back to Claudia. 'Answer one question.'

'Anything.'

'Why do you want to see him arrested? You said your-self, he saved your life. I can't imagine what you must be going through.'

Did she even know herself? The cold she'd experienced earlier deepened, cutting into her bones. Her body weak and overwhelmed as she was confronted with such a direct and emotive question.

'Why, Claudia?'

She raised her palms. 'He's my dad.'

Claudia's legs shook. She had to move soon, or she would collapse in front of Sharpe, and there was no way she'd do that. 'I failed last time.'

'He was—'

'It's too late.' Claudia paced across the room. Sharpe wasn't stupid, she'd see right through her, but Claudia only needed enough time to get out of the room, and Sharpe had a meeting with Connelly in a minute. She spoke fast. 'We deal with the now. I can't work the case against him. I can't even be involved in the arrest this time, but I let Ruth down in so many ways, and need to be present when he's brought in, to see it through. Plus, like I said, if I'm there, it might prove advantageous, if he plans on making it hard for the arrest team. He won't allow me to come to harm. No matter what the circumstances are.'

Sharpe checked her watch and moved towards the door. Claudia fell into step beside her.

'Catch up with Phil, but . . .' Sharpe paused and glared at her. 'You are at no point to be considered a part of the arrest or inquiry team. You do not enter the house during the arrest and search, unless Phil requests your support. You do as asked, then return to the vehicle. Do I make myself clear?'

'Crystal,' she said, mimicking Adam.

Sharpe opened the door. 'If you step out of line, Claudia, you do more than let Ruth down, you destroy any chance the CPS has of convicting Dominic of her murder.'

The barb hit exactly where Sharpe had aimed. The unwanted tears fell as Claudia stared at Sharpe's retreating back.

CHAPTER 52

The arrest and search teams were organised within ten minutes. Phil Carlyle and Trina McGregor worked in complete synergy to unify the separate units of uniform officers and plainclothes detectives, aided by a flow of incoming emails from Adam and his team of intelligence detectives.

Phil had received an email, not from Sharpe, but from Detective Superintendent Connelly himself, instructing Phil of Claudia's rigid restrictions and the penalty for failing to keep her in check.

As they strode out to the vehicles, Phil gave an apologetic glance. 'I'm sorry, I can't imagine what this day is like for you. My hands really are tied, though. Please tell me you'll stay in the car.'

Again with a colleague unable to imagine how she was. This would be her life for the foreseeable. Even her legacy. She'd better get used to it.

If she could put into words what it was like finding out your father was not only a murderer, but had framed another man for it, she'd voice it and put people out of their imagination-lacking misery.

As it was, she couldn't. 'I just want to see Ruth get the justice she deserves, Phil. It's been too long coming. Dominic took us all in, but I'm the closest to him. I should have noticed he was lying or he was hiding something or he was playing us. There had to be a visible sign.'

A train of vehicles drove the distance to Green Lane at Wharncliffe Side. Some marked, some plain, and a couple of dog vans.

'You can't beat yourself up,' Phil said. 'It won't serve you well.'

You didn't get to detective inspector without having a good head on your shoulders, and Phil was no exception.

'Easier said than done, I know, but once we're further down this process, do try to go easy on yourself.'

The words knotted themselves up around Claudia's throat. She couldn't respond to his kindness.

'I'll always be available if you need to talk it through.'

She stared out the passenger window as more tears fell. Was this her constant state now? The sky was incredibly blue and Claudia watched the birds take flight through the haze of overwhelming emotion.

The convoy was nearly there. The hope was that Dominic hadn't yet had time to run and South Yorkshire Police could contain the predicament of their own making.

Claudia wanted none of this to be true, but they were way past that now. All she could hope for was that Dominic came in peacefully.

CHAPTER 53

Dominic

The fingerprint on the glass wasn't the issue Dominic had initially thought it was. Not in terms of convicting him in a court of law, anyway. There was no way a jury of twelve people would convict a husband of killing his wife when they lived together, shared their property and some of that shared property had both his and her DNA and fingerprints on. Especially when a known and convicted serial killer had been found guilty of her murder. Not that they would be aware of the convicted serial killer information, if it got that far.

On the landing, Dominic pulled down the loft ladders and climbed up, switching on the single bulb as he did. The go bag he'd created for this very situation was safely stored up there, out of the way so Claudia, or any other guest, never stumbled upon it by accident and began asking difficult questions he didn't want to answer. Or rather, questions they really wouldn't want the answer to.

The bag was where he'd left it.

The memories there gave him a moment of hesitation as they washed over him. There were trinkets and cheesy knick-knacks from Claudia's childhood. When he and her mother had divorced, Claudia's childhood, securely stored in the loft of their family home, was split between them. Now he had to walk away from it all.

Dominic lifted the bag and returned to the landing. He crouched to check through the contents.

Even though, as a detective, he didn't deem the blood and fingerprint enough to prosecute him, Dominic understood his daughter and the force would come to make the arrest. He had to be quick.

He unzipped the large black carry bag and opened it wide.

The blood and fingerprint were all they had. Too much time had passed for them to complete a comprehensive investigation or to gather further evidence against him, such as mud from his tyre treads from the area Ruth was buried. He'd washed his tyres that night, as well as cleaning his car multiple times since then and changing the actual tyres, in case this day ever came. Being a cop was helpful.

Like packing the go bag. The clothes inside were all new and neutral. Clothes Claudia didn't know he owned, and ordinary enough that he'd blend in wherever he went. Dressed like every guy his age. No one would take any notice of him.

He'd loved being a cop, but it was too late for him. His daughter had the report from forensics on the glass. That, along with the constant claims from Tyler that he didn't kill Ruth, would be enough to cast doubt in her own mind and the minds of those above her. Those who made the decision about his future.

Dominic picked up the electric razor and weighed it in his hand. When his beard grew in, he'd shave his head. He'd look like a totally different man. Not the one police were searching for. He tucked it back into the corner on the bag, unable to believe it had come to this. That his mates and colleagues were coming for him.

The decision-makers wouldn't ignore the information they had. They couldn't possibly. Not with the furore in the press recently about how corrupt the police service was. No. Dominic would be hunted and publicly hung out to dry, if only to appease those who brayed for the blood of police officers.

It didn't cross his mind once that he'd actually killed his wife.

Last time, he'd had a plan on how to get out of the arrest with clean hands, but this time there was no way he'd walk away. The cloud would always follow him. This time, his career was over.

His whole life was over.

How the hell had this happened?

What had he said or done to make Claudia send the tumbler for examination? After Tyler's conviction as well. When Dominic had thought himself safe. When he'd thought it all over and done.

He wracked his brain, but nothing came.

His head hurt. How had it come to this?

He never meant for it to go that far. Ruth had known which buttons to push and she'd pushed them. She'd made his blood boil. The red mist had come down, and it was over before he'd even had time to think it through.

They'd had a good life, him, Ruth and Claudia. Hayley was just someone he was . . .

It didn't matter anymore. He had to move. And quickly.

Dominic picked the one item out of the bag he needed and walked downstairs into the kitchen.

CHAPTER 54

Claudia

There was nothing discreet about the convoy of police vehicles lined up in front of her dad's home. It couldn't be explained away as colleagues visiting for a cuppa. This was clearly a tactical visit. One he was not meant to escape from.

But were they already too late?

The car in his drive said Dominic was at home. But after the shock the day had already brought down on her, Claudia wasn't disposed to trust anything where her dad was concerned.

'You have to stay put.' Phil strapped his airwaves radio to his protective vest. The expression he gave her as he clambered out the car brooked no argument.

Claudia held up her palms. 'I don't want to see him in that position, Phil.'

He gave a quick nod and slammed the door shut before quietly issuing directions to officers also exiting vehicles. They moved into position, circling the house that was so familiar to her. They covered the front, back and sides. If Dominic made a run for it, there would be an officer waiting to scoop him up.

Phil, Trina and one of Trina's uniformed officers strode to the front door. From her position, Claudia could see the front of the house. Phil knocked, loud and strong. They weren't worried about needing a rapid entry, necessary if an offender might destroy evidence, as the house had already been searched when Ruth had gone missing.

There was no response. Phil tried the handle. There was no need to destroy a door if the occupant was inside and the door was unlocked. Television shows always missed this out for the sake of the dramatic entry that made for better television.

The door was locked, but Claudia had given them her key. Phil unlocked it and the three officers walked in. Everything was then out of Claudia's view. Her body flamed like an army of fire ants were swarming over her.

The clock on the car dashboard read two twenty-nine p.m. If it had been an old analogue clock, she would have watched the seconds tick by.

There was no movement from the officers around the house, which told Claudia her dad was either inside and securely arrested, or they'd missed him.

Then Phil was out of the house and walking towards her. He was alone. No one had brought her dad out yet. Claudia had no idea what this meant.

Would she be okay ever again?

She'd thought the trauma of losing Ruth had been difficult enough, but for her father to have been the one who killed her, it was the thing of nightmares. And after the nightmare . . .

Phil was getting closer.

After the nightmare was the emotional response of fear, anxiety, stress and depression. All of this would be put under a microscope by the press and ultimately the public, who would not take kindly to Claudia.

Though she didn't use social media, she knew enough about it to understand the vicious beast it could become. They wouldn't be satisfied in taking down Dominic, the guilty party, himself. That would be too easy. The beast would be awoken, and they would go for South Yorkshire Police. It would be their fault that one of their own had been a killer.

South Yorkshire Police should have known.

But Claudia hadn't known.

And that was the problem. South Yorkshire Police was a faceless organisation and the clamouring mob would need a real person to take the fall for Ruth's murder.

Who had helped him get away with it for so long? It could only be another police officer. And as his daughter, the one person linked to the investigation who shouldn't have been. She was the one, if anyone, who should have seen what was in front of her face.

Heat roared up Claudia's body as the thoughts raced around her head, and she jumped out of the car, panting, waving her hand in front of her face as though it could cool her.

Phil had reached her. 'Claudia?'

'What?' Claudia had no time to go around the houses. She wanted to know why he'd come out to her, and she wanted it now.

'Do you want to come in?' His tone was soft and gentle.

'He's not here?'

Phil shook his head. 'He's been and gone, Claudia. I'm sorry.'

Claudia strode out towards the house before he'd finished. 'His car's parked outside.'

'Yeah. Do you know if he bought a second vehicle at any point?'

They were at the front door now. 'No. But if he kept it in the garage, I wouldn't. I never went in there after . . .'

'Yeah. It's okay. The working hypothesis is that he bought a second vehicle in preparation for this day.'

It wasn't okay. It would never be okay.

'There's no sign of him packing in a hurry. No clothes pulled out of drawers or hangers on the floor. We think he probably had a go bag.'

Claudia's head was about to explode with the amount of information it was taking in today. And the one person she'd usually turn to would be Ruth. *Do not cry in front of these people. Do not cry in front of these people. Do not cry.*

The house was abuzz with activity.

'Kitchen.' Phil directed her into a room she was familiar with.

On the worktop was a clear plastic exhibit bag. Phil handed it to her. Inside the bag was a piece of paper with a note written in her dad's hand.

'It was in a sealed envelope,' Phil said. 'We obviously opened, read and exhibited it, but I think you deserve to read it.'

There were no words anymore; the tears flowed. She lifted the bag and read.

My Dearest Claudia,

This will be short, because, well, I'm not even sure if you'll ever read it. I love you. You have always been my whole world. And please know, no matter what happens next, that none of this is your fault.

The house is paid for in full. I transferred it into your name a little while ago, so it's yours now. They can't take it away from you and I don't need it anymore.

Please take care of yourself.

Dad x

THE END

ACKNOWLEDGEMENTS

I will attempt to keep these acknowledgements short. There is always a risk of these things running away with you and ending up being their own short story at the end of the actual book. The reason being, a published novel isn't a one-person event. So, let's see how I do.

I want to thank Hannah Weatherill for all her support and help over the last four years. It has not only been invaluable, but it has been a total pleasure.

Thanks go to my editors, Jodi and Robert, for their eagle-eyes, and their gentle touch when pointing out complex issues with the timeline, or the need for a character to be completely cut. The whole experience could have been a stressful nightmare, but was the opposite as they both brought calm with their explanations. To Elizabeth, for the once-over, proving that even in the proofread it's never too late to check your work again. And to Nick for the gorgeous cover. The one item that initially draws a readers' eye.

Thanks, of course, go to my editor at Joffe, Emma Grundy Haigh, who steered me calmly through a frantic time when I thought the whole manuscript was going to hell. I couldn't have got it over the finish line without her kindness.

My appreciation also goes to Nina Kicul and all at Joffe for making *Cold Hard Truth* the book it is today, and helping it reach you, the reader. They truly are a dedicated and incredible team.

For massive help in understanding how a press release is put together, I have to thank Sinead Crowley, Neil Broadfoot, Howard Linskey and Fiona Cummins. Any errors are completely my own — this is particularly true because the article was rewritten slightly in the edits, so I apologise for dragging their good names through the mud! To Graham Bartlett and Kate Bendelow for their expertise in sense of smell, particularly in the arena of a post-mortem.

Every author needs those friends who cheer her on, even when she wants to slide the manuscript into the desktop bin. Here I thank Jane Isaac — there are never enough hours . . . I really wouldn't like to put us to the test on talking the hind legs off a donkey!

To the cohort of crime writers who make up the genre. A most welcoming bunch you could ever hope to meet.

To readers, without you, this is just me talking to myself for a very long time, and I'm really glad I'm not talking to myself! You are the thing (people) that brings a book to life.

And to my family, for giving me the time and space to let the ideas rumble around my head, and tap away at my desk. This is always for you.

THE JOFFE BOOKS STORY

We began in 2014 when Jasper agreed to publish his mum's much-rejected romance novel and it became a bestseller.

Since then we've grown into the largest independent publisher in the UK. We're extremely proud to publish some of the very best writers in the world, including Joy Ellis, Faith Martin, Caro Ramsay, Helen Forrester, Simon Brett and Robert Goddard. Everyone at Joffe Books loves reading and we never forget that it all begins with the magic of an author telling a story.

We are proud to publish talented first-time authors, as well as established writers whose books we love introducing to a new generation of readers.

We have been shortlisted for Independent Publisher of the Year at the British Book Awards three times, in 2020, 2021 and 2022, and for the Diversity and Inclusivity Award at the Independent Publishing Awards in 2022.

We built this company with your help, and we love to hear from you, so please email us about absolutely anything bookish at: feedback@joffebooks.com.

If you want to receive free books every Friday and hear about all our new releases, join our mailing list: www.joffebooks.com/contact

And when you tell your friends about us, just remember: it's pronounced Joffe as in coffee or toffee!

ALSO BY REBECCA BRADLEY

DI CLAUDIA NUNN SERIES
Book 1: BLOOD STAINED
Book 2: SECONDS TO DIE
Book 3: SHE KNEW HER KILLER
Book 4: COLD HARD TRUTH

Milton Keynes UK
Ingram Content Group UK Ltd.
UKHW040733251023
431306UK00004B/147